PRAISE FOR *DISSONANCE*

"Kaledin's knowledge about music, the environment, and the law shine through in *Dissonance*, a suspenseful thriller with an end the reader will not expect."
— HARRY GROOME, author of *The Best of Families*

"A grand romp through the dunes of Cape Cod and the treacherous waters surrounding them. *Dissonance* features an irresistible mix of lowlifes in high culture, compelling courtroom drama, and a hungry shark. Kaledin's fast-paced and erudite debut will leave readers clamoring for the sequel."
— CONALL RYAN, author of *House of Cards*

"Twists and turns like a Cape Cod country road. Readers had better hold on for dear life, and watch where they're swimming too!"
— M. TODD HENDERSON, ESQ., author of *State of Shock*

"A fun, riveting, multi-dimensional read. Kaledin weaves spot-on social and environmental commentary through a nail-biting "who done it," creating a page-turner with a conscience. It is also an ode to a very special place for many of us: Cape Cod. *Dissonance* left me eagerly looking forward to the next tale in the Hennessey Cape Cod series—the highest compliment I could give it!"
— ELISA M. SPERANZA, author of *The Italian Prisoner*

"A tightly woven suspense and legal thriller. Kaledin shows off his substantial lawyer's chops in the trial scenes—richly textured, tension-building legal fiction along the lines of Scott Turow or John Grisham. And did you read the Boston Globe's recent Spotlight report on the incredible injustice of the felony murder rule in MA? Kaledin focuses in on it like a laser beam in his debut novel. Read *Dissonance* now!"
— HARRY S. MARGOLIS, ESQ., author of *Get Your Ducks in a Row*

"Detectives, crooks, intrigue, romance, and big-time surprises—all on picturesque Cape Cod! *Dissonance* is a compelling read."
— R.C. BINSTOCK, author of *Tree of Heaven*

D0061607

Jonathan Kaledin was born and raised just outside of Boston. Trained as a cellist and musicologist at Harvard University, he then attended New York University School of Law. His career has been as an environmental lawyer and non-profit organization executive.

Non-fiction work of his has appeared in *The American Prospect, USA Today, Boston Globe, Philadelphia Inquirer*, and numerous other journals and newspapers. He co-edited and co-authored the textbook *Water and Cities in Latin America* (Earthscan/Routledge, 2015).

Jon has spent many a summer on Cape Cod, swimming well offshore into Cape Cod Bay, Nantucket Sound, and even out into the open Atlantic Ocean. That, however, was before the arrival of apex predators to the Cape's waters.

Dissonance is his first novel.

DISSONANCE

THE HENNESSEY CAPE COD SERIES

JON KALEDIN

Publishing Coordinator – Sharon Kizziah-Holmes
Cover Design – Jaycee DeLorenzo

Paperback-Press
an imprint of A & S Publishing
A & S Holmes, Inc.

ISBN -13: 978-1-956806-53-3

For Clayton, Nina, and Sarah—
the three brightest stars in my firmament

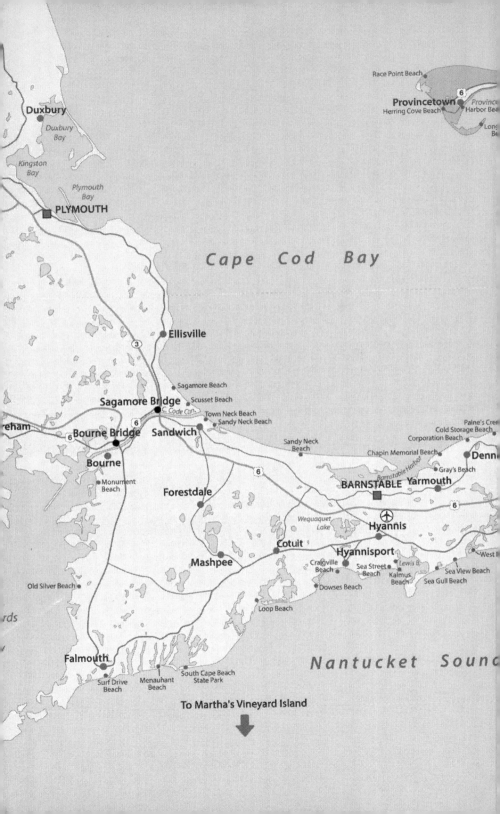

HENNESSEY'S CAPE COD

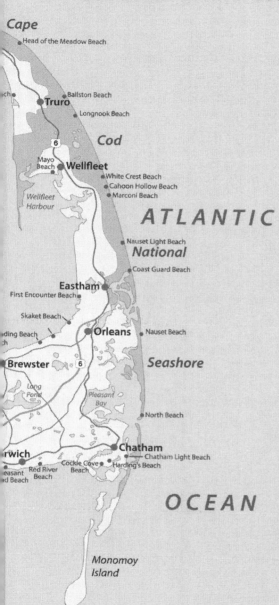

Cape
- Head of the Meadow Beach

ch •
• Ballston Beach
•Truro
• Longnook Beach

Cod

6

Mayo
Beach • •Wellfleet
• White Crest Beach
• Cahoon Hollow Beach
• Marconi Beach

*Wellfleet
Harbour*

ATLANTIC

• Nauset Light Beach

National

• Coast Guard Beach

Eastham •
First Encounter Beach•

Skaket Beach•

ding Beach •
h •Orleans • Nauset Beach

•Brewster 6

*Long
Pond*
*Pleasant
Bay*
Seashore

• North Beach

•Chatham
•— Chatham Light Beach
rwich • Cockle Cove• •
easant Red River • Harding's Beach
d Beach Beach

OCEAN

*Monomoy
Island*

To Nantucket Island

DISSONANCE

THE HENNESSEY CAPE COD SERIES

PROLOGUE

Saturday, August 14, 2021

Barbara gazed wistfully out the window as her husband Eric drove them home. It was a switchover Saturday, the day vacation renters on Cape Cod left in the morning and new renters arrived in the afternoon. The new arrivals eagerly anticipated a week or two of sun, fried seafood and *lobstah*, and all sorts of entertainment on the beach. The departing did so under a proverbial grey cloud. Most thought only about one thing: how they could leave the rat race behind and stay on the Cape forever.

Her thoughts took her many places, scuttling about like the fiddler crabs she and her seven-year-old son Billy chased together at Skaket Beach. Dissatisfaction with her accounting position at the tech firm, nagging doubts about her competency as a mother, the difficulties she and her siblings were having with their elderly, increasingly cantankerous mother, but most of all, the humdrum and lifeless character of her marriage, especially the almost total lack of intimacy within it.

He turned away from me in bed last night—after I told him I was in the mood!

How she longed for any sort of spark or excitement.

Pondering whether what she and Eric once had was irretrievably lost, Barbara realized she knew the answer and rationalized it away. Too painful to confront openly, she just lived with it, but it was always on her mind.

What's happened? How did the two of us get here?

In the back seat of the car, the kids sat quietly, opiated by their hand-held video devices. The silence was a relief, although Barbara would never admit it. She constantly harped on them to get off of the electronics. Eric, on the other hand, didn't seem to care.

Daughter Julia had been a real handful over the two-week break. She'd turned thirteen at the beginning of the summer, entering the tunnel of stupidity—her teenage years. Barbara had laughed and said, "Dad and I will be waiting for you with open arms and big hugs when you emerge at twenty." That went over like a lead balloon. Julia's pot smoking worried Barbara the most. Thirteen seemed awfully young to get going on the cannabis.

Billy, on the other hand, still provided joy in most ways. He'd become an inveterate beach and tidal pool comber, collecting shells, clams, periwinkles, crab claws, skate egg casings, minnows. You name it, Billy collected it, whether dead or alive. His beach bucket always smelled to high heaven. To avoid complaints and nausea, it ended up being jammed into the back of the station wagon at the very last moment, right before they left for home. A couple of years ago, in a fit of good parenting, they promised Billy his collection could come home with them before being winnowed out. Barbara regretted this now, especially with Eric doing the driving, as she'd have to clean everything off when they got home.

A few hours later, coming out of the house with her rubber dishwashing gloves on, Barbara set about lining up in the driveway everything needing dousing and fetched the garden hose. Beach toys, chairs, the bocce set, sand-filled bathing suits, everything got hosed off.

She turned to the bucket, set a short distance off from

everything else due to its special qualities. Picking out the few items she'd let Billy choose as mementos, the rest quickly found their way into a small, plastic garbage bag, to be sealed airtight and thrown away. She reached the bottom in no time.

What on earth could that be? Billy's found another razor clam?

Holding it at eye level between gloved thumb and forefinger, she brought the three-inch long item close to her face, looking at it the way a jeweler examines a diamond. She'd have never known what it was except for the deeply embedded, sand-encrusted gold band. Stunned and sickened, Barbara dropped it immediately. "Eric, ERIC... Come here... NOW!"

Billy had brought home a human finger.

CHAPTER 1

Tuesday, August 17, 2021

Timothy "Drink" Hennessey didn't enjoy getting up. Never had. And at age fifty-seven that wasn't ever going to change. But he'd just been hired by the Barnstable County Police Department (affectionately known to insiders as the BCPD) to look into the discovery of a human finger on a Cape Cod beach, and to help solve a series of arson attacks, all involving performing arts buildings. Strange. Weird. A felony murder too. Some poor guy was trapped in the Lowlands Theater in Falmouth when it burned down. So he made the extra effort this morning. There was a lot going on in Barnstable County. Hennessey was needed, and he liked that.

Kachunk Kachunk. His tires signaled he'd gotten on the Sagamore Bridge, that graceful ninety-year-old beauty of engineering connecting Cape Cod to mainland Massachusetts. Below, the rip-rapped Cape Cod Canal cut an Atlantic-blue swath. Off the bridge. *Kachunk Kachunk.*

Hennessey was heading to Wayland, one of Boston's hoity-toity suburbs, to pick up an unidentified human finger and chat briefly with the distraught family that found it. The Wayland police had already been all over them. Rounding up unleashed dogs usually highlighted the daily law enforcement activities in Wayland, so having a body part show up was a big deal.

Settling in on the back patio with coffee, and after the bare minimum of required small talk, Hennessey, Barbara, and Eric Wexner got going. For Barbara, nothing had ever destroyed the afterglow of their Cape vacation quite so quickly as discovering a decaying digit among the family belongings.

"Do you have any idea where Billy might have picked it up?"

"No, no idea at all," she said.

"Why do you say that?"

"Well, we split our time between several beaches. Skaket Beach and Nauset Beach mainly, also a few days at Hardings Beach, and a day on a small Pleasant Bay Beach. I don't know the name of it. It could have been any of those places."

"Does Billy have any idea, do you think?"

"No, he doesn't know. We've been over it with him. He picks up and keeps his favorite beach things with him while we're there. More and more stuff is added to the bucket the longer we're there. It could have come from anywhere during the two weeks."

"You found it at the very bottom of the bucket. Maybe he picked it up at the first beach you went to?"

"Sure. It's possible. Billy likes to take stuff out of the bucket every day, though, play with it, and then put it back. There's never an order to what's in the bucket at the end of our trips."

"I guess I'm wondering why you didn't find it before. Didn't you and your husband play with Billy and his beach things, spend time with him, when you were there?"

Barbara stared hard at Hennessey, really hard, before answering. She didn't need a semi-retired police detective from Cape Cod suggesting, and unsubtly at that, that she and Eric were bad parents. Maybe she was being overly sensitive—a tendency of hers, she knew. Glowering at Eric, who hadn't said a word after the introductions, Barbara thought she tried much harder than her husband to spend quality time on the beach with Julia and Billy.

Where is Eric when I need him? Boy, are we ever over.

The truth of the matter, though, was that Barbara used their Cape vacations almost exclusively for herself. Even when she was with the family, and active with them, she wasn't there. Whether out for an evening ice cream at Buffy's in downtown Chatham, or in the middle of an intense four-way bocce ball match on the beach, Barbara was a million miles away. That defined her state of mind these days.

"What a silly question. Of course we did. We played with him and his sister as much as we could, almost every day. I'm sorry to say I can't explain how it ended up in his bucket. Just can't explain it." She shuddered thinking about it. "Listen, if there's nothing else we need to go over, I'd like to get back to things."

Hennessey knew he'd bothered her with that question. He made good on the way out with some light, routine 'boys will be boys' comments about Billy's beach bucket collection. After all, he could tell some stories about his childhood and adolescence in South Boston that would widen their eyes.

Guaranteed.

Eric Wexner walked him out. Once inside his car, Hennessey unrolled the window, sticking his elbow out on the car window ledge.

"Good to meet you Eric," he said, an almost imperceptible toughness entering his voice. "Think, how cool? Your young son Billy spent the past two weeks on the Cape's beautiful beaches, letting his imagination run wild while playing with seashells, crabs, and… a severed human finger."

Hennessey moved to Brewster after being booted off the Boston Police Department. Fired. Terminated. Expunged. Deleted. He figured he'd regroup on Cape Cod—that sandy, hooked peninsula covered with pitch pine and scrub oak. His plan was to get his drinking under control, clear his head, and clean up his act while walking the Cape's idyllic beaches and taking in the fresh ocean air.

The fifteen-foot rental truck he hired for the move proved easy enough to maneuver. The drive down from Boston was easy too, except for that narrow, nail-biting section on the Sagamore Bridge.

CRACK! "What the hell?" Hennessey yelled, startled by the loud snap of shattering plastic and tinkle of breaking glass. Some yahoo in a white Suburban SUV, blasting over the bridge toward him, crossed the double yellow lines, clipped Hennessey's mirror, hit the brakes for an instant... and then kept going. There was no way to turn around or stop on the Sagamore Bridge, absolutely no way. So it wasn't possible to file any sort of accident report against Mr. Yahoo. Hennessey actually liked it that way. He told the truck rental office the next day that he'd taken the mirror off on a tree, backing into the driveway of his newly rented cottage.

"Sorry about that," he said, walking out of the rental agency. Quick and easy.

For once, he'd listened to one of his neighbors who helped him load up and saw him off. "It's extra, Drink, but if you get in an accident, or bump into something in the truck, you won't need to call on your own insurance." Hennessey bought the comprehensive insurance that rental companies fob off on their customers, although by and large it isn't needed. Coverage usually exists through auto or home insurance already, or through the credit card used to rent the vehicle. That never stopped the rental agencies, though, from pitching the need for another blanket of insurance.

More money for the rental companies.

That fundamental goal of America: more money. It infected everything and everyone. Some people pretended to care for colleagues, friends, and community... not really. Building a better society? Hennessey scoffed at that one. For a long time now, America stood for one thing and one thing alone: money. Just money. Every single thing was monetized these days. And while he didn't think about politics often, when he did, Hennessey always arrived at the same conclusion.

America. The best democracy money can buy. Yes, indeed.

During his first few years on the Cape, Hennessey told a few friends from his former life and his new buddies—the regulars at Land Ho! in Orleans where he watched the Red Sox, Bruins, or Patriots a few nights a week—that he was figuring out where to go next, what his next life chapter would be.

"It'll be something completely different," he said, holding onto that delusion even after purchasing a bungalow on the bay side of the Cape in Brewster and being hired by the BCPD as an on-call consulting detective.

He acquired the nickname Drink at sixteen. With a couple of his South Boston buddies, he'd broken into a package store in Brookline. It was far enough from their own neighborhood that the damage couldn't possibly be done to someone they knew, and couldn't come back to haunt them in any way. A wealthy part of Boston too; they knew the takings would be good.

Back at Carson Park in Southie, his buddies were in hysterics. They'd hustled a bottle of Hennessy Cognac V.S.O.P. without even knowing it. Ruminating over the situation, that Hennessey had stolen Hennessy, they arrived at an inevitable conclusion. Tim could no longer be Tim. His new name? Drink.

For years he enjoyed the nickname, even preferring it to his given name. Gregarious at one point in his life, Hennessey had great fun introducing himself: "Hi, I'm Drink Hennessey." The name was an instant icebreaker and relationship builder. Later, when his long, increasingly serious battle with the bottle emerged, Hennessey downplayed the nickname. For years now, he'd gone by his surname, although Drink would be with him forever and he'd always answer to it. He now also lived by a Pythagorean dictum: meaningful silence is better than meaningless words.

He'd grown up during the 1970s, a tumultuous time for Boston, and South Boston in particular. His father John, a mail carrier, was fastidious and proud of his work; good, unionized work that allowed him to provide for his wife Mary and three boys, and set him up with a pension that would do the trick at the end of his life. The family and community turbulence, intense at times, came from his parents being leaders in the South Boston anti-busing crowd. A federal judge ordered Boston's schools desegregated by busing kids, including Hennessey and his two brothers, all over the place. The close-knit South Boston community went wild. They viewed themselves as guinea pigs in a grand social experiment gone awry, one they hadn't chosen and would never voluntarily participate in.

Although anti-busing activism died down after a few years, the Hennessey family never quite shed the whiff of racism that settled upon them through their leadership in the movement. Hennessey often wondered whether he'd paid the price for growing up in a family that acted on its principles, especially principles as uncomfortable as those associated with the anti-busing movement. He admitted to himself later on, never publicly, that being bused to a school in Boston's Chinatown exposed him to new people and things, and opened his eyes in ways that never would have happened had he stayed in his insular, isolated South Boston world, yet he still resented being sent to school outside his own neighborhood.

What bothered him the most was that the hypocrites who advocated the loudest for forced school busing were bleeding heart liberals who didn't even live in Boston. They championed school busing from afar, from the wealthy and almost exclusively white suburbs they lived in. A classic example of words not deeds. Even decades later, Hennessey was bitter and disdainful of the Boston suburbanite do-gooders.

Screw 'em.

Outgrowing the injudiciousness and petty criminality of his adolescence, and more importantly, having gotten away with it, Hennessey joined the Boston Police Department after a couple of years of criminal justice studies at UMass-Boston, that concrete monstrosity on the edge of Southie. He did well enough in his studies, and the police department entrance exam, for the BPD to hire him just as he turned twenty-one. At twenty-eight, he became one of the youngest detectives in the entire department. His analytical skills, attention to detail, thoroughness, and laid-back, easy-to-get-along-with demeanor made anything seem possible for him in the BPD in the future.

That was thirty years ago. Now, other than the three bright stars of his universe, his children, most everything had gone south for Hennessey.

The Hennessey brothers—Tim, Doug, and Joey—had been a tight-knit bunch growing up. Two years separated Tim and Doug, and four years separated Doug and Joey. Each had a birthday in October, making the month an exhausting one for their mother. The three of them were close enough in age that they swung baseball bats at the park together, scraped knuckles against family foes together, and lived dreams and disappointments together.

Hennessey was a decade or so into his professional life when Joey fell in with the wrong South Boston crowd. There'd always been that fine line in Southie between the legitimate, which included small-time thievery like breaking into package stores in Brookline, and the illegitimate. The latter involved a life devoted full-time to crime. Serious crime.

Joey's taking up with the Locust Hill gang shouldn't have surprised anyone. In retrospect, his need for attention and respect flashed like a Cape Cod lighthouse. He was the baby of the family, and his two older brothers, whose love for him could never in a million years be questioned, always found a way to put Joey in his birth-order place, physically and emotionally.

Everyone knew getting caught as the getaway driver in a botched Charlestown bank robbery was a big deal. The bank had two security guards, not one. One of Joey's bank robbery partners was gunned down when the second security guard came out of the shadowy corner where he'd been posted. Although Joey waited outside in the car, hadn't stepped foot in the bank, and never wielded a weapon, he and the other bank robber were sentenced to jail for life. Without the possibility of parole.

The Hennessey family shattered, the bounce in their father's step and the ever-present sparkle in their mother's eyes disappearing the day of Joey's conviction. The family never showed it or talked about it though. That was an indulgence in South Boston back then, the showing or expressing of emotions. Drink, the oldest of the brothers, had taken seriously his role model responsibilities for Doug and Joey, so the silent pain ran deep.

Mary Hennessey died twenty months later. Metastasized breast cancer, growing like a pernicious weed in the summer sun. The boys didn't even know about their mother's cancer. Drink suspected she hadn't bothered getting it treated. She'd wanted to go, after the shock and shame the family endured, and the incredible injustice of Joey's prison sentence.

How could she?

John Hennessey retired a few months later, sold the family house, and moved to Florida to fish and golf. He became a shell of a man, numbing his pain with pills, alcohol, and superficial friendships focusing exclusively on the material, never on the spiritual.

Strike one.

The next dark hole Drink found himself in, and which he almost, but never quite emerged from, came out of the blue. Hennessey met his wife Jessie at UMass-Boston, in an American literature course of all things. He knew instantly. Halfway through the semester they read *The Bridges of Madison County* together, a study group of two. That sealed the deal.

Yet, after more than a decade and a half of marriage, and with three children on their hands, she'd let on that she wanted a different life, one that did not include him.

He'd been stunned. At first, he took the blame, berating himself for his complacency and for taking things for granted. During the agonizing period of their uncoupling he'd asked over and over, "Why, Jessie, why? How can this be? Am I not a good provider, a good father, a good companion? We've done great things together, not the least of which are upstairs sleeping."

"No question about it, Drink. You are a good man in so, so many ways. It's just not the life for me anymore. We both know it, and I need to do something about it."

Hennessey hadn't known. After turning blue in the face trying to get her to change her mind, including offering to go to a marriage counselor, which she declined with a "nah" and small shake of her head, that was that. Her selfishness, narcissism really, floored him. The pain never fully went away, the stark reality of an unexpected, terrible life event imposed on him, imprisoning him forever through its definitional quality. He was a divorcé, something he'd never seen coming, never imagined, never wanted.

His heart literally ached for a while. Real pain, not something read about in a pulp fiction romance. It magnified a hundred times over when Jessie quickly got involved with a lawyer at the big downtown law firm she administered, some hotshot ten or twelve years younger than her. Soon, she froze Hennessey out of her life almost completely, except for brief, terse exchanges about child rearing responsibilities. It led to many lonely, drunken nights for him.

Strike two.

The straw that broke the camel's back came when advancement within the Boston Police Department, which at first happened so effortlessly for Hennessey, ground to a halt. Perhaps it had something to do with the family's history as leaders of the anti-busing movement, or his youngest brother's criminal record. Remember, though, this was

Massachusetts, where one Bulger brother from South Boston could be President of the Massachusetts State Senate while another Bulger brother ranked right behind Osama Bin Laden on the FBI's most wanted list: a serial killer, and possibly the mastermind behind the world's most famous art heist at Boston's Isabella Stewart Gardner Museum.

Whatever it was, after being passed over for a captain position a third time—the last time it went to someone younger and less experienced, and the decision reeked of political correctness—Hennessey imploded. Within a year, two DUIs were on his record. The Boston Police Department looked the other way on the first. The second couldn't be overlooked; it resulted in several demolished cars, including Hennessey's unmarked police cruiser, and other serious property damage.

Hennessey was then caught abusing an informant. Donnie Zimmer always brought out the worst in Hennessey. He couldn't tolerate snitching. The issue wasn't those receiving the information, like him, a detective simply doing his job any way that he could. It was the snitches themselves, those out on the street who were expected to be loyal to their friends and colleagues in the underworld. It didn't help that Donnie Zimmer had introduced Joey to the Locust Hill gang years ago. Although his baby brother was an adult, old enough and responsible enough to make his own decisions, the fact that Zimmer opened the door for Joey to enter the gang stuck in Hennessey's craw.

By the time the 'memory refresher' was done, Hennessey handcuffed Zimmer to his new cruiser and dragged him alongside it, Zimmer had to have his right leg amputated at the knee. Not much remained of it. None of it made the news. The Boston Police Department's multiple walls of silence and smoke screens made sure of that, and since a hardened criminal was the victim of Hennessey's behavior, no one felt much sympathy.

But Hennessey's tenure as a Boston Police Department detective was over.

Strike three.

Over a thirty-year period, a dark veil descended, cutting Hennessey off from the world and the world from him. It didn't drop quickly, like a heavy velvet theater curtain bringing a show to an end. No, it came down slowly, in light, gauzy layers. The first layers added only a haziness to the brightness and clarity Hennessey felt as a young family man making his mark as a talented, hard-charging detective. His divorce, his battle with alcoholism, his brother's jailing, his inexplicable failure to get promoted—these life events brought down layer upon layer upon layer. An impenetrable and permanent opaqueness now surrounded Hennessey. Its ingredients: disillusionment, heartbreak, cynicism, numbness, rage. At fifty-seven, very little light entered Hennessey's heart, and very little shone forth.

CHAPTER 2

Saturday, May 15, 2021

Climbing the stairs at Charlie's Kitchen in Cambridge left George Slavin out of breath. Especially after the two-hour drive to get there. The email said to head to the back booth in the dimly lit left side of the second floor. Slavin tried to reply to the email with a simple 'confirmed.' It came back as undeliverable.

Pat Kimmell waited, hidden completely from Slavin under a strongly starched hoodie. Its front extended fully and slightly downward, like the bow of an upside down canoe.

"What'll it cost?" Slavin asked.

"$300,000." The voice, quiet and without any inflection whatsoever, came through an electronicized filter. No one could tell whose voice it was, not even world-class voice recognition experts. Male or female, young or old... who knew?

"C'mon... you're kidding, right? I'll pay you $100,000. That's more than enough."

Silence. For an eternity. The void made two things clear: nothing was negotiable, and there was no turning back.

"Email me when you're ready to pay. Each week I'll send you a new email address to use. I'll send information on the block chain cryptocurrency I want used too, how to purchase it and where to send it. You'll have four hours to act once I send you the cryptocurrency information."

"It's so much friggin' money. How about installment payments?"

"Fine. Before every payment I'll send new instructions. I'll take whatever that day's exchange rate is for the cryptocurrency I want."

"Down payment?"

"No need. Pay it all at once, or pay it in installments. Only one thing's critical: payment in full within thirty days after it's all done. This one's a two-part job."

As Slavin mulled over getting out of the exorbitant price tag, the voice continued.

"I know what you're thinking. You'll pay fifty percent, sixty percent through installments, and then call it a day. Let me tell you about your daughter living in Los Angeles, and your other daughter living in San Francisco. And your five adorable grandchildren, the three boys and two girls you and your wife dote over."

A pause ensued, then Kimmell continued.

"Do you know the addresses where your daughters work, or where they park when they go to work? I do. How about the addresses and names of the schools the kids go to, or the nannies for the two babies? Their daily schedules? Do you know? No? I do."

Slavin turned ghostly white.

"Full payment within thirty days. Follow my instructions. You can go now."

"I thought I'd have lunch…"

"Not here you won't. And don't even think about waiting outside for me, or trying to find out who I am. I'll destroy your computer faster than you can blink, after I've hacked your bank accounts and taken every cent you have. As to the three hundred grand, I don't care where it comes from or whose it is. My guess: it's not yours. Doesn't matter. You get it to me when and how I tell you.

"Be smart. Think about what I said. I know everything about you. I know everything about your family. Everything."

As the dates drew near, Kimmell reflected on the work that went into pulling it all off, work that included getting a tour of the Barnstable music school from Tiffany Tisdale, the director of Cape Now's music school program. Kimmell had signed the visitor's log as a parent of a child potentially interested in enrolling next semester. Funny, that one.

"While our building may be a wee bit tired, it is seventy-five years old, after all," said Tiffany Tisdale. Summoning new-found enthusiasm, she continued, "you folks shouldn't mind that at all. So the roof leaks here and there. Who cares?" Tiffany giggled, imagining what it would be like giving piano lessons from under an umbrella and with a raincoat on. "What's important is the eagerness and excitement shown by our students, children and adults alike."

Sure, there was plenty of energy filling the Barnstable music school building each day. Enthusiasm ran amok, although the dozens of students who came also unleashed agony and torture on the ears of the unsuspecting: the sound of beginning musicians hard at work.

The tour of the building took in the music school's rehearsal rooms, pianos, drum sets, the old harp that no one knew how to tune or play, and then finished in the music library. An entire room filled with loose-leaf sheet music, tens of thousands, maybe hundreds of thousands, of ripped, dog-eared, finger and coffee-stained paper. Pat Kimmell was thrilled.

Oh how interesting. Nirvana!

Strangely enough, seeing all the music made Kimmell think seriously about backing out of the job. Pat had been a good violist growing up. Good enough to get into the Greater Boston Youth Symphony Orchestra. Good enough to study chamber music for a couple of years at the Walnut Hill music school outside of Boston.

I've played some of this music. I love it. How can I destroy it?

Pat loved string quartets above all else. The intimacy of the genre spoke to Pat more than anything, the lively dinner table conversation of four musical voices interacting with each other. Pat especially related to the works of loner composers: Janacek, the Czech; Shostakovich, the Russian; Ives, the American. Janacek's *Intimate Pages* quartet was the favorite; a tale of ardent, burning, unfulfilled love expressed through wild and strange music. Music that seared the soul. Pat was thrilled to hear excerpts from it in the movie version of Milan Kundera's *The Unbearable Lightness of Being* several years back.

Now there's an enlightened movie director.

And how Pat loved that towering German genius, Beethoven, who also led an isolated, lonely life; never married, in love with his "Immortal Beloved" but a love not reciprocated, first hard of hearing and then stone deaf for years on end, his late music coming from deep within the inner recesses of his mind. He heard none of it. Talk about loneliness.

At different times in Pat's life, there'd been different favorites. Beethoven's Opus 18 No. 6, an early effort at the genre, had been Pat's best loved at first, the opening few measures filled with get-go impishness and muscularity. It was pure, youthful exuberance, filled with confidence and perfectly crafted—the cocksure young Beethoven saying 'look out, I've arrived,' to the party of august peers preceding him, including his teacher and the father of the string quartet, Franz Joseph Haydn.

Next, Pat favored Opus 127, the first of the last five quartets and written when the composer was totally deaf. The wall of sound at the very beginning of the piece, the exquisite turns of phrase in the slow movement that put Mozart to shame, the foot-stomping Texas barroom climax of the last movement. Fall off your seat music. It enthralled Pat.

Incredible stuff.

These days, Pat obsessed about Opus 95, nicknamed the *Serioso*, from Beethoven's so-called 'middle compositional period.' Filled with drama and intensity (hence the nickname), Pat loved the finale's surprise ending. The great master first telling fate, 'c'mon, come get me, c'mon,' and then turning on a dime into light-heartedness. Pat understood Opus 95's coda loudly and clearly.

Life is a joke... Better get used to it. Life is one big joke.

Finishing up the tour, a sense of professionalism took over. Job accepted. Thumbing through reams of Mozart, Boccherini, Brahms, and the overly prolific Dvorak left Pat with just one thought.

This is child's play, absolute child's play. Like igniting the world's largest leaf pile. One match. Nothing more.

◊   ◊   ◊

The practice of burning leaves, once a storied New England tradition signaling the end of fall and beginning of winter, initiated Pat into the ritual of fire. With the strike of a match, and if lit on the underlying pavement, a nice circle-of-life type touch, a hefty pyramid of leaves reduced quickly to ash. The lovely, nutty aroma of burning leaves, the slight tearing of the eyes, stayed etched in Pat's memory. At a young age—seven, eight, nine, the exact age didn't matter—Pat became a leaf burner. Leaf raking and the task's subsequent reward, leaf burning, became a much-anticipated and coveted event. An irrational attachment to it developed, or so everyone thought, as fall became Pat's favorite season by far.

Leaf burning had long been banned due to environmental and safety concerns. The end of the annual ritual left Pat bereaved and desperate in an animalistic, primitive way.

What bullshit. How about banning SUVs instead? They're much bigger polluters. And how many people die in them every day?

Without the intoxicating, hypnotic effect of fall leaf

burning, bigger and more destructive activities emerged. "No leaves, huh?" Pat muttered during the first few arson attacks. After years and years at the job, though, it wasn't until seeing and touching all that sheet music in the Barnstable music school library that leaf burning popped back into Pat's mind.

CHAPTER 3

Friday, July 16, 2021

The fires were spectacular. Both buildings blazed gloriously, separated by about twelve miles as the crow flies, and ignited forty-five minutes apart. The Mashpee Arts Center went up first, followed shortly by Cape Now's Barnstable music school building. At their peak, the combined intensity and size of the fires created a glow over the entire Middle Cape. Evening passengers on the ferries back to the mainland from Nantucket and Martha's Vineyard couldn't understand the spectacle. Looking north, the sky glowed orange, as if remnants of the day's earlier sunset had returned, repeating itself in a different direction.

The Mashpee Arts Center, known as MAC to those who held it near and dear, was well beyond the halfway point of its expansion project. The project aimed to turn MAC's modest set of buildings into what its executive director proudly claimed would be the "Lincoln Center of Cape Cod." With flammable construction materials all over the site, including the main performance hall's four hundred wooden seat frames stacked neatly on pallets, it was an easy job.

The MAC fire was just the kick-off, and a decoy at that. The true task at hand lay ahead, so Pat left without waiting to see if the MAC fire really took. There was no need to hang around; Pat knew it would succeed, and also knew the danger of lingering. The contract called for fifty to sixty percent destruction of the half-built MAC complex. Pat got paid if the percentage reached at least that level. Given the on-site conditions, especially the cheap wooden performance hall seats, it was a pretty low bar to meet.

A no-brainer, this one.

Pat developed the percentage burned approach years ago. Now it was an established industry standard for arsonists. "Why not use percentages?" Pat had asked fellow members of the arson underworld at their surreptitious annual get-together in Las Vegas. "Different clients have different needs, so it makes sense." For the business owner who simply wanted to pocket a little insurance money while keeping going, a low percentage burn made the most sense. For the former husband taking revenge on the 'ex' living in their nice house with her new beau, a much higher percentage always prevailed.

Pat never worried about getting paid. Never asked for payment up front, not even a down payment. The one client who stiffed Pat, claiming that the percentage reached in the burn wasn't what they'd agreed to—the client wanted his restaurant closed for a couple of months, requiring a twenty to thirty percent burn—learned the hard way. The percentage at the next fire, at the client's house: one hundred percent.

To get over to Barnstable from Mashpee, Pat first went north on Route 130, then in the village of Forestdale turned northeast onto a small local road leading up to Route 6. The main highway on the Cape, Route 6 ran west to east for its first half, and then at the Cape's elbow made almost a ninety degree turn and ran north up to the tip: Provincetown. As Pat headed east on Route 6, fire trucks in groups of two or three barreled by in the opposite direction, travelling the route taken by Pat and rushing desperately to help with the MAC fire.

Perfect, just perfect.

The plan couldn't have gone any better. Cape Cod's firefighting forces were lean to begin with. It wasn't New York City or Boston after all. With most of the Cape's firefighting power directed to the MAC fire, what came next would be devastating.

Cape Now's Barnstable music school didn't stand a chance. Not a chance. A good-sized crowd watched the flames engulfing the building from the adjoining property. Pulling into the parking lot of the Burger King and Mobil gas station at Exit 15 off of Route 6, Pat eased into the mob and fired up a cigarette.

Well done. Very well done.

Everyone watched the Barnstable music school inferno from a hundred or so yards away, letting forth "ohs" and "ahs" every time the flames flickered above the pitch pines separating the two properties. The burning building silhouetted the trees. The sight was mesmerizing and horrifying at the same time—that perverse, contradictory, yet common human response to witnessing tragedy.

Not Pat though. With the first half of the job done, Pat felt the most intense pleasure possible, almost sexual in nature, coming and going in waves as the spectacle unfolded. What a feeling. What a sight.

Burn baby burn.

Two weeks later, Pat Kimmell's arson artistry was on display again. The second half of the job proved more challenging. The geographic distance was much greater, with Wellfleet located on the Outer Cape and Falmouth on the Upper Cape, fifty-five to sixty miles away by car. There were also three buildings to handle this time, not two. The planning of this next part called upon Pat's strategic and creative skills in a big way.

Just the best.

The Wellfleet Theater arson attack called only for modest damage. One of Pat's buddies from the dark side of Boston received the assignment, getting careful coaching on what to do and when to do it.

"There's no room for fucking up on this, got it?" Pat said, with an intensity that made the consequences clear. "Got it? Let me know as soon as it's underway."

"Underway."

The one-word text came in at 9:13 p.m., giving Pat precise notice as to the moment the destruction in Wellfleet began. It came from a disposable cell phone that would never see the light of day following the removal and destruction of its SIM card. It buzzed through to a similar phone in Pat's pocket. By the time the Wellfleet, Truro, and Eastham fire departments put the fire out and called it a night, Pat's buddy was well on the mainland side of the Sagamore Bridge.

The more exciting and interesting challenge for Pat came from having to destroy Cape Now's Falmouth music school building and its Lowlands Theater simultaneously. Pat's sense of perfection yearned for a conjoined burn of some sort—an arc of flame—since the two buildings stood across a wide, shared parking lot from each other. A huge, sustained electrical impulse came to mind. That really excited Pat.

How cool would that be? Probably my best work yet!

After considerable research, Pat reluctantly concluded it couldn't be done. With the task soon at hand, practical thinking set in, and with it, more and more focus. Incendiary devices were chosen, enough to take out a small town, let alone two buildings, and one of them the wooden, rickety Lowlands Theater. Built in the 1890s, the Lowlands Theater was also stuffed to the gills with old canvas and wooden sets and props, and contained a leftover paint collection in its cellar similar to those found in the few remaining independent hardware stores left on the Cape.

The road into the two buildings helped, a narrow, twisty, unlit passageway. Fire trucks and other emergency vehicles negotiated it slowly and with care, especially at night. With the destruction started, Pat approached cautiously up Falmouth's Beebe Forest hiking trail from a parking lot half a mile away. Getting close, and wearing the omnipresent hoodie, Pat took to the woods and stood a short distance off the trail, peering through the trees as the conflagration took down both buildings. Watching the music school and theater succumb to the flames filled Pat with great satisfaction, an authentic, deep emotional response to a job well done. Happiness. Joy. Unrivaled pleasure.

BURN BABY BURN.

◊　◊　◊

Arson is notoriously difficult to solve. The percentage of arson attacks ending with an arrest is fifteen to twenty percent. You have to be a real dope to get caught at it. One way is to be a gawker, to admire one's own work too closely, and to do so repeatedly. Several of the most famous serial arsonists got caught like that, watching their own handiwork up close. Using the same materials and heat stress points on every job sometimes gets you nabbed too, because doing so gives the FBI, police, and insurance investigators too much information. It allows them to work with patterns. Some solved arson attacks came from linking patterns to people.

Meticulous work went into each and every job Pat undertook, in part because of almost being caught once. Pat never found out what led to nearly being nabbed; what saved Pat's ass, though, was a text from a buddy in their apartment building, saying that the police had let themselves into Pat's apartment and were waiting inside. Pat never went home again. Not to that apartment.

After kicking back and taking some time off, Pat got back to business, adding a new item to the due diligence checklist for each job. In addition to researching the target building's history, construction materials, contents, estimated time of fire department response, best incendiary devices on the market, and client motivations, Pat now also looked at local police and insurance investigation rosters, so as to gauge what the post-arson response might be.

"Well, well, well," Pat chuckled, after looking into the

Cape's arson investigation capabilities. "If it isn't Hennessey, good old Hennessey. It's incredible... all these years... what a connection. Something lousy must have happened to his career, to go from being an up-and-comer in the Boston Police Department to looking for consulting breadcrumbs on the Cape. What a loser."

Small world. Hennessey had been in the Boston apartment years ago, leading the team waiting to arrest Pat. A rendezvous that never happened. Slouched down and watching from the car, Pat took cell phone pictures of the three cops emerging hours later, empty-handed and defeated. It took no time at all to identify which law enforcement members had been in on the attempted arrest.

Several weeks later, a fire broke out at Hennessey's house in South Boston. A small fire, it damaged only fifteen to twenty percent of the rear of the house, and was attributed to Hennessey's carelessness with the grill that evening.

"A few too many scotch and sodas with the steaks, huh, Drink?" a neighbor joked.

"Yeah, yeah. Must've been that," replied Hennessey.

Everyone ribbed him about it. Red-faced, he picked up the insurance check a few days after the adjuster assessed the damage. Neighborhood contractors had the house back in one piece, better than ever, in a month. All's well that ends well.

Hennessey knew better. There was absolutely no chance he left the grill on, or in a place where it could start a fire. He let his shaken and furious ex-wife believe it was his fault, could still hear her saying, "How could you, Drink, how could you? With the children asleep upstairs?" She wouldn't be able to deal with the truth about the dark, sordid world Hennessey inadvertently pulled his young family into.

From there on out, he always knew how high the stakes were. Always knew. And year after year, one person was at the top of his 'get even' list: Pat Kimmell. Threaten Hennessey's family, his children? His steel-trap-like mind would never let it go, even if it took decades to resolve in his favor. The treatment the snitch Donnie Zimmer received at

Hennessey's hands was nothing compared to what was coming Pat Kimmell's way.

I'm tracking you down. You better believe it. And when I do, look out. You'll need a lot more than a prosthetic leg when I'm done with you.

CHAPTER 4

Tuesday, August 17, 2021

Kachunk Kachunk. After meeting with the Wexners, Hennessey took the Bourne Bridge, not the Sagamore, on his way to check out the arson scene in Falmouth. Better late than never. The less travelled of the two gateway bridges to Cape Cod, the Bourne led to the Cape's southwest reaches. Less travelled, relatively speaking. Traffic on the bridges was a nightmare almost all the time these days. *Kachunk Kachunk.*

The focus of his upcoming visit perplexed Hennessey. While the Mashpee Arts Center needed to start all over again with its half-completed "Lincoln Center of Cape Cod" project, it was Cape Now, known as CAN, and the largest arts and culture group in the region, that bore the brunt of the craziness. A month ago, CAN's Barnstable music school building went up in flames. Completely destroyed. Then, two weeks later, its Falmouth music school building and Lowlands Theater were reduced to ash. Hennessey was befuddled.

Why would anyone burn down Cape Cod performing arts buildings? Utterly inexplicable.

The gravity of it all came home to roost with another loss

experienced by CAN: Peter Warbles.

The building and house manager of the Lowlands Theater, Warbles epitomized one of those lost souls who acted impetuously on the dream of never leaving the Cape after spending a magical summer there. His important, if minor, summer stock roles at the Lowlands Theater during his junior and senior college years had convinced him, as did his revelatory experiences with his first-ever girlfriend, Susan Smith, who'd spent one Memorial to Labor Day stretch educating Peter while Kate Bush's "The Sensual World" played over and over again in the background.

Overstaying his time on the Cape by decades, not years, Peter devolved into a balding, paunchy middle-aged guy whose dreams destroyed him. CAN hadn't had the heart to let him go, so he managed the box office during the summer, and the building year-round, the latter amounting to a glorified janitor's job. In exchange, Peter received a couple hundred bucks a week and the Lowlands Theater's uninsulated attic apartment, where he sweltered in the summer and shivered in the winter.

He woke gasping and coughing on his old Sears Roebuck bed the night of the fire, smoke pouring under the quarter-inch gap at the bottom of the door to the apartment. Opening it, Peter looked down into an inferno, flames climbing the steps toward him. An unfathomable terror gripped him as he realized the back staircase was blocked, filled with theater sets and other paraphernalia he placed there through the years. Completely impassable. Calling out the window was hopeless. The closest neighbors to the theater were a good half-mile away. He made the effort nonetheless. He then peed his pants.

Peter heard the fire truck sirens in his dazed semi-conscious state. Death imminent, he heard other sirens too, the Sirens of Odysseus. They sang to him with indescribable beauty about the meaning and preciousness of his small and insignificant life, of his largely unrealized existence. Fear disappeared. Bitterness and remorse as well. Vivid, instantaneous images put Peter at ease, of a family never had with Susan Smith, and children who filled his heart with a warmth he'd not experienced before: paternal love.

A committed thespian to the bitter end, Peter died rallying his troops, exhorting them onward, the great King Henry on a brilliant St. Crispin's Day:

> This story shall the good man teach his son;
> And Crispin Crispian shall ne'er go by,
> From this day to the ending of the world,
> But we in it shall be remember'd;
> We few, we happy few, we band of brothers;
> For he today that sheds his blood with me
> Shall be my brother.
> William Shakespeare, *Henry V*

With the location of his body still taped off among the charred ruins, Peter's actual last role at the Lowlands Theater, and a lonely, horrible one at that, was as a victim in the felony murder case staring Hennessey in the face.

Felony murder as a legal doctrine dates back to the thirteenth century. Like the English language, it came to us from across the Atlantic. Following England's lead a few decades back, the United Kingdom and all other members of the British Commonwealth struck the felony murder rule from their criminal statute books. Use of the rule is now uniquely American and invites emotional, vigorous debate.

A surge of anger coursed through Hennessey as he confronted the case. Peter Warbles died when an arsonist burned down the Lowlands Theater, so, regardless of intent—intent, or *mens rea*, in all other situations being the keystone component of any criminal act—his death was a murder. It didn't matter a whit if it was completely unintended. In states like Massachusetts it didn't even matter who died or who caused the death. You commit a felony and someone dies during the crime, you get charged with murder. Completely unforeseen or accidental deaths happening during felonies trigger murder charges for those unlucky criminals caught in the maw, in the vise-grip, of the felony murder rule.

What the hell? Another felony murder. How screwed up is that?

It wasn't only law professors and other eggheads who pondered the fairness and role of felony murder in our criminal justice system. Hennessey's life had been touched directly by it. His brother Joey was convicted of felony murder after one of his partners in crime died inside the Chester Savings Bank that fateful afternoon in Charlestown. Joey received a life sentence, with no chance of parole, merely for driving the getaway car.

Like England, a few progressive states had already abolished the felony murder rule when Joey ran afoul of the law, but not Massachusetts. And what was worse, Massachusetts used the toughest approach to felony murder, the proximate cause theory as opposed to the agency theory. Hennessey thought about it every day.

That's why Joey was convicted of murder even though it was the security guard who shot and killed one of Joey's buddies. Joey wasn't even in the bank when the shooting occurred. WTF!

Yes, Hennessey knew all the intricacies, all the arguments for and against the felony murder rule. He also knew that the Massachusetts Supreme Judicial Court recently limited how prosecutors could use the rule, in a way that would've made it inapplicable to Joey. He dwelled on it constantly.

◊ ◊ ◊

"Detective Hennessey! Well, I'll be. What a pleasant surprise running into you." It was Ben Maisky, the head of the Archduke Insurance Company's investigations unit. Police and insurance company investigations often entwine themselves, competing and feeding off each other like vines coiling and growing around the same tree trunk. So it was going to be in the investigations of the CAN arsons. When

Hennessey worked in Boston, where Archduke Insurance was headquartered, he often collaborated with Maisky. As a young detective in the Boston Police Department, he learned a great deal from Maisky and had great respect for the guy.

Maisky lowered his glasses to the tip of his nose and looked out over the top of them. "It's been years. I knew you were down here on the Cape. Heard it somewhere, can't remember when or where. Consulting these days, right? They're lucky to have you, whoever's got you on this one."

Maisky defined eccentric genius to Hennessey. The two of them caught up on the Red Sox, the Patriots, and the Cape's best fishing spots. They debated whether Maisky should hop on the retirement train and head down the track to the Cape.

"I enjoy it here," said Hennessey. "Seriously. Life's quiet and smooth, except for the summer months. Move down here with us."

When Maisky demurred, Hennessey took his leave. "It's been great to see you, Ben. I've got to head Mid-Cape, out to the BCPD, or I'd stay and catch up longer. Let me know if you come up with anything. Call, or text, or email me. Or call my colleague at the BCPD, Detective Phil Lipman, and let him know."

Excessively jovial, Maisky's persona hid a formidable character and mind. Archduke faced an $8-10 million payout for CAN's destroyed music school buildings and Lowlands Theater. He was all over it. He'd come up with a few interesting leads when poking around the burnt-out shell of CAN's Barnstable music school building and the surrounding area, including the Burger King and Mobil gas station property next door. One thought stuck with Maisky.

Maybe the fires are tied back to CAN? If it's an inside job, Archduke won't be on the hook. Who knows? It's way too early to say.

Maisky was deep into his third hour of scouring the Beebe Forest woods when something caught his eye.

"Well, I'll be. A funny place to find a cigarette butt, no?" he said to himself. He picked it up gently with gloved fingers, stuck it into a plastic bag, and continued rambling: "I'll match it against the butts found in the parking lot in Barnstable, where all the gawkers watched the fire. If there's a match I'll take it further, see if I can get DNA off of them."

"My bet, there's a link," he went on. "Better than even odds."

"You're on," Maisky retorted to himself.

CHAPTER 5

Tuesday, August 17, 2021

The BCPD headquarters sat at the back of a non-descript county office building, a dreary one-story thing with 'built in the 1960s' written all over it and begging to be demolished. Arriving mid-afternoon, Hennessey found the comely, gracious, somewhat reticent department administrator, Kelly Coughlin, at the front desk. He chatted with her longer than he should have, then headed in to see the BCPD's only detective, Phil Lipman. Lipman had hired Hennessey and was one of the few members of the Barnstable police force Hennessey actually liked.

The Wayland police had put the finger in a small modern styrofoam container filled with dry ice. It looked like a tiny insulated beach cooler.

"Someone's lunch. Fish food, or finger food?" Hennessey cracked, handing Lipman the container. Lipman looked forward to putting the finger through a forensic analysis, even though the Wayland police had already done so. The Wayland report confirmed the following: It was a male finger, the fourth finger from a left hand—of course, since the wedding band came with it—and in a state of decomposition indicating it had been separated from its owner one to three weeks earlier. Wayland even got a print off of the finger; unfortunately, no match existed in either the Massachusetts State Police or FBI databases. As for a DNA test, without anything to match the finger against, it didn't make sense to do one. The purpose of DNA testing was to link potentially incriminating evidence, hair, blood, saliva, or semen to a particular individual. No individual existed in this instance.

That no one with a cut-off finger had rushed into a Cape hospital emergency room or urgent care center intrigued Hennessey and Lipman. They inquired, first on the Cape, then throughout Massachusetts, and finally throughout New England. No construction accident, no boating accident, no cooking accident, no mishap of any sort had been reported. Nothing.

Lipman thought he knew the answer. Some poor fisherman lost it while fishing illegally. In this age of rapidly diminishing natural resources, and the bitter, vindictive squabbling it produced, the fines for illegal fishing were astronomical. Criminal charges could even be brought.

"That's gotta be it," he said to Hennessey with conviction. "Who else would let a cut-off finger and lost wedding band go unreported?" Lipman figured that a fisherman decided it wasn't worth getting medical treatment, despite the physical agony of losing a finger and the emotional agony of losing a wedding band with it. The risk of getting nailed was too great.

Hennessey wasn't so sure.

Lipman walked Hennessey out. Kelly remained in her entryway administrator's seat. As the three of them spoke out in the reception area, Hennessey vaguely noted her fetching smile, her winsome voice, her innate intelligence, the tautness of her shirt across her breasts, parking it all somewhere in the deep recesses of his male mind. Halfway down the long corridor when the front desk phone rang, Hennessey slowed ever so slightly. Lipman glanced quickly at Kelly, then picked it up. After listening for a few seconds, he cupped the mouthpiece and shouted: "Hennessey… come back here."

◊　◊　◊

Millie Nickerson found the foot. She discovered it during the Monomoy Island Bird Inventory Club's bird counting and exclosure set-up work that afternoon. The group went by the acronym MIBIC. Uttered quickly, and in a staccato, repeated manner, it sounded like the call of the sanderling, a shorebird MIBIC monitored carefully. Club members often greeted each other with "mibic mibic" whenever they ran into each other on Chatham's Main Street, or at the Stop and Shop in Orleans. The "mibic mibic mibic" response, when overheard, invariably left those outside the caste scratching their heads.

The chilling mist and poor visibility meant most folks overlooked the day's MIBIC bird counting and exclosure set-up work, even though it'd been scheduled for the afternoon. Millie and her husband Robert never passed on their assigned days. The Nickersons were two of the few founding MIBIC members still alive and took their bird stewardship responsibilities seriously.

Robert wore a button-down shirt when undertaking his MIBIC duties; he had for the past fifty years and always would. As he buttoned up his thread-bare Brooks Brothers Oxford slowly, and to the very top out of deference to the weather, he reminisced fondly about his and Millie's years as active citizens of Boston's Beacon Hill, as part of the city's upper crust.

Ah, once a Boston Brahmin, always a Boston Brahmin. I love living down here on the Cape, but how I miss Louisburg Square.

On the trip out, they quibbled testily about bringing exclosure materials. Millie thought the timing was right; Robert thought it too early to find any piping plover nests. Millie almost always got the upper hand in these arguments, no matter that history proved her wrong more often than not. The exclosure materials were with them.

"What a waste of time and energy, lugging all this stuff out here for nothing," he huffed, carefully speaking upwind so that Millie wouldn't catch it.

Coming off the skiff, the Nickersons headed north along the beach, while the other MIBICers went in the other direction.

"Careful now, Millie... careful now, my spring chicken," he chortled, as his octogenarian wife bolted from the boat. "Millie, Mildred! Don't get too far out ahead of me," he said forcefully.

"You're always bossing me around, Buster," she shouted back, storming ahead and not caring if he heard her or not.

As they took their cell phones out to snap pictures of the different shoreline bird tracks they came across, Robert thought about his beloved Monomoy. The small island, a sand spit really, represented the mainland's last defense before the mighty open Atlantic Ocean. Transformations were afoot, the result of more intense storms and rising sea levels, increased human traffic (the Chatham Town Board, who controlled it, frequently received Robert's caustic views on visitation to the island), and changing fauna.

In the past, seeing a harbor or gray seal on Monomoy, or in the waters around the island, brought an emotional high from experiencing one of nature's rarities, at least to those with the sensitivity for such things. After several decades of protection under the federal Marine Mammal Protection Act, which made it a crime to kill or harm seals, the seal population was totally out of control. The seals were almost as common as seagulls, with tens of thousands of them living on or around the small island. They ruled supreme, much to the consternation of the Nickersons and others. MIBIC members rooted for the birds.

Millie, ever intrepid at eighty-one, insisted on a step or two advantage over Robert. Walking slightly in the surf, she sang the opening of Orff's *Carmina Burana* boldly to herself. It was her favorite piece of music, even though she knew it was schlock. Taking pictures of the shore-side bird tracks and absorbed in her work, she was only a few feet away when she noticed a grey non-descript blob half buried in the sand.

What's that?

At first she thought it a dead mew, a common seagull whose carcasses were frequently sighted on Monomoy and Cape beaches. It was only upon using her walking stick to poke and prod—curiosity always got the better of Millie—that she realized she'd unearthed something quite remarkable: a human foot. Robert called it in, since the uniqueness of her find caused Millie to drop her cell phone in the surf.

Hennessey and Lipman met the folks from MIBIC at the Chatham pier. The group was agog about their discovery. Fortunately, MIBIC always carried a plastic bag or two on the boat for the odds and ends found during Monomoy outings. Usually the bags filled up with trash; today the main catch was a human foot. It made for an abbreviated MIBIC work outing, although a couple of people, including Millie, argued against cutting the afternoon short and going back simply because of what they'd found.

Robert Nickerson was proud of his bagging work. Millie, who usually took charge of everything, had been a little too flabbergasted to handle the task.

Handing the decimated foot to Lipman as he stepped off the boat, Robert looked quizzically at the detectives, "You gentlemen want to go back out to Monomoy, so I can show you where we found it?"

"Probably not a bad idea," Lipman responded. "Hennessey, what do you think?"

"I agree. But the tide's come up quite a bit since Robert called us. I wonder whether it'd really be useful."

Robert jumped in. "Well, I anticipated that, so I built a cairn of shells and beach stones well above the high tide line, marking the spot."

By the time Hennessey, Lipman, and the now somewhat

calmer Robert made it down the beach at Monomoy to where the improvised cairn stood—Hennessey wondered if it was only people who wore button-down shirts to the beach who built cairns—the incoming tide had obliterated the exact location of Millie's find. Much like a footprint or sand castle at water's edge, the spot where the foot had been dug out of the sand was completely smoothed over. After digging and splashing about for ten or so minutes under the expert direction of Robert, the two detectives called it quits.

Robert captained the MIBIC skiff back, allowing Hennessey and Lipman to put their heads together on what was going down. They stood at the bow of the boat with their backs to Robert so he couldn't hear what they were saying. Lipman shook his head slightly and leaned in toward Hennessey with a grim look on his face.

"I don't know what to think," he said. "Body parts showing up on our beaches. We've got something terrible on our hands."

"Wish I could disagree with you, Phil. I can't," said Hennessey. "This is one of the weirdest things I've ever come across, that's for sure. I'm stumped by it."

Lipman would've howled except for the seriousness of the situation. Hennessey brought a wicked irreverence to the work they did together. Nothing unprofessional in the least, just a perspective, an eye, that always saw the irony and intrinsic dark humor to the situation before them.

"We've got to try to keep the news under control," said Hennessey. "It'll be terrible for it to get out that human body parts are washing up on the Cape's beaches."

"Yes, indeed," said Lipman. "The problem is, that as far as today's discovery goes, we're not the only ones who know. The MIBIC folks know too."

After huddling a little longer, the two of them turned back toward Robert and made their way to him as the skiff bounced lightly on the calm sea.

"Robert," said Lipman, "we're thinking that we've got quite a delicate situation on our hands, with what you found today. We wanted to see what we might do about it with you and your MIBIC friends. The last thing we want is to turn off visitors to the Cape, scare them away, with a story about a foot being found on one of our beaches. Do you think you and your friends can keep quiet until Detective Hennessey and I get a handle on it... until we figure out how a foot could've possible ended up on Monomoy Island? What do you think?"

Robert grinned back at the two of them. Still spry at eighty-three, he wasn't giving up on life yet, and he hadn't had so much fun, hadn't had so much adrenaline blasting through him, in God knows how long.

"Well, Millie and I can keep it under wraps. I know that. My guess is that our fellow MIBICers can too. I'll get on the phone with them as soon as we get back. And I'll call our daughter and two grandsons too. I sent them photos of our prize find from the scene. Pretty good with all this darn technology stuff, aren't I?" chuckled Robert.

By the time the three of them were back on shore, the Monomoy Island Foot was well on its way to becoming a social media sensation. Robert and Millie's teenage grandsons made sure of that. The boys took the few photos Grandpa sent and worked technological miracles on them of the sort only their generation knew how to do. The thirty-second meme of the half-buried foot digging itself out of the sand, then hopping away by itself toward the east end of the island, like a pogo stick, spread like wildfire on the internet. Hennessey and Lipman's cell phones tipped them off to it as they were getting back to shore.

Several reporters awaited them on the Chatham dock, a mob by Cape Cod standards. Reminding Robert of what he'd agreed to, the two detectives turned to the media at hand.

"Can we see it?" asked one of them.

"I assume you're talking about what appears to be a human foot, found out on Monomoy Island earlier this afternoon," Lipman responded tersely. "No, we don't have whatever it might be with us. And we are not, I repeat NOT, making any assumptions as to what it is."

Luckily enough, before he and Hennessey headed out to Monomoy with Robert, Lipman called Kelly at headquarters. She'd come over with a locking cooler filled with ice bags, and taken the foot back to the station with her. So much for the reporters' prying eyes, at least for the time being. Hennessey appreciated Kelly's above and beyond act.

What a good egg she is.

Sensing that Lipman might get himself into trouble by continuing in an aggressive and hostile manner, Hennessey stepped in. "You know, we're as curious about what our bird-loving friends found this afternoon as you are. It's too early to say anything though. We will certainly share information with you as it develops. The one thing we'd ask is that you be responsible, and sensitive, about any reporting you do before hearing from us about what we have on our hands."

As the two of them wended their way off the pier toward land, a reporter blurted out for all to hear, "there's a rumor that other body parts have also been found on Cape beaches. Any truth to that? What do you know about that?"

Lipman kept walking.

Hennessey whirled around quickly. "Where'd you hear that?" he asked, staring at the reporter who posed the unfortunate question, and who in a nanosecond opened a veritable Pandora's Box. After what seemed like an eternity, Hennessey replied, "I've no comment. No comment at all."

◊ ◊ ◊

Back at the BCPD, a strange group awaited the detectives: Nancy Springer, a MA Department of Environmental Protection environmental police officer; Darlene McCoy, the State's marine biologist stationed on the Cape; and Reggie Smith, a local fisherman out of Eastham. Springer was the only one Hennessey recognized.

"Gentlemen," she said. "It's good to see you. I'm glad you've arrived. We've got quite a situation on our hands." Hennessey knew instantly that Smith had been nabbed at something. A quick look at his face said it all. It portrayed shame and defiance in equal parts.

"Mr. Smith here caught himself one heck of a specimen," continued Springer. "Come take a look."

The DEP's Ford F-250 was parked out back of the building. Laid out in its flatbed was the largest fish Hennessey had ever seen: a great white shark. It wasn't big as far as great whites go, but it was still ten or eleven feet long. To get as much of it into the truck's flatbed as possible, the shark was put in diagonally on its side. A foot or two of the shark stuck out the back and the truck's tailgate couldn't be shut. So a ridiculous little red bandana had been tied around its tail. The regulatory system at work. Although the drive to BCPD headquarters was ten miles or so from where the shark was brought in, there was no danger of it bouncing or falling out of the flatbed of the pickup truck. Not something that tipped the scale at around 1,100 pounds and that needed hoisting onto the truck by a fishing pier pulley designed to get boats out of the water.

All the commercial fishermen worth their salt on the Cape knew that catching and killing a great white shark was strictly verboten. As of 1997, federal law prohibited it, around the same time federal law began protecting seals and other marine mammals. Massachusetts designated great white sharks a protected species in 2005.

Reggie Smith was unrepentant, and spoke with a coarse, hardened New England accent. "Take my commercial fishing license if you want," he spat out. "Fine me if you want too. As if I've got any dough to pay the State.

"These damn things are killing our fisheries. There's more and more of them, and less and less fish. You all could give a rat's ass, but for the handful of us still making a living at sea, or trying to, what you're looking at right there is public enemy number one."

Smith laughed bitterly and continued. "What a life it is. What... a... life. Birds protected, seals protected, whales and dolphins protected, and even these killers protected," he said, waving a hand in the direction of the dead shark.

"When am I gonna get 'protected status,' huh? When's my wife and two kids gonna get it? Her bustin' her butt at the Holiday Inn in Hyannis, the two kids doing just ok in school and in the community. My catch goes down and down every month. More and more rules, regulations, and other bullshit to deal with. Who's going to pay our house mortgage, the boat mortgage? Huh?"

As he vented, Smith stared right at Springer. He viewed her as the environmental do-gooder responsible for the mess he was in. Wouldn't he love to land a grappling hook in her and pull real hard. "Screw the DEP," he said defiantly. "You're a bunch of elite, self-righteous do-gooders."

Lipman and Hennessey got it. They commiserated with the life Smith faced, even though they believed what scientists like Darlene McCoy told them: that the Cape's fast-growing great white shark population had a negligible effect on its fisheries. Hennessey felt for the Reggie Smiths of Cape Cod. He identified with them all, understood the predicament they faced as their way of life disappeared—slowly, surely, relentlessly.

This guy believes completely in what he's done, thought Hennessey.

Lipman took Smith gently by the elbow and gestured him toward the BCPD office. "Come inside with me, Mr. Smith. We'll talk about it and see what we might be able to do about this unhappy situation." Sensing a light touch was about to be applied and damned if she'd let that happen, Springer started objecting, moving toward the two men. Faster than one might expect, Hennessey, who was still a very good athlete after years of indolence, stepped right in front of her, putting himself between Lipman and Smith. Springer fumed, knowing she'd boxed herself in. She was the one who brought the matter to the BCPD rather than to the state police. The matter was now in Lipman's hands.

Hennessey stayed outside with Springer and State Marine Biologist Darlene McCoy.

"The State wants a necropsy performed on the great white," said McCoy, explaining her presence at the awkward, unfortunate scene. It also explained her attire. McCoy wore girlie rubber boots, a one-piece surgical outfit, and heavy skin-tight gloves.

"Hand me up that box, please," she said to Springer and Hennessey, nodding toward a heavy equipment box filled with a combination of carpenter and surgeon's tools, and with a bumper sticker on the top reading "BITE ME." McCoy's attitude: no-nonsense. Wielding a large knife, she knelt next to the underbelly of the shark and expertly opened it up.

First, the shark's liver came out. It needed to be taken back to the State marine lab to be weighed and analyzed. Then, McCoy proceeded further into the animal's gut. The shark's most recent prey came out in bits and pieces—cod, striped bass, a plastic bottle, all sorts of fishing gear, tuna, and more. Great whites were voracious, no doubt about it.

"What's this?" said McCoy, cutting the shark open further down toward its tail, and pulling a gelatinous blob the size of a basketball out of the shark's lower intestine. "Oh, my God. Oh-My-God!" she exclaimed, loudly and excitedly, a touch of horror in her usually unflappable voice. "It's part of a human torso. I'm sure of it."

Sea Interlude #1

While there's still lingering debate about it, the growing consensus among scientists is that, since around 1950, we've lived in the Anthropocene Epoch. Anthropocene translates from Greek as the "recent age of man." The name of our current geologic age is a center stage bow to Homo sapiens. Its distinctive characteristic, its uniqueness, is as an era in which one species, and one species alone, dominates and is substantially changing all aspects of the Earth.

Earth has never experienced anything like us. We now number 7.9 billion and counting, and inhabit every corner of the planet. A lucky few of us, from a numbers perspective at least, get to roam at will wherever we want.

Virtually all other species are at our beck and call, at our mercy. Should we want to ignore the political, economic, intellectual, and moral dimensions of doing so, we could easily eliminate any number of species through a concerted, specifically-aimed campaign. The African elephant? Gone in a year or two if we wanted, maybe sooner. With the push of a few buttons, we can also by and large wipe out our own species. The resulting severe destabilization of the planet would usher in the next geologic age in short order, the post-Anthropocene Epoch.

We are the ultimate apex predator.

Yet other apex predators remain. They live an uneasy co-existence with us. Without any of the tools derived from our intelligence and ingenuity—guns, knives, spears, pepper spray, escape vehicles—we are no match for them. Ask anyone who has survived an attack by a grizzly bear or a cougar. The only thing we have going for us when confronting one of these apex predators in the wild is that we are a terrestrial species too. Putting brains and feet together and backing away slowly from a grizzly or cougar has saved a life or two.

As a terrestrial species, though, we are disadvantaged in the ocean. The ocean is not our home and never will be. And we must always remember, always, that the ocean contains apex predators. The great white shark is among them.

CHAPTER 6

Friday, August 20, 2021

All hell broke loose during the few days it took to get the DNA and other forensic test results back on the various body parts arriving, one by one, at the BCPD.

The press didn't know about the human torso. No one knew except for a handful of people. After the shock of McCoy's discovery wore off, Hennessey convinced both McCoy and Springer that it was in no one's interest to share with anyone else what had been pulled out of the dissected great white shark—at least what it looked to be—until testing confirmed the grimness of what they had on their hands. Neither of them took much convincing.

"Thanks, you two," said Hennessey. "I'll call you with the forensic results as soon as we get them."

Nancy Springer left in a complete daze, forgetting entirely about the sizeable fine and weekend in jail she'd envisioned for Reggie Smith.

Since there was rarely daily news of substance on the Cape, the discovery of what appeared to be a human foot out on Monomoy Island, and dark rumors about additional body parts washing up on other Cape beaches, sent the fourth estate into a frenzy. It didn't help that the Monomoy Island

Foot meme already had 400,000 hits, from all around the world.

After receiving three calls and umpteen text messages in fifteen minutes, Hennessey turned off his cell phone. Lipman let his office answering machine handle the duty. At the very end of the day, though, they took the time to meet with Larry Sylvester, the executive director of the Cape Cod Chamber of Commerce. Larry came over to the BCPD from his office in Hyannis. He called Kelly. She let them know he was on his way over to visit and wouldn't take no for an answer.

"What do you mean you have nothing to tell me?" Sylvester asked incredulously. "Phil, it's me. How long have we known each other, huh? Since high school?" he went on.

"Larry," said Lipman, glancing quickly at Hennessey, "we really can't say anything at the moment. Rest assured, you'll be one of the very first people we call when we know what's going on, and when we've got something to share."

Sylvester wasn't going for it. "Can I see what you brought back today? Is it identifiable? And is it true you've found other body parts on other Cape beaches?"

Lipman and Hennessey gave him the silent treatment.

"Okay, don't tell me. The two of you not saying anything... that tells me everything. Know that. What a stinking disaster for the Cape," Sylvester moaned. "Think about what it'll do to tourism, our heart and soul. People will stay away in droves. A romantic stroll down the beach, a Kennedy Family-like touch football game, a power walk to help work off the week or the year, and then—'oh, hello foot, hello arm, hello head.' Gives me the creeps. It's a disaster. And it couldn't come at a worse time. Just as we're getting through the goddamned pandemic."

Lipman looked at Hennessey, who nodded almost imperceptibly.

"Larry," said Lipman, "I'll tell you something serious and discreet. Extremely discreet, understand? I'll charge you with something—anything—and throw the book at you if you share it with anyone... anyone at all."

"What was brought in from Monomoy sure looks like a human foot," continued Lipman. "And yes, a finger was definitely found. Taken home to Wayland by some young kid at the end of the family vacation."

"Oh boy," said Sylvester.

"There's more," continued Lipman. "The DEP brought over a dead great white shark in its flatbed truck. Caught illegally by one of our few remaining commercial fishermen. Poor guy. Nancy Springer from DEP enforcement wanted us to throw the book at him. We didn't."

"When Darlene McCoy, the State marine biologist, opened it up—they do that when anything big is caught, fish or mammal—she pulled out what appears to be part of a human torso. She's convinced of it. Hennessey and I think she's right."

Larry Sylvester looked at the wall above Lipman's head for some time, as if in a trance. His foot tapped the floor nervously, his slight quivering noticeable.

"Unbelievable, just unbelievable," he finally blurted out. "Someone else killed by a great white shark. The second death in a couple of years, on top of the non-lethal attacks too. The fools, the goddamn fools," Sylvester spat out, thinking about swimmers, surfers, paddle boarders, and others foolish enough to try their luck in waters teeming with great white sharks.

"This is apocalyptic for us," he continued. "We've got to keep as tight a handle on it as possible. Can you two deny it to the press, to the public?"

Hennessey and Lipman spoke simultaneously. "Absolutely not," Lipman said.

Hennessey said, "No way. Unethical for us to lie about it or otherwise cover it up."

"The cat's already out of the bag anyway," Lipman continued. "Millie and Robert Nickerson and their bird watching buddies know. The family in Wayland that found the finger knows, and God knows how many people they told. Half the world knows about the foot, thanks to that blasted meme."

"I can't believe it," Sylvester said, a look of defeat on his face. "What a string of bad luck we've had down here. A way of life, our way of life, is really at stake. The Cape of the past is gone. Commercial fishing is no longer a serious industry. It's a shell of what it once was. The Chinese have taken over the cranberry market with their government subsidies... those jerks. What's left? Tourism, where we cater and suck up to vacationers and the imperious wealthy. At least it puts food on the table for those of us lucky enough to call this magical place home. These blasted shark attacks are going to destroy us."

Getting up to leave, Sylvester sighed and asked, "Who was it?"

Lipman shrugged quizzically. Hennessey responded: "We're working on that, Larry, we're working on that."

Reporters came from New York City, Philadelphia, Washington, D.C., and other East Coast hubs, arriving the day after Millie Nickerson's discovery. The Monomoy Island Foot meme had already become a global social media sensation, and half of the reporters who flew into Hyannis summered or vacationed on the Cape anyway, making the trip to Barnstable a coveted assignment, especially at the tail-end of the high season. Hennessey couldn't stand them.

Turkey vultures. They're like those big ugly birds pecking away at carcasses on the side of the road, feeding off of anything.

With the BCPD unwilling to provide any specifics, and the Nickersons and other MIBIC members actually upholding their agreement not to discuss publicly what they'd discovered, the pickings were lean for the reporters.

That didn't stop them from trying. "I know nothing... nothing at all," Robert Nickerson said during his time with a few of them. The ear-to-ear grin on his face and the huge wink he gave seemed at odds with the definitiveness of his statement. The Boston Globe and the Cape Cod Times wrote it up speculatively. The Globe buried the story in the middle of its regional section. The Times, while placing it on the lower half of the front page, headlined it in such a way as to cast doubt: "Human Remains Found on Our Beaches?" The Chamber of Commerce's Larry Sylvester was relieved.

Good. Thank God, thought Sylvester. *It won't be taken seriously.*

No one asked the Wexners up in Wayland, though, not to talk to the press. Hennessey hadn't thought to when he interviewed them about the finger. Why would he? The other body parts hadn't been found by then. It was too bad that Eric Wexner read the online Globe cover to cover. Upon finishing the story, he clicked on the email contact for the Globe reporter at the end of the piece, a newbie named Madison Jones, and wrote her a one sentence email: *"My son found a human finger on a Cape beach during our recent vacation."*

With her boss's permission, and after talking to the Wexners, Jones careened down to the Cape. She knew that Hennessey had met with the Wexners, knew they'd turned the finger over to the Wayland police, and knew the Wayland police gave the finger to Hennessey and the BCPD. She also knew that what looked like a foot had been found out on Monomoy Island. Although a rookie at the Globe, Jones surmised that the story loomed larger than it appeared; she was excited about it.

That Monomoy Island Foot meme? thought Jones. *Hype! I'd really like to meet the guys who put it together.*

"Detectives, what can you tell me about the finger and foot?" she asked, after waiting patiently for an hour to get in to see Hennessey and Lipman.

"Ms. Jones," said Lipman, "we're not a hundred percent sure it's a human foot. The forensic analysis isn't finished. At the appropriate time, we'll release a statement to the media. You should have called us, rather than driving all the way down here for nothing."

"So, you know you have a finger, but you don't know if

you have a foot?" she asked, sarcasm dripping off the question. "I think you two middle-aged white guys resent me. You resent dealing with a young woman reporter digging around on an important story. Sexist of you, don't you think?"

Silence. Hennessey's long, handsome face became stiff and blank. Chiseled. Anger rose up in him like a wave swelling up before breaking on the shore.

"Ms. Jones," Hennessey said. "You know, that's the most screwed up thing I've heard in a long time. I'm sure Detective Lipman agrees with me. Who are you, coming in here and speaking to us like that?"

Flummoxed by the unfortunate turn in the conversation, yet trying to show moxie, Jones plowed ahead. "Sorry guys, but I know you're stonewalling me big-time on this. I wonder what your motive is for doing so. You don't get the Woke Movement or something?"

That was it for Hennessey. That was it.

"Get outta here, you goddamn twerp, before this middle-aged white guy picks you up and throws you out," he said, steel and menace in his voice. He advanced toward her in a threatening way. "And tell Meg Blanchard that Drink Hennessey says to never, ever send your sorry ass this way again. Understood?"

Three hours later, Jones sheepishly shared with Blanchard, her boss and one of the senior editors at the Globe, that she'd gotten nothing new on the human body parts story from her trip to the BCPD. Jones shared the message too. Blanchard, who grew up in Southie and had been bused to school with the Hennessey boys for years, smiled ruefully. "Well, that's your last trip to the Cape on this one," she said to her novice reporter.

So *that's where Drink is,* Blanchard thought.

At Archduke Insurance Company's downtown Boston office, located on Federal Street, Ben Maisky put two sandwich bags on the large oak table next to his desk. *Click.* He turned on the fluorescent examination light that hung overhead.

The first bag contained eight cigarette butts, collected in the Burger King parking lot next to the destroyed Barnstable music school. The second bag held just one, found by Maisky a hundred yards deep in the woods adjacent to where the Falmouth music school and Lowlands Theater once stood.

Forming an eighteen-inch by eighteen-inch square on the left-hand side of the table with paper towels, Maisky carefully used a pair of tweezers to pull out the eight cigarette butts from the first bag, lining them up neatly in a row so the background whiteness of the paper towels highlighted their features. Then, he took the solitary butt out of the second bag, placing it below the others.

Wanting to ensure his complete focus on the task at hand, Maisky took a bathroom break. Five minutes later, he hunched over the table again. The tweezers in his left hand held the single butt found in the woods; he had a magnifying glass in his right hand. He moved down the line of eight butts still on the table one by one, stopping at the sixth for a long time. Placing the one found in the woods back in the front row, he then moved the sixth butt from the top row down right next to it, always using the tweezers, never his fingers.

"Well, I'll be," Maisky said to himself, going to his filing cabinet and pulling out a yellowed, dog-eared document whose appearance spoke to its age and frequent use. "Thank goodness for Bob Bourhill's *Guide to Cigarette Butts.* I'm sure we have a match here. Let's see what Bob comes up with."

"Lucky Strikes? That's luck in itself. Not many people smoking those anymore."

After putting each Lucky Strike cigarette butt in a separate and new plastic bag, Maisky continued chattering to himself. "Time to send these fellas out for a DNA reconnaissance trip. Which company this time... 23andMe, or Living DNA?"

"Who won the bet?" Maisky asked. "You did!" he said to

himself proudly.

Years earlier, Hennessey chuckled frequently during the mandatory DNA forensics training class he took as a Boston Police Department detective. But he also took the training very seriously. After moving to the Cape, he kept abreast of all DNA developments as they related to his work. Hennessey found the details and history of DNA fascinating.

Deoxyribonucleic acid. DNA. The nucleic acid containing genetic information that allows all forms of life to function, grow, and reproduce. Watson and Crick's famous 1953 paper is largely thought to mark the beginning of work on DNA. Not so. Efforts to unlock the secrets of our genes go all the way back to 1869, a few years after the American Civil War ended. The work started in Europe, where a young Swiss scientist named Friedrich Miescher got the ball rolling in the brand new field of tissue chemistry, now called biochemistry. Building on Miescher's pioneering work was Steudel, who modeled a DNA strand in 1912. The Russian chemist Levene came next, in the 1920s and 30s, and then Linus Pauling, modern-day champion of the dietary importance of vitamin C and winner of not one, but two, Nobel Prizes. Pauling's DNA model didn't get it quite right. What Watson and Crick did was hit upon the correct 3-D model of DNA. They built on decades of brilliant work before them, added their own genius to it, and received significant assistance from a woman, Rosalind Franklin, whose x-ray crystallographic studies were critical to answering the final questions about DNA structure. She died before sharing in the accolades.

Advanced work on DNA these days has scientists thinking that its building blocks—adenine, guanine, and related organic molecules—might very well have formed extraterrestrially, in outer space. The complex DNA organic compounds of life are now formed in laboratory conditions that mimic outer space, building with chemicals found in meteorites, such as pyrimidine. It amused and fascinated

Hennessey.

From outer space? Get outta here! Those wackos out west, searching the sky for UFOs every night, they must get their jollies off on that. Marfa, Texas, here I come!

What Hennessey really couldn't get his head around was the fact that each and every human inhabitant of planet Earth shared 99.9 percent of their DNA.

How can that possibly be?

DNA profiling of individuals came about in the 1980s, and up to about a decade ago was used almost exclusively in criminal forensic work. The first patent covering the direct use of variations in DNA for forensic purposes went to an American, Jeffrey Glassberg. Much of the foundation for today's DNA forensic efforts was developed by British geneticist Sir Alec Jeffreys; like the felony murder rule, another gift from across the Atlantic Ocean.

While rarely used to exonerate innocent people languishing in jails, the use of DNA to identify criminals really took off in the 1990s. Civil libertarians rang alarm bells about constitutional and other legal issues surrounding the growing national DNA database—the Combined DNA Index System, known as CODIS. As usual, the civil libertarians lost that one. Local, state, and federal law enforcement agencies contribute to and share CODIS information. It now holds over nineteen million DNA profiles, one out of every seventeen Americans.

Hennessey grimaced when thinking about Joey, his locked-up young brother. Now that was nothing to chuckle about. Not at all.

Joey's in that CODIS system for sure. Wonder if my DNA profile is too.

◊ ◊ ◊

No one was ever more relieved to receive DNA and other forensic test results than Hennessey and Lipman. The few days of ducking and weaving, of providing evasive answers to questions from all quarters, had put them on edge. The detectives were surprised, though, when Bernie MacKenzie, the Massachusetts southeast regional crime lab director, arrived to share the news with them. Usually, it was an underling who came to discuss the report, or called with the information, and then followed up with an email about it.

"To what do we owe this honor?" Lipman joked, as MacKenzie entered his office.

As to the forensic results, the two detectives were skeptical yet resigned to what MacKenzie told them. The gelatinous basketball McCoy pulled out of the great white shark was indeed a good chunk of a human torso, in fact, the entire upper half of one. What's more, the torso, finger, and foot were from the same person. A one hundred percent match. No quibbling possible.

"Truth be told, we were lucky to be able to do the analysis," said MacKenzie. "The body parts were in sad shape, really sad shape. The foot and finger contained degraded DNA, due to exposure to the elements. And the torso... well, you can imagine. Digested in good part by the monster that preyed on it. We ended up with both shark and human DNA to analyze. Distinguishing between them was no problem though.

"Nuclease enzymes had a field day on all of it—that's the stuff that breaks down DNA. They munched away on the DNA the way we used to munch on fried clams and onion rings out at Liam's on Nauset Beach, before that nor'easter destroyed the place."

MacKenzie chortled at his own wit. No one else laughed.

"None of the body parts were found together," Lipman said. "How can they possibly match?"

"My guess," Hennessey interjected, "is that in its feeding frenzy, the shark separated the finger and foot from the rest of the body. Probably somewhere off of Eastham, or Orleans, or Chatham. The family from Wayland told me they went to Nauset as much as any other beach during their vacation. It's right up the road, so to speak, from Monomoy Island."

"Gentlemen," continued MacKenzie, "I understand your

confusion, but there's no mistaking the genetic science. While there wasn't much DNA left to analyze, what was there matches. There's absolutely no question about it. All the body parts are from the same person."

MacKenzie's next bit of information totally confused them. It was a mind bender. Big time.

"Are you sure about that?" Lipman asked, after MacKenzie delivered the news.

"Yes, I'm sure," said MacKenzie. "I found it so strange I ran all the tests twice to confirm it."

Hennessey spoke slowly and clearly. "You're telling us there were traces of alcohol and GHB in the torso and foot? GHB... the date rape drug? It's a male body, not a female, which makes that highly unusual, no? And what about the finger—no traces there?"

"The finger didn't have enough blood residue in it for us to test for anything other than DNA. You don't need blood for a DNA test. The bigger body parts, no problem. We ran the titers and found alcohol and GHB in the foot and torso."

MacKenzie went on: "Men are probably raped by slimy creeps using GHB too. It's a drug that works on whomever you give it to. It's not gender specific in any way. People also take it themselves. It's a form of ecstasy, you know."

After an awkward pause, Hennessey said, "You're also telling us that the lung in the torso indicates that whoever it is, whoever it was, might have drowned?"

"Yup, that's my hypothesis," replied MacKenzie. "None of it makes sense to me. It's hard to say, detectives. There's so much unknown still, and it's all so unclear. But unless I've got it wrong, which is possible, although I don't think so, that great white shark ate an already-dead human being. It didn't attack and kill anyone."

"Wait a minute, wait a minute, wait a minute," interrupted Hennessey quickly. "Wouldn't the lung get water in it after or during the shark attack?"

"Who knows? In all likelihood, no," replied MacKenzie.

"Here's the scenario," continued MacKenzie, "if this guy

was killed by a great white shark. The poor soul is swimming, or lying on a surfboard waiting to catch a wave. This monster comes out of nowhere and essentially cuts him in two, taking out a huge chunk of his torso in one bite, including a big piece of lung. Boom—it's inside the shark. The lung doesn't have time to fill with water."

"Can't it fill with water once inside the shark?"

"C'mon, Hennessey. Do you have water sloshing around in you? Sharks swim in the stuff, they don't have it inside their bodies. Just like us. Our bodies are sixty percent water, give or take, but we don't have it sloshing around inside us.

"Think about folks killed in the ocean, hit by lightning while swimming, or stung by a poisonous jellyfish or snake. Their bodies float, and it's not only because of the salt water. It's also because their lungs still have air in them when they die, adding to their buoyancy."

Getting up to leave, MacKenzie concluded: "I don't know what to think. The portion of lung was completely saturated, like a sponge that can't hold any more water. It makes me think that whoever it was might well have drowned, and didn't die at the hands of a great white shark. But who knows?"

"Listen," said Lipman. "Don't discuss your findings with anyone until we figure out what we want to do next." MacKenzie nodded in agreement, shook hands with the two detectives, and left.

Hennessey and Lipman sat there. Just sat there.

"What can it possibly mean?" said Lipman, thinking out loud. One person's body parts on their hands, the remnants of someone savagely torn apart, and still absolutely no idea who it was. Then bizarre information, truly bizarre information, from MacKenzie: GHB and alcohol detected in the body? Drowning and not shark attack a possible cause of death? What the hell... How to process it all?

Lipman picked up the phone. He was about to make good on his promise to the Chamber of Commerce's Larry Sylvester that he'd be among the first to know when the

BCPD had news. Hennessey gently pushed the receiver cradle button down, stopping any call from being made.

"Wait a minute, Phil. I'm not sure it's a good idea to share what we know with the outside world yet."

"Why not? We told Larry and the press we'd pass along information as we got it."

"Yeah, but what do we have? The DNA report makes sense. Body parts found in proximity to each other. This beach or that beach, or in a great white shark caught close by, that doesn't matter. It makes sense they're from the same body, no matter how weird the discoveries or timing. What's grabbed me by the cojones," Hennessey continued, "is the second part of Bernie MacKenzie's report. GHB and alcohol found in two of the three body parts? The lung showing that a drowning might have occurred? Too much."

"So, what are you saying?"

"I'm saying that while we probably have another shark attack death on our hands, there's an outside chance, a slim one, we have something else on our hands. Best not to share it with anyone until we know more. Including who the hell it is."

Sea Interlude #2

Even as their overall population decreases, great white sharks now inhabit surprising places, and in what seem to be plentiful numbers. Cape Cod is one such place. A rarity in the Cape's waters in the past, the great white shark has arrived in force and is here to stay. Two of its favorite prey, harbor and grey seals, are now plentiful, and there are enough other victims of its incessant hunting—cod, bluefish, bass, tuna, seabirds—to keep it around.

But, what has really brought this fearsome apex predator to Cape Cod and other new environs, aside from burgeoning seal populations?

Climate change.

A mass movement of marine life, especially in coastal waters, is occurring everywhere these days. Ocean and coastal ecosystems are changing almost literally before our very eyes, as waters once too cold for certain species warm and become hospitable to them. Other ocean areas are becoming too warm, driving away species that called them home for millennia. Data tracking shows it.

What swimmers, surfers, kayakers, and others must know is this: Scientists see that, because of the effects of climate change on our oceans, the overall range of the great white shark has shrunk considerably, forcing predator and prey closer together. How unnerving.

We humans passed laws protecting seals—a noble endeavor—and seal populations boomed. Climate change, also a human product, made North Atlantic water temperatures much more suitable. So the great white shark descends en masse. The unforeseen by-product of these two human activities: a much greater risk of encountering a great white in the waters of Cape Cod, including in really shallow waters. How ironic.

Caution is certainly called for. Perhaps a healthy bit of fear. The great white shark knows no fear. None whatsoever. Nothing resembling that primal emotion can ever be seen in its vacant, dull, robot-like eyes as it searches for its next meal.

CHAPTER 7

Friday, July 9, 2021

Nastiness hung in the air. Thick and pervasive, like the ugly brown haze urbanites flee from when the deep summer heat arrives, at least those urbanites able to do so.

All the recent board meetings of Cape Now ended similarly. Distrust. Rancor. Divisiveness. Angst. Anger. Board committee meetings played out the same way.

It took a lot to rattle Jason Karp, but after a year as the executive director of the organization, 'flummoxed' was his middle name. Cape Now housed the prestigious Cape Philharmonic Orchestra, the Cape Music School and its Barnstable and Falmouth buildings, and the Lowlands Theater, also in Falmouth. Cape Now was considered one of the preeminent arts and culture organizations of the region.

Years earlier, when the symphony, music school, and theater merged, the Cape Cod Times applauded. According to the Times, Cape Cod was overrun by small non-profit organizations, all producing adequate local fare, all competing with each other for precious dollars, and all led by starry-eyed directors whose idealism and unique management skills made their institution unquestionably superior to others. The bringing together of the symphony, music school, and theater was viewed as a step in the right direction, a way to harness disparate energy and effusiveness into a single operation: Cape Now. CAN, as in 'CAN-DO,' proclaimed the Times's editorial about the merger.

That was then. Now, behind closed doors, Karp faced total disarray.

This place is a disaster.

None of the original goals behind setting up CAN— administrative efficiency, artistic integration, and most importantly, financial solvency—had been achieved. Solutions weren't anywhere in sight either. Of course, inefficiency can be overlooked or downplayed under any number of circumstances, and particularly when money isn't tight. CAN couldn't afford to do so. It was losing a lot of money every year. The draw on CAN's relatively modest endowment increased annually. Dipping into endowment to cover operating losses had started some time ago. At the current draw-down rate, the entire endowment would soon be gone. Karp gave it another two or three years.

He arrived after turning around another arts organization in Kansas City, and was supremely confident of his ability to get everything running smoothly at CAN, even on quirky, parochial Cape Cod. He wasn't cocky about it anymore though. Some of the discord and turmoil was his own doing, even though he'd been there just a little over a year. His bad habit of cutting people off, and of dismissing ideas quickly, came across as arrogant and impatient, as imperious, leaving CAN staff and board members muttering under their breath after almost every interaction with him.

The real problems, the deeper, more fundamental problems, all predated Karp. He'd inherited a group with confused, ill-planned organizational goals, and whose implementation of its goals was lame. A schoolteacher would have graded it a D. To Karp, one word defined the key personalities at CAN: toxic. The organization's leaders were like jigsaw pieces from different puzzles that had ended up in the same box. No cohesive, unified picture could ever emerge. Pervasive dysfunction defined CAN. Karp wasn't nearly experienced or talented enough to work his way through it.

Proud of his Turkish heritage, Emre Aru Massahol, the conductor and music director of the Cape Philharmonic, never tired of correcting the pronunciation of his last name. The two "ss"s sounded as a "z," the middle "a" was silent, and the last "o" sounded like the two "oo"s in "poodle." Spoken phonetically, it was "Mazhool." No one got it right.

After a dozen years as the Philharmonic's leader, Massahol was the most identifiable arts and culture figure on the Cape. Denise Douward, the doting octogenarian CAN board vice chair, referred to him affectionately as "our rock star." Massahol milked that for everything it was worth. He was also pleased with the nickname she'd given him—Double M—for Maestro Massahol, although he made fake, immodest efforts to stop its use. It was now ubiquitous. Everyone, from board to administrative staff to musicians to patrons, called him Double M.

He did have another, somewhat unfortunate nickname. Like many rock stars, Massahol used to wait a fashionably long time before springing out onto the stage, sometimes up to fifteen minutes. The effect of starting concerts late heightened audience desire and enhanced, psychologically, his attraction and command over attendees. The musicians hated it.

He'd learned to be right on time, though, from an experience at one of the rare concerts played out on Martha's Vineyard—a place that, due to the cost of getting a full-sized orchestra out to the island, rarely received a visit from the Cape Philharmonic. Getting impatient after the performance time came and went, the several dozen Martha's Vineyard high school students in attendance started chanting the iconic, somewhat profane term reserved for overly aggressive drivers in Massachusetts, which an out-of-stater like Double

M, from San Antonio, Texas, was completely unaware of. The chant started and continued for several minutes, despite the "shushes" and "stop its" of the elderly. "Maaassshole, Maaaassshole, Massa-Hole, Mass-A-Hole, Mass-A-Hole." Double M finished tying his bowtie quickly, and never again started a concert on the Cape more than a couple of minutes late. Despite his changed ways, the chant made its way to the mainland via the kids from Martha's Vineyard who attended Cape Cod Community College in Barnstable. Double M was resigned to hearing a few "Maaaassshole, Mass-A-Hole" catcalls at almost all concerts, including from a couple of tenured musicians in the orchestra as he came out onto the stage.

A true peacock, as many conductors are, Massahol cut a dashing physical appearance: lean, six-foot-two, and with piercing blue eyes that warranted the contact lenses he wore. No one wanted to hide those eyes behind glasses, certainly not CAN's publicity department or Massahol himself, even though wearing contact lenses made reading musical scores difficult. Massahol got lost in the music more than once in his career. It proved a point he jokingly made sometimes at rehearsal, that orchestras didn't really need their conductors.

The musicians could indeed play most of the orchestral repertoire without anyone standing in front of them waving a stick, especially someone like Double M. His ictus—his conducting technique—was lousy, making beats difficult to follow and often leaving orchestra members guessing where he was at any particular moment. Massahol also used, ad nauseam, his famous hemiola waist wiggle, showing when two groups of three beats broke down into three groups of two beats through an exaggerated, sexually charged side–to-side hip movement. It never failed to delight the female septuagenarian symphony concert attendees. The musicians thought something else entirely.

"Makes me want to puke," said one of the French horn players during a concert, almost loudly enough to be heard by Double M.

Over time, Massahol built the Cape Philharmonic into a decent regional orchestra. It didn't matter that it performed in the Barnstable High School Auditorium. Double M was mighty proud of his music ensemble, and thought about it all the time.

We're really on par with the London Philharmonic, and here on Cape Cod, of all places! We've got to figure out a way to get the Cape Philharmonic on the road, over to Europe if possible, to show what we're really made of.

Massahol had washed up on the Cape's shores years earlier. The Cape Philharmonic represented a remarkable turnaround in his career as a conductor. Before it, he'd been on professional life support. Now, at age sixty-seven, his current Cape Cod gig represented the end of the run for him. Amazingly enough he'd managed to extend it for well over a decade. With nothing else in sight, it was no wonder he clung to the Cape Philharmonic as if his life depended on it.

He had once been the music director of the Dallas Philharmonia, a much more substantial symphony orchestra than the Cape Philharmonic. Wanting to increase its importance in the field and its international stature, and knowing Double M couldn't possibly take them there, the Dallas Philharmonia parted ways with him. In a fit of pique, he also abruptly quit his music director position with the Fort Worth Chamber Gigsters, which paved the way for the organization's bankruptcy and created ill-will that hung like a grey cloud for decades and from thousands of miles away.

Now, other than his Cape Philharmonic responsibilities, Massahol was reduced to spending a week or two teaching at third-rate universities. In these settings, he spoke unfailingly and with a burning intensity about the two attributes necessary for performing music well—unbridled passion and irrational commitment—to students who would never become musicians and weren't at all serious about it. These characteristics defined Massahol. Every thought he had, or thing he said, oozed with unbridled passion and irrational commitment. Karp had been startled when a CAN senior staff member whispered in his ear a few weeks in, "you'll come to hate him." A year later, Karp understood completely.

That afternoon's board meeting descended into cacophony. Someone pounding on a piano keyboard with both fists over and over. Board members argued loudly among themselves about what to do with CAN. At the root of it lay the fact that the Cape Philharmonic annually made money. The Cape Music School and Lowlands Theater each lost bundles, and needed to be propped up every year by the symphony's income and by dipping into the endowment.

Things got heated when Massahol and board member George Slavin proposed a vote authorizing a study on how to break CAN back up into three separate non-profit organizations.

"That wasn't even on the agenda," Karp said through clenched teeth, glaring at Massahol and Slavin standing together at the dais, then looking at Board Chair Greg Hemshaw, who sat next to him, for support.

"Are you declaring this out of order, or tabled?" he asked Hemshaw.

Hemshaw shrugged and offered timidly, "What can I do about it?" As usual, the board chair was completely ineffectual.

"Jason," said Slavin, speaking above the chatter. "We've got to face reality. We'll never get our new performing arts center built, let alone keep going in the future, if we don't break our programs back out into separate entities. They've got to stand on their own two feet, like children ready to leave the nest. And you know that once the new center is built, the music school and theater will have homes there as rent-paying tenants. We're already planning for that."

Karp looked away for a moment. What Slavin said had a laughable 'what's wrong with this picture' aspect to it. Karp didn't want to telegraph his contempt. He opened his mouth and closed it. Inhaled deeply and then exhaled.

"George," he responded finally. "You know how unrealistic that is. I'm surprised you've even brought it up again. Our orchestra, our music school, our theater... as stand-alone, non-profit organizations in today's world? When they couldn't make it on their own in the kinder, gentler world of fifteen years ago?"

Karp went on. "How will they break even, let alone pay rent to a new performing arts center? I haven't seen any sort of number crunching or projections from you showing how any of it would work. You said you'd have that work done months ago."

"It's coming, it's coming, it's almost done," muttered Slavin.

The call for hard, reliable data invariably shut Slavin down. Karp, keeping a strict poker face, delighted inwardly at Slavin's tried and true reaction to being challenged about the new performing art center's financing: He flushed. Sometimes it was the beet red that people show when called out or caught in a lie, other times a slight darkening of the face that came and went, a cloud passing in front of the sun and then departing. Sometimes it stuck around for a while, other times not. Once Karp was onto it, he never tired of trying to provoke the Slavin flush.

Look at that—red as a rose today!

A semi-retired investment guy, the phrase 'he's a character' didn't really fit Slavin. Too benign. All those years of sucking the bone marrow out of America through private equity deals and his morally questionable transactional work—the good, the ugly, and the really ugly—took its toll. No one would ever use words like gentle, or diplomatic, or nuanced to describe George Slavin. Not even bright. There were huge numbers of investment folks like him, members of the venture capital and private equity communities, who were completely and unjustifiably full of themselves. Their aggressiveness made them more brawn than brains.

Although he'd initially supported the creation of CAN, Slavin now thought the symphony, music school, and theater should split up. He couldn't really explain why, except to think it would make it easier for the new, sorely needed performing arts center to become a reality. Slavin dominated the CAN board for years. More often than not, he got his way on issues of importance to him through a combination of belligerence and bullying. Supposedly as a reward for his years of devotion to the organization, but in reality due to his heavy-handed lobbying, Slavin was named the first board president of the performing arts center subsidiary set up by CAN: the Sea Heights Living Arts Center.

SHLAC had been a dream of Slavin's and other CAN board members for decades. And what a dream: a twelve-hundred-seat concert hall, a three-hundred-seat theater/black box, fine dining, and accompanying music education, arts, and administrative buildings. After all, the fact that the Cape Philharmonic played in a high school auditorium with amped sound was a bit of a travesty. It put the sound mixer at the back of the auditorium, and not Double M, in ultimate control of the orchestra. The Cape Philharmonic deserved better—much better. Massahol had to use a converted windowless janitor's closet as his dressing room, more like a prison cell than warm-up and wind-down space befitting a talent like his. And it certainly couldn't be used to host the rare VIP who came down to the perform to perform with the orchestra.

Despite its serious financial problems, CAN pumped significant funding into the SHLAC project, a red flag that immediately caught Karp's eye when he took charge. He objected strenuously, to no avail. The result? After years and years, and hundreds of thousands of dollars put into the SHLAC project, it had gone nowhere. That never stopped Slavin, though. Not a chance.

I'll get SHLAC done if it's the last damn thing I ever do. How sweet it will be. And I'm not putting a dime of my own money into it. CAN's still got plenty of money to put into the project. If we can only get the damn music schools and theater out of the way... those losers.

As the argument heated up, Slavin fantasized again about walking into the George A. Slavin Hall, named after him for his yeoman, tenacious, and successful effort at bringing a twenty-first century performing arts center to Cape Cod. Truthfully, Slavin was clueless about how to develop a thirty- to forty-million dollar performing arts center. He had convinced himself and others, however, that he had the background to pull it off.

Slavin wasn't the only clueless one. So was his partner in the SHLAC project, Conrad Redlich. Redlich was Jason Karp's predecessor at CAN. Forced out as CAN's executive director, Redlich had been thrown a bone: He became the first executive director of SHLAC. It came with a nice salary, despite the conflict of interest it posed and Redlich's equal lack of experience in developing performing arts centers.

A former import-export executive, Redlich hadn't succeeded as the executive director of CAN. While his instincts about CAN were good, he butted heads mercilessly with Massahol time and time again. Every other month he announced his resignation due to some power struggle lost with Double M, and changed his mind so many times that people gave up caring, like the boy who cried wolf. Redlich's departure came about only when Massahol issued a 'him or me' ultimatum. Tears welling up in his eyes, Double M said, "I love you, man, I really love you. But, there's no way we can continue working together. You're way too much in my space..."

So, Jason Karp followed Redlich as CAN's executive director. He'd been hired to establish CAN more fully as one organization, to integrate the symphony, music school, and theater completely, and to lead the conceptualization and development of the SHLAC project. These tasks, and others, had been listed as his principal job responsibilities. After all, Karp had been involved with performing arts center development work before, and non-profit turnaround work too.

Almost immediately upon arriving, Karp had a bead on

the situation. Slavin and Redlich hadn't raised a dime of the tens of millions of dollars needed for the project. They hadn't even acquired a site for SHLAC yet. The latest thinking about where SHLAC should be built was on a golf course in Hyannis. The location: on a small two-lane road, adjacent to a residential neighborhood, behind a hotel, and kitty-corner from the Cape's largest outdoor seasonal concert venue.

Touring the golf course site with Slavin, Karp quipped, "you're not serious, are you?"

"We're dead serious about it, Jason," Slavin said solemnly.

SHLAC was sinking rapidly into quicksand.

"Enough already... enough. Quiet please, everyone. QUIET!"

Waving Massahol and Slavin back to their seats, Board Chair Greg Hemshaw whacked his half-sized gavel over and over again on the Hyannis Sheraton Inn's conference room table, finally grabbing the board's attention and bringing the meeting back to a semblance of order for presentation of the final agenda item.

It turned out to be a blessing for Karp. Up last came Tiffany Tisdale's update on state funding for the desperately needed renovations to the Barnstable music school building. The news was good.

Tiffany, the slender, attractive, talented director of the CAN music schools, exuded bitterness. Arriving on the scene several years after Massahol, she'd been treated like a second-class citizen from day one. A gifted pianist, she didn't have much opportunity to show that side of her. Karp thought her a more talented musician than Massahol, and many others agreed. To her credit, she focused like a workhorse on her teaching and administrative responsibilities, which she viewed as critically important in this day and age of declining arts and music education. It put Tiffany at a distinct disadvantage when compared to the Liberace-like Double M.

She was also disadvantaged when trying to build the case to the board that CAN's music schools should be treated equally to the Cape Philharmonic. No luck on that one. It came as no surprise to her when CAN's board decided to pursue SHLAC, making plans to close down the two music schools and move their operations to the new performing arts center, without even asking for her input or opinion. Anger coursed through Tiffany when she thought about it.

That says it all. Could they possibly treat me more shabbily? I can't wait to get away from this male-dominated, incestuous, insular, mediocre place.

Making matters worse, she couldn't stand Karp, her boss of the past year. Tiffany yearned to be free of his supervision. It had really pissed her off when, early on in their time together, he asked her to make sure her staff got to the office right at nine in the morning.

Why should I do that? she thought. *They're all adults. Let them start their workday when they want. What a pretentious jerk and control freak he is.*

Totally pissed off during one of their tense meetings, Tiffany told Karp, "You know, I've got other professional options than hanging around CAN. I can easily go someplace else, where I won't be treated like a second-class citizen."

"Please go ahead and act on those options then, Tiffany," Karp responded. "Let's announce your departure tomorrow. We'll tell everyone you're leaving in two weeks, or in a month. I'm sure that after some time off to recharge your batteries, you'll land right back on your feet."

Ouch.

Tiffany's news to the board that afternoon was good. Karp hoped it would quell the 'split-them-all-up' rebellion, at least temporarily, and perhaps once and for all.

"The Massachusetts Cultural Center," she reported excitedly, "just agreed... drumroll please... to give us a $150,000 grant to renovate the Barnstable music school building. YEAH!"

"It's a three to one matching grant," she went on,

"meaning we have to raise or otherwise put in $50,000. We also have to meet typical reporting requirements for State grants. Other than that, though, we can spend the money on whatever we think the Barnstable music school campus needs the most. My vote is for the new roof first."

"What great news!" exclaimed Karp, who knew it already. "I think that…"

"Jason, could I please finish?"

"Of course, Tiffany, of course," Karp said graciously.

"The $200,000 covers only a third of what needs to be done at the Barnstable campus. Still, I'm sure you all agree with me it's a wonderful start. We should pounce on this generous offer."

Before any other board member could speak, Slavin stepped in.

"Tiffany, what sort of long-term commitment do we need to make to the State in order to get these funds?"

"I'm not sure I understand, George," she replied.

"Well, if the Massachusetts Cultural Center gives us $150,000 to renovate the Barnstable music school, do we need to stay there for any period of time? Do we need to keep the building, and keep our music education programs there? Or can we still do what we want with it? Give it to another non-profit group, or even sell it if we want?"

Tiffany and Karp knew exactly what Slavin was getting at. He wanted CAN's Cape Music School moved to SHLAC as soon as possible—yesterday, today, tomorrow. Investing hundreds of thousands of dollars in renovating the Barnstable campus building would make pulling off the SHLAC project that much more difficult.

"I don't know George," Tiffany replied icily to Slavin. "My guess is that Jason can give you the details, the answers to all those highfalutin questions you just asked. But as far as I'm concerned, the music school campuses in Barnstable and Falmouth won't be going anywhere anytime soon."

"Wait a minute," growled Slavin.

"Ohhhhhboy," the exasperated Massahol groaned simultaneously, loudly enough for half the room to hear. The decibel level shot up immediately, as board members expressed their varied opinions in unison. It sounded like the world's worst chorus. All eyes turned to Karp.

What an unbelievable mess, he thought glumly.

CHAPTER 8

Years Earlier

For the first couple of months, Joey panicked when he opened his eyes each morning. Overwhelming panic, like being in a horrendous car accident, the vehicle spinning and spinning out of control with its passengers helpless to do anything about it. Gut wrenching. The reality of his situation explained the cold sweat he found himself in every morning.

Joey of course understood how driving a car for his Locust Hill gang buddies during a busted bank robbery led straight to his incarceration at Massachusetts Correctional Institution-Walpole. But he thought it would only be for a half dozen years or so.

Here for life? No possibility of parole? How can that be? None of it makes any sense.

Reading up on all aspects of life without parole sentences made it even worse. For a maximum-security inmate, Joey was well educated. Initially, he spent all his time in the jail's library, boning up on everything he could find on prison sentencing guidelines. He knew, through the print newspapers and magazines he read—and his on-line access wasn't bad either—that a number of states were reconsidering all aspects of life without parole sentences.

In some southern states, if you stole groceries to feed your family, or tools from a hardware store to use to make a living, and got caught and convicted three times, you got a life sentence without parole. Louisiana, known as the 'penitentiary capital of the United States,' now worked hard to get rid of that unfortunate moniker by changing its prison sentencing laws, including its life without parole sentencing guidelines. Prison sentencing reform was underway in many states. Joey took careful note of it.

God, I hope Massachusetts does it soon.

After the shock of incarceration wore off, Joey found his existence strangely bearable. In some ways, he enjoyed living the severely regimented and spartan life of an MCI-Walpole inmate. He told himself it wasn't that different from what he'd experienced at home; his loving but controlling parents, his brothers who ruled the roost, sometimes with their fists. Particularly his oldest brother, Drink.

The only difference was there was no love inside the four huge, razor-wired walls of MCI-Walpole. None whatsoever. Whoever thought of calling such a hell-hole a 'correctional' institution mocked everyone whose life it touched: inmates, guards, administrators, public defenders, and most of all, the family members of those locked up. There was absolutely nothing correctional about MCI-Walpole. Who was getting corrected, the inmates? Not happening. Not the bunch of murderers, rapists, armed bank robbers, and other hardened felons Joey found himself in with.

Built in the 1950s, MCI-Walpole once held the dubious honor of being the most dangerous place in the country to be in jail. Albert DeSalvo, otherwise known as the Boston Strangler, ended up there. Another inmate stabbed him to death. Tony Costa, Cape Cod's most famous serial killer, was there too. Rather than waiting for Mother Nature to dictate when he'd take his last breath inside the razor-fenced walls at MCI-Walpole, Costa hung himself.

The Locust Hill gang members remained a tight knit bunch through thick or thin, inside or outside of jail. It was as if they were members of a criminal college fraternity. A couple other members of the Locust Hill gang called MCI-Walpole home too, and their presence saved Joey's ass, literally and figuratively. Without them there, he'd have been in huge trouble. At five-foot-nine and weighing 175 pounds, Joey had 'fresh meat' painted in capital letters on his back.

"I like what I see," said another lifer out in the rec yard, talking up close to Joey. Way too close. The guy was much heftier and without an ounce of redemption in him. "Here's my new jailpony... just what I needed."

"You can fuck off," Joey replied, without much effect.

Instantly grabbing Joey as hard as he could by the throat, the thug responded, "No kiddo, it's 'fuck me... please.' That's what you say to me. Understood?"

It all ended quickly. Jack Ford, the senior Locust Hill gang member at MCI-Walpole, and there for the rest of his life for committing three murders, got the thug tormenting Joey into a corner of the rec yard that didn't have security camera coverage, and with a padlock stuffed inside a sock, made clear to him that anyone who messed with Joey Hennessey had Jack Ford to answer to. Joey was a blessed man in that regard. Truly blessed.

As the end of Joey's second year at MCI-Walpole approached, Drink and his other brother, Doug, brought him the terrible news. The worst news possible. Their mother had died.

"What? How can that be? Mom's gone?" Anguish and disbelief filled Joey's voice in equal measures. He stifled a sob and put his face in his hands, elbows on the table, while his two brothers sat across from him.

"It's on me. We all know it. I've killed Mom with my bullshit behavior. Oh God, please God... It should've been me. C'mon, say it... Say it, you two. Say it: Look at what the fuck you've done."

Neither Drink nor Doug would go there, would ever go there with Joey. To what end? They might agree with what he'd said, they might think it day and night, but the code of conduct they followed, handed down by family and the South Boston community, would never allow them to say so.

"Joey, it wasn't you," said Drink. "Mom had cancer, breast cancer. It took her real quick, before she or any of us could do anything."

"With Drink and me out of the house," Doug interjected, "workin' stiffs now, we didn't see Mom or Dad much. We had no idea Mom was sick, let alone dying. It was a complete shock to us. Know that."

"I talked to her a while back… two, three weeks ago. She sounded fine. A little tired, that's all."

Speaking to his brothers, Joey's voice trembled. He'd almost convinced his mother to come visit him at MCI-Walpole in that last call. She hadn't been able to do it, not for the year and a half Joey had been there. Phone calls and emails, which were always screened carefully, were as close as Mary Hennessey allowed herself to get to her youngest son.

She'd still been trying to wrap her head around what happened, was still trying to figure out what her response should be as an outstanding member of the South Boston community, and as a mother who'd tried her best to teach her sons the virtue of good behavior. During that last call, filled with compassion and motherly love, she said she'd visit Joey soon. It put a huge smile on his face, lifting his spirits unlike anything else in the previous eighteen months.

Mary Hennessey's health worsened drastically right after her call with Joey. She was dead in a matter of weeks. Ironically—tragically really—she'd been sincere about visiting him in jail. At long last she was ready to do so. Mulling over his mother's death, Joey misinterpreted what she'd told him. He, the youngest child, with youngest child sensitivities and perspectives on life. He, the baby of the family, his mother's last and favorite. It changed him; his thoughts became tormented and tortured.

Unbelievable, just unbelievable. Mom lied to me about visiting. She never meant to do so. She never wanted anything to do with me anymore.

The sight given by hope disappeared. The sight given by spirit and soul disappeared too. An all-encompassing, unforgiving blackness took over. The new Joey emerged.

CHAPTER 9

Friday, July 16, 2021

CAN's executive committee meeting followed the disastrous full board meeting by a week. A much smaller and discrete number of board members sat on the executive committee, including Board Chair Greg Hemshaw, Vice Chair Denise Douward, George Slavin, and four retirees with time on their hands and some interest, sincere or not, in dabbling in the arts. Emre Massahol and Tiffany Tisdale attended in their *ex officio* roles. Conrad Redlich was present too. He, Slavin, and Massahol had been invited to give the executive committee a detailed update on the SHLAC project, much to Jason Karp's chagrin.

From his seat at the head of the table, Karp took in the executive committee. It could have been a retiree bridge club gathering. From the discussion so far, he knew that Slavin, Massahol, and Redlich were playing the long game, masters at inflecting long-term strategy with short-term opportunism. Unfortunately, they were winning the war.

"As Conrad mentioned in that terrific summary of where things stand, and thanks for that, Conrad, by the way, at long last we've got a clear path ahead. SHLAC will become a reality." Slavin gave heavy emphasis to the last phrase, articulating each word forcefully and separately. "The golf course property is ours for three and a half million dollars. A steal, given what it's worth on the open market."

Denise Douward looked at Slavin affectionately. "George, when do we need to close? Isn't that the real estate term, 'close,' on the property?" she asked.

"That's the beauty of our arrangement, Denise," said Slavin. "While normally a transaction like this has a thirty day closing period, the seller here, a big supporter of our orchestra, has given us ninety days to acquire the property."

"Fantastic!" exclaimed Douward.

"Yes indeed!" pitched in Greg Hemshaw simultaneously. As board chair, Hemshaw often felt the need to have his voice heard, although he rarely had anything of substance to say.

"Where's the money for the property going to come from, George?" Karp asked suddenly, catching Slavin off guard and eliciting an 'I don't know and I don't care' shrug. Slavin's telltale flush emerged. Karp caught it immediately and smiled inwardly.

Too bad. Not as red today as last time.

"Folks," Karp continued, "I'd like us to step back for a second and think hard about what's been presented to us. Yes, thanks, Conrad and George for the presentation, and for the interesting news about the terms of a possible purchase of the golf course property. However, is this really what we should be doing?" Karp went on. "At this time in CAN's history? Don't we want to spend our time and resources building CAN into the multi-faceted arts organization dreamed about when the symphony, music school, and theater merged?

"Taking on a hugely ambitious performing arts center project will take all our time and resources for years to come. It will detract from our unfinished work at CAN. I can guarantee it. And where *is* the money to buy the golf course going to come from, let alone the millions needed for the rest of the project? Conrad and George have tried for several years to raise funds for SHLAC. I'm sorry to say, they haven't succeeded.

"Bear with me, please, and let me read to you the strategic memo I've written about CAN. You can all read it at the end of our meeting. I've copies for all of you.

"So... for the reasons set forth above, and because we must look to the future and not the past, I recommend, emphatically, that we not separate the music school and theater from CAN. Instead, let's figure out a way to get our three entities working even more closely together than they have in the past. We can do it. Let's build a great, unified organization: CAN."

Karp read the close of his memo with a flourish, convinced he'd persuaded executive committee members of the merits of the strategy.

Stone silence. No one applauded or expressed any enthusiasm whatsoever for what Karp said, save for the "hear hear" from Tiffany Tisdale, sitting in the row of seats behind the board table on the right-hand side.

Tiffany remained pissed off about not being consulted during the initial planning for SHLAC, a project involving the music schools she ran, her music schools. Worse, she knew that building SHLAC meant closing the Barnstable and Falmouth campuses. CAN couldn't afford to keep them going, and who would want to attend classes or lessons at either of the run-down places when a state-of-the-art facility beckoned, even if it was a fifty-five minute drive from Falmouth? She fumed as she thought about it.

That's not happening. Not if I have anything to say about it.

Ignoring Tiffany's support, Massahol took his turn. "I agree with you, Jason. SHLAC is hugely ambitious."

"But our Cape Philharmonic deserves a better home," he continued. "A much better home than the high school we currently play in. By peeling off our money losers, the music schools and theater, we could devote the resources necessary to make SHLAC a reality. And it's a reality that George and

Conrad have worked so hard on, and have the skills and experience to pull off, now that a property is lined up."

Massahol was on his conductor's podium, figuratively speaking, deftly leading the troops with great panache. "The music schools, and the Lowlands Theater too, can relocate to SHLAC as tenants. We've designed it that way. It's only right to offer it to them."

"Only right to offer it to them!" exclaimed Karp sharply. "What a thing to say. We're all one entity. You make it sound as if their separation from CAN already happened, or is a done deal. What do the rest of you think?" The inability or unwillingness of other board members to express an opinion infuriated Karp. There was an unthinkingness to the group that astonished him. A sheep-like mentality pervaded each and every one of them.

A few days earlier, when Vice Chair Denise Douward stopped by CAN's office with a Tupperware container full of her famous brownies—she put salt-water taffy in them, of all things—Karp invited her into his office for a quick chat.

"Denise, tell me what you really think about the SHLAC project, and even more importantly, what you think about this cockeyed idea of splitting CAN back out into three separate non-profit organizations? I won't share what you tell me with anyone, so please, speak your mind."

"Oh, I don't know, Jason," she said with an owlish grin on her face, her eyes crinkling behind her round wire-rimmed glasses. "I guess I'm up for anything!"

"Denise, when you add it all up, we've already spent around $400,000 on SHLAC. We've carried all of the project's expenses so far. And the commitment the board made last year has CAN on the hook to SHLAC for another $300,000, to pay Conrad's salary and cover George's expenses.

"Have you looked at the site selection report done for SHLAC, Denise? The one that came up with the golf course property as the preferred site? It's pathetic. Middle school children do better analyses than that consultant did. It cost a fortune too."

"Yes, I know, Jason, I know." Silence descended while Denise pondered things. "I'm game though! Give George and Conrad the money! Let's see what magic they can make with it!" Her owlish grin returned.

Hearing the same thing from other board members left Karp wondering if there was more to it than simply the collective urge to get along by going along. He couldn't believe the lack of thinking, of analysis, that went into responses to his inquiries about SHLAC, and about the future of CAN. Duplicity? Malevolence? Ulterior motives? Karp couldn't figure it out.

The executive committee meeting continued like a tennis match, Karp on one side, Massahol and Slavin on the other. Tisdale and Redlich played supporting roles for their respective sides. The other meeting participants were not even line umpires or ball girls. They were spectators.

Board Chair Greg Hemshaw served as chair umpire. Hemshaw's problem was that he liked everyone, even the intensely unlikeable Slavin. He found himself bewildered by the animosity filling the room, by the intensity and cut-throat aspect of the proceedings, and had just one thought.

I wish they'd all quit it and get along.

Hemshaw's role was one of authority. His wishy-washiness resulted in him holding no authority at all. To Karp, Hemshaw was in many ways the worst of the lot.

"Greg, you and I should be working together like pen and paper," Karp said at one of their recent one-on-one weekly meetings. "And you should always have my back, always. You hired me, after all. What kind of legacy do you want for your chairmanship? Don't you think George Slavin and Erme Massahol ride roughshod over CAN, and over you and Denise?" Karp's exasperation was evident. All this was taking place under Hemshaw's chairmanship. Time and time again he failed to step in, leaving Karp dangling in the wind.

Hemshaw saw things differently. He was more than a little miffed at how the relatively new executive director spoke to him. Hemshaw thought about it frequently.

I've simply got a different approach to things than you do, Jason Karp, and maybe it's better than yours.

The executive committee meeting wrapped up with two votes: one to hire a consultant to analyze breaking CAN back up into three separate organizations, and the other to make available to SHLAC all of the funds previously agreed to under the previous year's commitment, the commitment Karp so bitterly objected to. The money would now be made available to Slavin and Redlich as they needed it.

"I don't and can't agree to either," said Karp, almost yelling. He stood up abruptly, looking at his watch. "I've got a plane to catch. Remember, I'm off the next ten days. Greg will wrap things up nicely, I'm sure. What you've all approved is a big mistake in my opinion. I'm glad the full board will have the final word."

Not that the full board will do anything about it, Karp thought bitterly.

◇ ◇ ◇

Karp headed to Logan Airport in Boston to catch his flight to Geneva. Despite the utter malarkey he'd just dealt with, he felt happy. He was off to be with his Swiss wife, Ulrike, who'd gone over two weeks earlier to spend time visiting with her ailing mother. Karp always missed Ulrike when they were apart. Much more than he let on. Tall and willowy, sharp and witty, blonde and beautiful, and with a smile that instantly and always showed sincerity, she was his best friend, lover, and counselor. Ulrike invariably gave him spot-on advice when he needed it. Through the years his behavior had sometimes been less than admirable. Nevertheless, they hung together. His love for her, he realized, was a deep one. The thought of being with her again, in the idyllic Jura Mountains at her family estate, brought a warmth and peacefulness to him.

His cell phone rang. Greg Hemshaw.

"Hey Jason. You make it to the airport alright?" Hemshaw

83

sounded nervous.

"Sure Greg. Thanks for asking. What's up?"

"Listen," Hemshaw blurted out, summoning more courage than he'd ever shown before. "I've got bad news."

"After you left, the executive committee talked about your tenure with CAN. Everyone is super disappointed with you. We can't have you treating board members the way you do, flustering George all the time, belittling Denise in your office the other day. It simply won't do.

"What's more, it's clear your vision for CAN is very different from where we seem to be heading. You don't seem to get that.

"A vote was taken and it came out unanimous," Hemshaw continued. "The executive committee is recommending to the full board that you be terminated as of today."

Karp was stunned. In his moments of frustration and despair about CAN, frequent moments, he thought about resigning. He fantasized about it and even once typed up a letter of resignation to deliver to Hemshaw and Douward. He never in a million years expected it to come to this.

"It's nothing personal, Jason. Just that you're not right for CAN. We'll honor all the financial terms of your contract, which runs another eight months, and provide you with the health insurance it calls for. Please don't return to the office. We'll deliver your personal belongings to your home in Hyannisport in a few weeks, when you're back from your trip." Hemshaw's voice faltered and cracked a bit, withdrawing like a hermit crab back into its shell. He recognized the import of his message.

Before Karp could say anything intelligible, the conversation ended. His thoughts boiled over like an out-of-control cooking pot.

I'm contacting the most aggressive employment law lawyer I can find and suing the bastards. How dare they treat me this way? I've busted my butt professionalizing the place, and quickly too. This is the thanks I get? The reward I get? I'll show them.

Swissair Flight 220 took off right on time at 9:50 p.m. It was a through-the-night trip, like most trans-Atlantic flights. Taking off out of Boston's Logan Airport in a southwesterly direction, at 10,000 feet the Airbus 350 banked east. Starting the long journey across the Atlantic Ocean, it flew straight over the entire lower half of Cape Cod. Passengers looking out the window, including Karp, saw fires burning, one on the Upper Cape—it looked to be in Falmouth—and another Mid-Cape.

How strange, thought Karp. *What can those fires possibly be? Landfills?*

Eight hours later, the plane started its descent into Geneva. Looking out at the Alps, and at incredible Lake Geneva, Karp left his anger and frustration behind.

I'll find something else pretty easily, and it'll be much better than CAN, that dysfunctional heap of... As to SHLAC, I'll bet anyone a million bucks, a million bucks, it'll never, ever get done.

CHAPTER 10

Tuesday, August 24, 2021

Hennessey now had an assigned desk at the BCPD station, out in the vestibule ten yards or so away from where Kelly sat at the front administration desk. No privacy at all, but better than nothing. He actually enjoyed the arrangement. Not for work reasons though. Kelly and he got into the flow of talking to each other now and then, short, intermittent chatter. Boy, did he like the sound of her voice, no matter what she said.

Anytime, or anyplace, he hummed. *Hmm... what song is that from?*

What Hennessey didn't like was the fact that, after almost a week, he and Lipman had made no headway at all in determining whose body parts were out back in the BCPD freezer. With the State's DNA and forensic work done, it was now up to the two of them to figure out who it was and what happened to him. They knew one thing: It was a man and not a woman. The other reason Lipman brought Hennessey in as a consultant, to help solve the Cape's recent string of arson attacks, would have to wait. Lipman first needed Hennessey to tackle the 'mystery man' matter.

The CODIS database, containing the DNA profiles of

nineteen million Americans, didn't help. There was no match in it for the DNA identified in the finger, foot, and torso. Hennessey and Lipman then got permission to request an international search from DNA Interpol, a database containing DNA profiles from more than eighty countries. The cost made the BCPD Commissioner balk. Lipman convinced her it was the appropriate next step to take in trying to identify the body parts they had on their hands. No match existed in the DNA Interpol database either.

"Damn." Hennessey slammed his hands down lightly on his desk upon getting the news.

"What's the matter?" Kelly asked, looking up from reading the Cape Cod Times's weekly police blotter, a duty she found boring and unproductive.

"We've come to the end of the line in our DNA database search. National and international searches. Nothing. I've also done a detailed missing person alert, and followed up on it every way I can. It's the most thorough work I've done in thirty-five years. Nothing. I don't see how it can be. No one reported missing, no one identified through any forensic work or databases."

Kelly looked at Hennessey in a bemused yet sympathetic way.

"How about the watch?" she asked.

"What watch? What're you talking about?"

"You know, the watch found in the shark's stomach."

"Where is it?"

"Lipman locked it up in the vault in his office, along with all the other stuff the marine biologist pulled out. That beast was like a swimming landfill—license plate, fishing tackle, shish kabob sticks, whiffle ball, watch, chunks of fish, human torso… you name it."

With Lipman down in Florida visiting his parents for a long four-day weekend, and completely offline during his time away, Hennessey thought he was stuck.

That's that. Need to twiddle my thumbs yet again.

"I know the combo to the vault," said Kelly. "And I've

always had permission to go into it as I see fit."

Hennessey cocked his head slightly and gave her his best 'would you do that for me' look.

"Wait here. I'll be back in a few," she said.

She returned with a big see-through freezer bag. They emptied it on the table next to the security gate.

"Phew, what a stench!" Hennessey exclaimed. "Wasn't this stuff hosed down before being put away?" The odor came pretty close to making him gag.

The bag's contents contained all of the inorganic junk from inside the great white shark. What an assortment. On top of what Kelly remembered, the shark's stomach contained a miniature nerf football, a Budweiser can, and a domino—sixes and threes.

A friggin' domino, thought Hennessey.

There, in the middle of it all, was a watch. A gold men's watch with a gold wrist band. All things considered, it seemed in pretty good shape, although it wasn't running.

Hennessey picked it up and peered through the clouded crystal. He could barely make out the brand: Philippe Jurgensen. Although not one for the finer material prizes of life, Hennessey nevertheless knew that if the watch was real—and there were loads of fake high-end watches out there—it was a valuable item. Thousands, if not tens of thousands, of dollars' worth of watch if it was an authentic Philippe Jurgensen.

It embarrassed Hennessey that Kelly had brought the watch to his attention. Without her mentioning it, he'd have never even known about it. After Darlene McCoy, the State marine biologist, pulled the human torso from the shark and handed it over to him, he'd carried it inside like a football captain carrying the Lombardi Trophy around. McCoy finished up the necropsy work by herself.

Shame on me, he thought. *What a faux pas... and after all these years. Shame on Phil too. He should've known better.*

Lipman had locked the items up without giving them a second thought or telling Hennessey about them.

"Thanks Kelly," he said. "This might really lead somewhere. I'd have never known about it without you."

She beamed, then, deciding it was high time to get back to work combing through the Cape Cod Times's police blotter, said, "you're welcome" and sashayed back to her desk.

According to the best jewelry and watch store in downtown Hyannis, the watch was a real Philippe Jurgensen. Really expensive watches have their own serial numbers, like a VIN number on a car. In most cases, they can be traced to the original owner, even to subsequent owners if re-registered properly. Companies like Philippe Jurgensen, making the highest quality watches in the world, do so proudly. Their products are a combination of art, jewelry, investment, and functionality. Keeping an ownership registry is an important part of these businesses, part of their heritage, and allows them to keep track of their work through the years if it's necessary to do so.

Getting information out of the Swiss-based Philippe Jurgensen company proved complicated. It didn't matter to the company that it was the BCPD, a U.S. law enforcement agency, requesting information about the eighteen-karat gold watch with serial number PJ 2019-4005. The company balked, saying it needed approval from the Swiss national police before releasing the information. It would take three business days.

"That doesn't make sense!" Hennessey yelled. "We've got an urgent matter on our hands, a missing person who might well be linked to the watch we're asking about. I know, I know... privacy laws. Bend the rules for once, will you?"

"Ahh, they are so anal," Hennessey griped, slamming the phone receiver down. He'd failed at getting the good folks at Philippe Jurgensen to see things his way, and continued on for thirty seconds or so with a stream of not-so-nice generalizations about the Swiss personality and culture.

Kelly caught every word. "I didn't know you were so cosmopolitan," she said to him when his venting wound down. "Didn't know you were so knowledgeable about the

Swiss, Mr. Hennessey. Where'd you pick all that up? Southie? U-Mass Boston? The Boston Police Department? I want to hear all about it."

Hennessey took the next couple of days off, playing golf and tending to his garden. He went into the office on Friday, spending most of the morning puttering around. Late in the morning, he mustered up his nerve.

"Um, Kelly, if you're not busy tonight, ah, would you be interested in, ah, in going to the Cape Philharmonic concert?"

"Hennessey, I haven't been to a concert like that in a long, long time." Silence.

"So, not interested?"

"No, actually I'd love to go. Thanks for asking. Used to be a bit of a pianist myself."

Hennessey couldn't quite understand why he felt so good hearing that from her.

"Me too. My ivory-tickling days are behind me. I've still got my Baldwin baby grand though. I'll pick you up then. Seven-fifteen sound good? Concert starts at eight."

"You know, I've got a long-standing appointment at six tonight. Let's meet at the Barnstable High School auditorium. I'll get there twenty or thirty minutes beforehand. Why don't you wait out front for me? Don't worry, you know what I look like," she said impishly from across the room.

"Remind me again," said Hennessey.

Since the Cape Philharmonic rarely sold out, tickets were easy to come by. The concert was Mozart and Ravel; one piece by the former, two by the latter.

Kelly's arrival took Hennessey's breath away. She'd clearly had time to run home and gussy herself up a bit. She had her hair up and wore an interesting, beautiful mid-length dress, covered by a summery white jacket. Charming and pretty in a totally natural way, as if she'd stepped out of an Andrew Wyeth painting. Hennessey tried his best not to burn his eyeballs.

Look at her... Gorgeous.

Massahol, who never allowed the Philharmonic to be conducted by guests—he was too narcissistic and insecure for that—first led the orchestra through Mozart's insipid *Eine Kleine Nacht Musik*, a perennial crowd favorite. One of the most popular classical music pieces of all time, Double M played on its familiarity, conducting as if he had Mahler's mighty Ninth Symphony before him, not a slight piece ranking as second if not third-rate Mozart. Hennessey was unimpressed.

Before the intermission came Ravel's *Bolero*. The orchestra played it well. Everyone in the audience knew it or had heard snippets of it before. Like Mozart's *Eine Kleine Nacht Musik*, *Bolero* was a true crowd pleaser. During Ravel's lifetime, its popularity detracted so much from his other music he rued composing it. What an ending it had! Everyone was in great spirits at the break.

The second half featured Ravel's magnificent *Daphnis and Chloe*, a large orchestral tone poem that unfortunately showed some of the Cape Philharmonic's thin spots. Not that anyone noticed. It too ended with a bang. A better Friday night was not to be had on Cape Cod.

Hennessey walked Kelly to her car. Their cars were parked almost a quarter-mile apart in the huge Barnstable High School parking lot. As they approached her Subaru Outback, he asked whether she'd liked the concert.

"Hmmm," she responded, inflecting up and down in an interesting way, and with an inward look on her face, as if she was connecting the music to something else, some past feeling or memory.

Taking his hand in her small, supple one and holding it for a moment, she said, "Yes, I did. You surprise me Hennessey. A classical music aficionado, huh? It was a lovely evening, one of the best I've had in a long time. Let's talk music—soon."

Strolling back to his car, Hennessey thought about it.

Where did my connection to classical music, my passion

for it, come from?

It came from his parents. Mary Hennessey, nee Greenwood, couldn't get enough music in her life and infused her deep interest in all things musical in her three boys. She had a lovely mezzo-soprano voice and brought with her to America a wide repertoire of folk music, and a deep and abiding love for the classical music of Great Britain and Ireland. The composers Vaughan Williams and Elgar were her favorites.

John Hennessey surprised everyone. He loved classical music too. Not only that, he got around beautifully on the violin. Before the boys were born, once or twice a week he took off his postal uniform and headed out after dinner to play in the Boston Philharmonic Orchestra, an ensemble that included some of the city's best amateur musicians. He laughed at the good-natured joshing he got about it from co-workers and neighbors who couldn't quite get their heads around it.

One of his colleagues once told him, "John, don't carry dog pepper-spray on your postal route. Take your violin and charm 'em with an Irish tune or two when they come for you."

Hennessey had been a pretty good pianist, making his way through the easier Brahms Intermezzi and Debussy Preludes before calling it a day at his musical studies. Doug and Joey did percussion. One summer, John Hennessey built a soundproof room down in the cellar.

"Go at it down here... and only down here!" he told his two younger sons. "Your mother and I don't want to hear you wailing away on those cymbals anymore!"

Hennessey enjoyed one thing in particular about *Bolero*, and *Daphnis and Chloe* too: utterly sensual music. *Bolero* was one big crescendo, one big climax. That's why it had been used in movies about sex. *Daphnis and Chloe* also had several huge climaxes in it. The one that closed off the first section of the piece was pure bedroom music. Hennessey loved all of Ravel's music, always caught the overwhelmingly sensuous nature of it, like the first movements of *Gaspard de la Nuit* and *Chansons Madecasses*.

He thought about Kelly's reaction to what they'd just heard. *Maybe that's what she was getting at with that 'hmmm' of hers. I'm going to play more Ravel for her someday. Funny—that Ravel was a life-long bachelor. How did he know?*

The morning after the concert, Hennessey woke up at 10:45, the day well underway. Heading out to grab a coffee and an egg sandwich, he stopped suddenly as he bounded down onto the wooden front porch he'd built a few years back. Sitting there was a half-gallon glass milk bottle with a lovely bouquet of flowers in it. Not store-bought flowers. A bouquet from the side of the road: Black-Eyed Susans, Queen Anne's Lace, Day Lilies, Beach Plum Blossoms, an open yet completely intact milkweed pod.

A note folded in two wrapped itself around the bottle, held in place by a rubber band. Hennessey removed it.

The top half read "Thanks!" written lightly and neatly in cursive. The bottom half was also written out in cursive:

> It's all I have to bring today,
> This, and my heart beside,
> This, and my heart, and all the fields,
> And all the meadows wide.
> Be sure you count, should I forget,
> Some one the sum could tell—
> This, and my heart, and all the Bees
> Which in the Clover dwell.
> Emily Dickinson

Hennessey stood there for a long time. Transported to a place he yearned to be. Confused by it all, he accepted and embraced it nevertheless. Basked in it. Relished it.

CHAPTER 11

Mrs. Ulrike Baten-Karp had bought the Philippe Jurgensen watch as a tenth-year anniversary present for her American husband, Jason Karp. Hennessey was right. The watch's value was in the tens of thousands of dollars. Ulrike came from an extremely wealthy family. Her great-grandfather had founded one of Switzerland's notable private wealth management banks, a bank that for generations helped the wealthy from around the world hide information about their financial worth from the clutches of government, until the U.S. and other countries put their collective feet down and made it a requirement that all Swiss banks report client income information to them. No exceptions.

The Philippe Jurgensen company knew Ulrike had purchased the watch as a gift. They delivered it directly to her husband, along with a flowery note from her referencing emotionally richer and more exciting times ahead for them.

The internet led Hennessey quickly to Karp. He'd been named the executive director of CAN almost two years ago, the umbrella organization that was home to the Cape Philharmonic as well as other local arts organizations.

What a coincidence, Hennessey thought. *We heard the*

orchestra last Friday night.

Hennessey called CAN's office. "Yeah, ah, could I speak to Jason Karp?" CAN's office manager hung up on him. Blew him right off. Calling back, Hennessey let her have it. "Listen, I'll be there in ten minutes with a BCPD officer and have you arrested for obstructing an investigation. Who the hell do you think you are?"

Hennessey made clear he was working on behalf of the BCPD, which got her talking.

"He doesn't work here anymore."

"Since when?"

"I don't know, a month or so."

"Why did he leave?"

"He was terminated by the board. I don't know any more than that. You'll have to ask the board chair, Greg Hemshaw, for the details of what happened."

"You've got nothing more to tell me?"

"Look, Jason told us he was going to Europe for two weeks. A vacation. His lovely wife Ulrike—I really like her—was already there. The next thing I know, the following Monday, late July if I'm remembering right, Greg comes to the office and tells us Jason's no longer with CAN, and that Greg would act as interim executive director until they hired someone new."

"Have you seen Karp since he was fired?" Hennessey asked. "Did he come to say goodbye to everyone, stop by the office to pick up his stuff?"

"No, I haven't seen him. He never came by. They told me to box up his stuff and send it to the house the Karps rented in Hyannisport. A nice place, not far from the Kennedy compound."

"It doesn't surprise me that we haven't heard from him," she continued. "He went to Europe, Switzerland I think, for a couple of weeks. That's where Ulrike was from. Maybe he stayed there—I would've. My guess is he's still there. I knew they were away, so I took his stuff over to the house and put it on the enclosed back porch. Easy to do and safe enough.

There was nothing valuable in the box, just family photos and work mementos."

Hennessey's next call was to Greg Hemshaw, CAN's board chair.

"Yes... we let him go," Hemshaw sighed. "Truth be told, Detective Hennessey, everyone found Jason a little too much. Slightly abrasive and arrogant. He seemed to go out of his way to get himself in trouble, with the board and his staff. His relationship with our conductor and music director, Emre Massahol... Uggh—that's all that I can say about it. The same for his relationship with Tiffany Tisdale, the music school director. And she's such a sweetheart deep down inside."

"Anything else?" asked Hennessey.

"Not really. It just didn't work out. A real shame. I liked the guy. Not many other people did. He had good ideas, and a good presence, and was a good communicator, but boy... too full of himself. Not really a Cape kind of a person either." Hennessey swallowed hard when he heard that statement.

Gee... I'm not a 'Cape kind of a person' either. I'm Southie through and through. What of it?

"Do you know where he is?" asked Hennessey.

"No. No idea. Last I spoke to him, a while ago now, he was at Logan Airport, getting on a flight to Geneva for his vacation. The phone call when we let him go... a super tough call for me." Hennessey heard the discomfort in Hemshaw's voice when speaking about firing Karp.

"Did he come back on the flight he was supposed to come back on?"

"Detective Hennessey," said Hemshaw, slightly exasperated. "I have no clue. How should I know that? Why are you looking for him anyway? What's going on? Is he in trouble?"

Hennessey brushed off Hemshaw's questions like a horse swishing a fly off its rump. Thanking the CAN board chair for the information, he started thinking things through.

The Philippe Jurgensen watch is from Geneva. Karp's Swiss wife bought it for him a couple of years ago. They moved to the Cape recently so he could run CAN. He was on his way to Switzerland for a few weeks and was fired right before leaving.

"It has to be him," Hennessey said out loud to himself.

"How was the visit with your folks?" asked Hennessey.

"Like root canal surgery," responded Lipman. "An unpleasant part of life. Florida gives me the creeps, the heebie-jeebies. I can't stand the place."

Hennessey rarely went down to Florida to visit his father. Maybe once a year, or not even. He found it too depressing—the ghosts that swirled up from the past when he made such visits, and the rapidly declining state of his once-vibrant father.

Getting an update from Hennessey about the lead developing from the Phillipe Jurgensen watch, Lipman bit his lip. "My mistake," he said. "I threw the bag into the vault without thinking about it. Couldn't focus on the inanimate stuff, when we had body parts on our hands to deal with." Hennessey's affectionate clap on the back, an unusually warm gesture for him, put it all behind them quickly.

"What's our next step?" he asked Lipman.

"I think we need to call Ulrike Baten-Karp and find out if her husband is over there with her. And if not, find out from her where he is. Why wait?"

"Let's spend an hour or so checking out their rental home first," suggested Hennessey. "Maybe the guy's in there with a week-old beard and a bottle of scotch, watching Seinfeld reruns to cheer him up after his unfortunate stint at CAN. Let's do that before reaching out to his wife, no?"

The real estate agent who rented the place on behalf of the owners had the keys. Lipman tracked her down easily enough. "Don't get alarmed," he told her. "We need to take a quick look around the place to see what's up, without us having to get a warrant to do so. It's a potential missing person matter."

"Of course," she said, reassured by Lipman's statement. "I'll wait outside for you in my car. Take your time, detectives."

Hennessey noticed it immediately. The stagnant and still air of a vacant and sealed-up home. He stood beside Lipman as the door was unlocked and pushed open. The air rushed outward. He smelled it. The entire mixture of smells humans leave behind when they go away. Especially men.

"So, what are we looking for?" asked Lipman.

"Who knows? Jason Karp? Let's look, see how things are, see what we find. See if anything at all helps us."

The house came fully furnished. The owners struck a deal every year with whoever rented it during the off-season, from Labor Day until Memorial Day. Part of the house was off-limits and locked up, used as storage space by the owners. The closets were half full with the owners' stuff. The kitchen was built for a master chef: a six-burner Viking oven, Sub-Zero refrigerator and freezer unit, and state-of-the art space saver microwave. Without paying much attention to what he was doing, Hennessey opened the doors to everything—the oven and microwave doors, the freezer door, the refrigerator door.

"Phew, what a stench!" he exclaimed loudly. Lipman, in another room, didn't respond. The smell of food gone bad smacked Hennessey. Holding his breath, he took a closer look inside the refrigerator. Some of it, the hummus and milk, was open but barely consumed.

Man, that's the sourest smelling milk I've ever run across. Goddamn.

The worst smell came from the dish of leftovers on the top shelf. Chicken parmigiana with a side of broccoli? The mold covering it all made it anyone's guess as to what it was. Hennessey grimaced and closed the door quickly. Then breathed.

That's enough, thank you.

The furnishings and belongings of the owners dominated the interior of the house. The two detectives discerned the few household belongings and clothing belonged to the Karps, such as the wall hangings with pithy German quotes and phrases that hung in the living room. Since the last name of the owners was O'Donahue, the wall hangings most likely belonged to the German-speaking Ulrike Baten-Karp.

The garage held a snappy pink VW Beetle convertible. Hennessey and Lipman found a dozen or so unassembled moving boxes in the garage, stacked on top of each other. Small and medium sized ones. Moving tape and a Sharpie marker too. Three of the boxes were already assembled. Nothing was in them.

"Looks like the Karps are getting ready to move," said Lipman. "Think Jason Karp did this before he headed over to Europe? After being fired?"

"Nah, it couldn't have been him," responded Hennessey. "The board chair, Greg Hemshaw, told me that Karp went straight from the executive committee meeting to Logan Airport. He left the meeting early. There's no way he came back and did this before his vacation. Maybe they hired someone to pack up for them while they were away. But you'd have to know their stuff from the owners' stuff. Who would know that, except for them? And all the rotten food in the refrigerator... too much! It's strange."

Lipman went outside to tell the real estate agent they needed a few more minutes. Hennessey sprung up the garage steps back into the house. There were four bedrooms. He headed to the one the Karps used. It was dominated by a tightly made-up king size bed.

The clothes draped over the two reading chairs and the pile of bunched up underwear thrown into the corner of the long window seat meant nothing to Hennessey. *Not unusual... It's the stuff people leave behind when they rush out on vacation. They'll deal with it when they get back.*

Hennessey sat down on the edge of the bed up toward the pillows, and took in what was on the bed stand. A couple of books, one about spousal sexual compatibility and another by Brene Brown, an opened package of stick-ums, and a pocket size 2021 diary. Picking up the diary, Hennessey flipped to the inside front cover, where the owner's ledger was found. It was embossed with 'Property Of.' Written in ink on the line after the embossing was Jason Karp's name.

Hennessey jammed the diary into his rear pants pocket as he left the room.

◇ ◇ ◇

With the two Swiss cantonal police who'd come to her front door now standing in the vestibule with her, Ulrike Baten-Karp Zoomed with Hennessey and Lipman. They'd been introduced to her as a couple of police detectives from Barnstable on Cape Cod.

"Of course Jason returned to the U.S. as originally planned," she said. "Those ignorant small-timers at CAN, they didn't deserve him. Someone with his talent, brains, and vision," she went on, assuming the detectives were calling about his ignominious dismissal. "Those hicks, those rubes," she spat out contemptuously.

She's got a great command of English, thought Hennessey.

"No, I haven't talked to him, not since he settled back into Hyannisport. He sent a text message when the plane landed. An uneventful flight. Then we spoke briefly when he was back at the house."

When asked if she thought their sparse communications unusual, Ulrike replied forcefully, "No, I don't. Not at all. Busy professionals with lives all over the place, especially on different continents, are like that. And my sister and I have been travelling for much of the month."

Jason was cleaning out the rental house, she explained, putting their stuff in storage and then coming back to Switzerland. They'd figure out their next move from there. She listened carefully. Human body parts... dead great white shark... a Philippe Jurgensen watch traced back to her.

It all sank in. Ulrike sobbed. Then she began to half wail, half scream, an indescribable guttural sound coming from who knows where in her body. From her anguished soul perhaps. The sound of someone dispossessed—randomly, suddenly, violently—of what was and would always be the most precious part of her life. Profound bereavement swept over all of them, the four policemen spread over two countries and two continents, and the utterly exposed and alone widow.

Experienced as they were, Hennessey and Lipman were deeply affected. You'd have to be inhuman not to be. Expressing their condolences, they promised to determine as best they could what happened.

"We'll get DNA test results on a few of your husband's belongings at the house, ma'am," Hennessey told her. "And we'll match the results against the DNA results we already have."

"I'm sorry, ma'am, so, so sorry," continued Hennessey, "but prepare yourself for the worst."

Ulrike Baten-Karp fainted. She hit the vestibule side table hard as she went down. It was horrible to watch on Zoom.

It took three stitches to her forehead, put in by one of Switzerland's most skilled plastic surgeons, to close the wound. It was nothing like the wound to her heart though.

◊ ◊ ◊

Hennessey and Lipman headed straight back to the Hyannisport house after the Zoom call. Taking evidence bags with them, they picked the lock this time. Hennessey was a pro at it.

"The hell with dealing with the real estate agent," said Lipman, shaken to the core by the call with Ulrike Baten-Karp. They took the one toothbrush out of the holder in the bathroom attached to the master bedroom, and the hairbrush that was there too. It looked like a men's hairbrush. Both were put carefully into evidence bags to be delivered to the State's regional criminal forensics lab for yet another DNA analysis.

"We don't need more DNA work done," said Lipman

when they were back at the office. "We know who it is. Who else could it be?"

"Yeah, I agree," replied Hennessey. "We have to put it to rest though, Phil. I don't feel comfortable changing Karp's status from missing to dead, and you shouldn't either, until a matching DNA analysis is back. Seems unlikely it won't be the case. But let's make sure the toothbrush and hairbrush DNA results line up with what we already have."

"Ah, what horseshit," said Lipman, who rarely swore. His expletive wasn't directed at Hennessey; he agreed they needed to put it to rest with more DNA work. It was directed at the grim situation, the bitter reality of what they had on their hands.

"Time to call Larry Sylvester at the Chamber and tell him the full story, no?" continued Lipman. "The press too, no?"

"You know, Phil," Hennessey said, after a long silence. "If you think that's the right thing to do, then do it."

"You don't seem convinced."

"I'm not, not at all. But I don't know what else to do, how else we should go about it. What will you tell Sylvester? And the press?" asked Hennessey.

"I'm going to tell them what we know," responded Lipman. "An expensive watch was found in the body of a great white shark, along with part of a human torso. The torso hasn't been identified yet but the watch's owner was traced through its serial number. DNA work is now being done that will allow us to make a definitive ID on the torso. We think the dead person is Jason Karp, the former executive director of Cape Now, the regional performing arts group. The watch is Karp's. His wife over in Switzerland confirmed that he returned to the States several weeks ago after vacationing there with her. He hasn't been seen or heard from since."

"Makes sense to me," said Hennessey.

"Anything to add or change?"

"No."

Karp's death shocked Cape Cod. The news spread like a California wildfire blown by the wind; gossip flew about, buzzing and darting like bees in a summer garden. Chamber of Commerce members were aghast, knowing how vacationers would react to the horrifying story. Jason Karp's torso and very expensive watch found in a great white shark; a finger and foot of his found on different Cape beaches.

Counting Karp, it was the second great white shark attack death on the Cape in the past few years. Third, if you include the July 2020 death at Bailey's Island in southern Maine, nautically speaking just a stone's throw away from Cape Cod.

Meeting again at Lipman's office, Larry Sylvester proclaimed "this is the END" so dramatically that Hennessey burst out laughing. Neither Sylvester nor Lipman saw the humor in it. The Chamber of Commerce put its game plan into effect to ensure visitors felt comfortable coming across the Sagamore and Bourne bridges. A "Cape's Open/Cape's Safe" campaign spread across social media, print journals, and the airwaves. In the weeks following the release of the sensational news about Karp, lodging and weekly rental cancellations were up a bit, affecting all aspects of the Cape's economy—restaurants, bike rentals, attendance at cultural offerings, ice cream stores, and whale watching trips. But not enough to really matter. The perennial labor shortage the Cape faced every summer was much more of an issue for the local economy.

Sylvester and his colleagues at the Chamber were incensed at The Boston Globe's handling of the Karp tale. Madison Jones, the young reporter reamed out by Hennessey on her first trip down, dug into the story voraciously. She reported in graphic detail all aspects of Karp's demise—the who, what, and when, and especially the where in regard to the discovery of his body parts. Her article ended with an interview with marine biologist Darlene McCoy on what it was like to cut open a great white shark. Simultaneously, the Globe ran an editorial titled, "Cape Cod and the Great White:

Here To Stay." The piece provided sound science about the apex predator, and some good safety tips about what to do when visiting the Cape and swimming there.

"Those jackasses," Sylvester said out loud to himself, reading the paper in his office. "They had to rub it in, didn't they? 'Great White: Here To Stay.' What jerks." Hard work lay ahead for the Chamber of Commerce and the Cape's municipalities: figuring out the best way to protect people from great white sharks. Sylvester wouldn't mind shooting them all. He considered Reggie Smith, the commercial fisherman who caught the shark with Karp's torso in it, a hero. Sylvester now had to spend time and energy convincing people that the Cape was still a great place, a unique place, to unwind and let the kids have some fun. Thinking about it buoyed him though.

We'll get it done, no doubt about it.

Sylvester actually found himself feeling pretty upbeat. Australia and other parts of the world had by and large solved their beach and shark problems. So would Cape Cod. He prayed, though, that no other gruesome local news involving great white sharks came his way for a long time.

Sea Interlude #3

Marine biologists tell us sharks have been roaming our oceans for close to four hundred million years. They are much older than dinosaurs, and have inhabited the earth for millions and millions of years longer than humans. As a result of their longevity, their instinctual hunting and killing skills are highly refined.

The great white shark is a fearsome, perversely beautiful sight to behold. Shaped like a torpedo, it reaches lengths of up to twenty feet and can weigh up to a ton. Scientists aren't in agreement as to how fast they can swim. It is thought they can swim, in bursts, somewhere between twenty to thirty-five miles per hour. Olympic swimmers clock in between four and eight miles per hour. The great white's mouth contains dozens and dozens of huge, razor-sharp teeth, and its jaws are forceful enough to cut through just about anything. Its eyes are dull and reveal nothing.

There are certainly other apex predators in the ocean. The killer whale, for example, is one of them. Although the great white is often considered the top marine predator, killer whales, known as orcas, give it competition, and may actually rule. Orcas hunt in packs and are known to kill great whites; there is no record of a great white taking down an orca. Orcas are also mammals, the largest member of the dolphin family, and possess considerable intelligence. Orca communities have a fascinating, matriarchal hierarchy to them. Put succinctly, orca grandmothers rule.

Through a human lens, though, one fact is paramount: Orcas have never been known to attack and kill a human being in the wild. Never. The only human deaths attributable to orcas have occurred in those horrible, perverse settings where they've been locked up and forced to perform like circus animals. In those settings, an orca or two has taken its revenge.

The great white shark, on the other hand, is a fish. One of the ocean's largest and most dangerous. A solitary creature except when breeding, it never sleeps, never stops moving, never stops hunting. From a human perspective, it is the ocean's ultimate apex predator.

CHAPTER 12

Wednesday, September 1, 2021

Hennessey's attention to his garden paid dividends. Bumper crops of tomatoes, zucchini, bell peppers, and rainbow chard. The flowers—bounteous and magnificent. His raspberry crop, which he grew against the back fence, was much tastier than anything you could buy at the grocery store. He froze big zip-lock bags of them for consumption in the winter months. The strawberries had been great too, although the birds got their fair share of them.

Maybe the cow manure added to the garden soil helped after all. Then again, maybe not. The brussels sprouts were a bust. The little buggers stopped growing at the size of marbles, even after he cut many of the leaves off of the main stalk, something an article he read on the web told him to do. Hennessey never gardened growing up. He realized what a shortcoming that had been in his life.

Once done with his gardening chores, Hennessey headed to the hammock, a reward for work well done. He'd brought Karp's diary home with him for the weekend. After pocketing it, he worried it might be needed to identify Karp, using the DNA on the outside covers and inside pages. The other personal belongings Hennessey and Lipman collected did the trick though, the toothbrush and hairbrush. What did Hennessey and Lipman now know? They indeed had some of Jason Karp's body parts on their hands, the biggest one pulled from the guts of a great white shark.

The miniature lock on the diary was child's play. Hennessey smiled at it and thought about trying to pick it with his eyes closed. Once open, he noticed the diary was really high quality. Every page had a gilded date on the top; it functioned as a calendar diary, not as an unpaginated journal for jotting down dreamy, random thoughts. Hennessey thought about the quality of what he had in his hands.

Of course it's a good diary. The guy owned a Philippe Jurgensen watch, after all.

Not every date had an entry. Sometimes more than a week went by without anything being written down. Often the entries were short, other times Karp went beyond the two-page limit, writing over into the next day in the diary and not seeming to care about it. Some of what he'd written about Ulrike touched Hennessey deeply.

The May 16th entry, now months old, read in part:

> She's demanding and rigid, like many Swiss. Doesn't deal well with ambiguity—life is always this or that, never both. Always yes or no, never yes and no. But what a true marvel my Ulrike is. So good for me and to me. It's taken me a long time to recognize it, dope that I am. I'm planning to grow old with Ulrike Baten-Karp.

That put a big lump in Hennessey's throat. The next page, May 17th, was blank, and then came weeks and weeks of nothing. The next entry, an even bigger one, was on July 10th:

> Assholes Double M and GS pushed hard at board mtg yesterday. Again. There'll be no CAN if they have their way. They are so selfish it's unbelieva-

ble. Hemshaw? Utterly useless. "Hem & Haw" is what we should call him. Nothing I say seems to be taken seriously. Of course CAN, can function well with all three parts together, even be profitable, if well-managed. I need more time to plan and implement everything though. And check egos at door! The money spent on the SHLAC project so far: WTF! GS and his buddy CR pocketing it as salary. Nothing to show for it. WTFx2! Their favored golf course location: couldn't be worse. WTFx3! They have no idea what they're doing. GS putting the new performing arts center project right in the toilet. Unbelievably frustrating. Love the flush though! Always happens when called out on his malarkey.

Hennessey didn't understand most of what he read. He thought hard about it. *Their favored golf course location? Love the flush though?*

Flipping forward, he looked at the two most recent entries.

August 3rd.

Those assholes. Left my stuff on the back porch. Not enough integrity or courage to deliver it to me in person. What happened to the music schools?? To the Lowlands Theater??? Not my business any more thank God.

August 4th.

What an invite!?! Why not!! Cooking Gus and Dottie Lang dinner this Saturday. Such good eggs, the two of them.

Again, Hennessey didn't understand much of it. What he did understand: Karp was alive on Wednesday, August 4th, and that he made plans for dinner with a Gus and Dottie Lang on Saturday, August 7th. Maybe that explained the rotten food in the fridge. Time to find and talk to the Langs.

Gus Lang was one of those immensely likeable people. Professorial in looks and by nature, he pulled you into his special universe and sphere of gravity, like entering a warm bath. Hennessey felt it and appreciated it immediately.

"Jason and I really hit it off," he told Hennessey. "I'm a retired consultant. Used to do strategic planning and organizational growth work for non-profit institutions. I thought Jason had excellent ideas about CAN. He was on the right track with the organization after its many years of problems. What headwinds he faced. I tried helping him think things through. He had an incredibly difficult situation on his hands, given the dysfunctionality of the place."

Gus and his wife Dottie didn't know why Karp never followed through with their dinner plans for August 7th. They tried his cell phone a couple of times, but never got through to him and he didn't call back.

"We assumed he was too embarrassed and pissed off about getting fired by CAN to want to get together, so we let it drop," Gus told Hennessey.

The news of Karp's death shocked and saddened them to the core. They now assumed he'd died before being able to finalize their dinner plans. Hennessey agreed with that assessment. Dottie Lang couldn't even talk. Too upset and emotional about it, she sat with the two men and wept silently, while her husband spoke about their brief, meaningful moments with Jason and Ulrike.

Hennessey now understood why no one reported Karp missing. Newcomers to the Cape, the Karps knew very few people there. And no one from CAN would touch him with a ten-foot pole after Karp was fired. Hennessey's thoughts darkened.

He died all alone, his wife thousands of miles away. What a way to go.

Hennessey took Kelly to a Cape Cod League mid-week baseball game that night. It was a cheap date. The league's games were free to anyone who cared to watch. Founded in the 1860s, and the training ground for over a thousand major league players, college kids from all over the country, and an increasing number of young foreign baseball players, came to the Cape every summer to hone their skills, trying to catch the eye of a major league scout and ride their dream to the top.

Hennessey enjoyed Cape Cod League games more than anything. It was authentic and unadulterated baseball. No outrageously priced food courts; no distracting and deafening and really bad music; no luxury boxes filled with groveling politicians and where no one watched the game. All professional sports were the same now: Mega-rich team owners called all the shots, master puppeteers manipulating everyone else. Hennessey could live without it. Give him Cape Cod League baseball instead, any day of the week.

They were in Orleans at Eldredge Park field, right off of Route 28, watching the Orleans Firebirds take on the Falmouth Commodores. Hennessey made them a picnic dinner. For him, that meant buying lobster rolls at the Lobster Shanty right up the road in Eastham, along with potato salad and fruit too. He got peaches, something he'd never do on his own, and brought a basket of his homegrown raspberries too, thinking they might be to Kelly's preference. The two of them spread out on a beach blanket on the small rise a little beyond the left field fence, a four-foot-high chain link fence that could be seen through and leaned against.

The game started strangely. In the bottom of the first inning, Falmouth's fireball-throwing pitcher unleashed a ninety-eight mph fastball a little too high. It nicked the top of the catcher's glove before plonking the home plate umpire on the face mask right between the eyes. Over he went on his back, arms and legs sticking up and out as if rigor mortis had set in. He stayed that way for an uncomfortable period of time. With everyone huddled around the umpire, making sure he was still breathing, the Orleans runner on second base skipped to third and then tiptoed home. After determining the umpire would live to see another day, a lengthy discussion ensued as to whether the run counted, whether the ball was still live after beaning and almost killing an official in the field of play. In other words, a ten-minute-long wild pitch. Hennessey loved baseball's arcana. He looked at Kelly with a sheepish grin. She rolled her eyes.

In the top of the fifth inning, with the game settling down nicely, Kelly suddenly said, "I was married once," catching Hennessey off guard with the import of it and with the directness and tone of her voice.

"My husband Sam and I moved here when our daughter Rebecca was a baby. We'd been in Somerville and wanted to live where the beauty of our natural surroundings reminded us of what was important in life. Wanted our children to understand that too, wanted them brought up in a community small enough to know you, really know you, and humane enough to not care what college you got into or whether you even went to college, as long as you were a decent person and contributed some way, large or small, to life.

"Sam and Rebecca and I went to the cinema in Yarmouth. Becky, we called her Becky, had recently turned six. She was full of pep and curiosity and kindness and goodness. She begged and begged to go see Mulan, the latest Disney movie. Driving home, I couldn't even tell you what happened. There we were on Route 6, in a million pieces. They said Sam and Becky died almost instantly. Wish I'd died too, but I didn't. Ended up with a miscarriage, a small rod in my back, and a shortened left leg."

Her sky-blue eyes glistened, wetted by tears that slowly filled, then rolled down her cheeks, falling gently onto the empty paper plate in front of her. "It's been five years now. Some days it still feels like it was yesterday. Many days, actually."

Hennessey knew. Without ever talking about it, he knew. She'd endured a shattering misfortune, like him, a misfortune gifting and strengthening and ultimately giving her courage. Courage came with less struggle for some than for others. He sensed Kelly struggled mightily to possess it, asking herself all the time whether she had it and also how could this possibly be? How could any of it be real? Over time, her courage grew slowly and steadily, never faltering or disappearing, taking root like a mighty oak and not like a lovely lilac shining brilliantly for a few short weeks before disappearing.

By the time the game had ended and Hennessey had driven her home, they understood the story of each other. Individuality of loss respected fully. Hennessey's wife abruptly leaving a marriage he never once questioned, that had so fundamentally defined and grounded him, different from what Kelly left on Route 6 that night. Those who suffer great pain of injury or loss are often joined to one another with bonds of special authority: the bonds of grief. The grief of Hennessey and Kelly now joined them together while setting them apart from others, a space as great and vast as the Grand Canyon.

◊ ◊ ◊

The next morning, Hennessey got up early and returned the half-gallon glass milk bottle to Kelly. He knew where she lived well before their baseball game dinner date; he looked it up weeks ago and drove by a few times, like a teenage boy scoping out the house of his first crush. It was down Route 6A, five or so miles to the west in Dennis. He cut the flowers from his own garden—snapdragons, zinnias, yellow and purple bearded iris—and in the center put a trio of large, about-to-bloom sunflowers.

His note was in two parts too. The top half read, "I know you're desperate to get the twenty-five cent deposit back, so here's the bottle." The bottom half took him much of the night to find. He had first stumbled upon it during the darkest days following his divorce, and now wanted to share it with Kelly:

"Hope" is the thing with feathers,
That perches in the soul,
And sings the tune without the words,
And never stops—at all.

And sweetest in the Gale is heard,
And sore must be the storm,
That could abash the little Bird
That kept so many warm.

I've heard it in the chillest land,
And on the strangest Sea—
Yet, never, in Extremity,
It asked a crumb of me.

                    Emily Dickinson

CHAPTER 13

Thursday, September 2, 2021

Finding the lunatic torching Cape Cod's performing arts buildings proved easier said than done. Hennessey and Lipman had their hands full. CAN music school buildings in two locations, Falmouth and Barnstable, a theater in Wellfleet, an almost-finished multi-purpose arts center in Mashpee, and CAN's renowned Lowlands Theater, also in Falmouth, were all targeted. The seemingly indiscriminate destruction spanned the entire Cape. Thinking about it, Hennessey couldn't begin to piece together a motive.

Why? What's going on? To what end?

"It's clearly a highly cultured person," quipped Hennessey, sitting in his now-favorite chair in front of Lipman's desk. "Probably an aesthete upset at the artistic quality of their experiences here on the Cape."

All kidding aside, they faced a vexatious, extremely serious matter. Arson was a big deal. And the intentional burning of the Lowlands Theater resulted in a death; they had a felony murder on their hands. That it was arson was clear to them, especially to Hennessey, who'd spent years with the Boston Police Department handling arson cases. He knew all the signs. He noted the strategic burning of some of the buildings, enough to damage but not destroy them. Other buildings were torched beyond saving and could not be restored or rebuilt. They found scant evidence of flashpoints, and little in terms of incendiary device remnants. It troubled Hennessey tremendously—all of it. He'd seen similar arson attacks, almost identical, in his previous life. Not wanting to jump to any conclusions, he didn't tell Lipman what he was thinking.

These arson attacks have been pulled off beautifully. There's almost no evidence at all. Who could've done it so well? Pat Kimmell? Can't wait to get my hands on that fucker.

"Don't you find it strange that most of these buildings, three out of the five, were owned by CAN?" said Hennessey, spreading photos of the damaged and destroyed buildings out on the corner table in Lipman's office.

"Can't say that I do," said Lipman. "Nothing strange about it to me. They're all performing arts buildings. Some weird, specific vendetta against the arts, don't you think?"

"Yeah," replied Hennessey. "But the only buildings destroyed, completely destroyed, were CAN buildings. The theater out in Wellfleet... not much damage really. It'll be up and running before we know it. The damage to the Mashpee Arts Center? It was under construction, not an operating performing arts complex, and when all's said and done, it wasn't too bad either."

"So?" asked Lipman.

"So... the only organization that got closed down, that really got hit, was CAN."

Hennessey thought about the notes in Karp's diary. They nagged at him. Excusing himself for a minute, he went to retrieve the diary from his desk drawer, not really giving a hoot that it should either be returned to Ulrike Baten-Karp or kept somewhere more official in the BCPD offices. He glanced at Kelly and gave her a big smile. She smiled back and winked.

"OK, listen to this," he said, once back in Lipman's office.

Reading aloud from Karp's diary, Hennessey commented as he went, guessing as to the meaning of passages and inviting Lipman's input.

> Assholes Double M and GS pushed hard at board mtg yesterday. Again. There'll be no CAN if they have their way.

"There's clearly bad blood between Karp, on one hand, and Double M and GS, whoever they are, on the other," said Hennessey. "Board members is my guess. It reads as if these board members want to get rid of the organization, close it down." Lipman nodded in agreement.

"Listen to this next part," Hennessey said. "To me, it's Karp defending the organization, don't you think?"

> Of course CAN can function well with all three parts.... Hemshaw? Utterly useless.

"Hemshaw's the chairman of the board. Karp didn't get along with any of them," Hennessey told Lipman, noting Karp's sharp disdain for CAN's board chair.

"I spoke to Hemshaw about Karp being fired," Hennessey told Lipman. "He told me that no one liked Karp or could work with him. I didn't ask Hemshaw about any of the stuff in the diary though. He'd probably be able to explain some of it." Hennessey read further from the diary.

> The money spent on the SHLAC project so far: WTF! GS and his buddy CR pocketing it as salary. Nothing to show for it. WTFx2! Their favored golf course location: couldn't be worse. WTFx3! These guys have no idea what they're doing. GS putting the new performing arts center project right in the toilet. Unbelievably frustrating. Love the flush though! Always happens when called out on his malarkey.

"So now," continued Hennessey, "Karp is writing about GS and CR, whoever that is, not Double M. We know about the SHLAC project, CAN's new performing arts center. The Cape Cod Times writes about it now and then; all its troubles too. It'll be the new concert hall for the orchestra and the new location of the music school and theater. According to Karp, it's going right down the tubes.

"There's a lot going on at CAN. The couple I talked to about Karp, Gus and Dottie Lang? Gus said that CAN is a dysfunctional mess. That's what he picked up from his talks with Karp, and that's what I'm getting from these diary entries. I've no idea what this 'flush' thing is. No idea. To me it's a poker hand."

Together, Hennessey and Lipman reviewed the last two entries in the diary.

August 3d.

Those assholes. Left my stuff on the back porch. Not enough integrity or courage to deliver it to me in person. What happened to the music schools?? To the Lowlands Theater??? Not my business any more thank God.

August 4th.

What an invite!?! Why not!! Cooking Gus and Dottie Lang dinner this Saturday. Such good eggs the two of them.

Neither detective thought these diary entries added up to much.

"Now I get why you wanted to read Karp's observations and thoughts to me," said Lipman, curious as to why Hennessey hadn't shared them earlier but letting bygones be bygones. "Karp's anger with some of the other important players at CAN is clear. Who knows whether it's justified. And then to be terminated, on top of it all. Too much."

"Yeah, look," said Hennessey. "He knew the music schools and theater were destroyed. Seems as puzzled by it as we are. There's also a reference to his dinner with the Langs that never happened. A strange reference to an invitation too. Maybe it's the Lang dinner, although it reads as if Karp was invited out somewhere, not the other way around."

"Let's talk to the folks at CAN some more," Lipman replied. He was all in after hearing the diary excerpts. "Since Karp writes about board meetings in his diary, let's get copies of CAN board and executive committee minutes too. Time to dig in deep on these guys. We'll get warrants for whatever we need if necessary."

The divide-and-conquer routine worked well for the two detectives. Lipman made his way to Cotuit early the next morning for a quick meeting with Greg Hemshaw. He also scheduled an 11:30 a.m. with Denise Douward in Chatham. Meanwhile, Hennessey visited CAN's administrative offices, located in one of Yarmouth's non-descript strip shopping centers.

Tiffany Tisdale worked out of Karp's old office, looking for alternative space in which to hold group music classes and individual lessons. She'd reached out to all the churches on the Cape, many of them used sparsely save for Sunday, with mixed results. Hennessey found her sitting at Karp's customized desk, tapping and occasionally biting her wild red fingernails, with a yellow notepad in front of her. Alphabetized church names were listed in a column on the left, a corresponding "Yes" or "No" next to each name on the right.

"I'm sorry about what's happened to the music schools," said Hennessey after introducing himself.

"Ah, yes. I'm doing all this work finding new places of joy and inspiration for our students." She laughed nervously. Talking to men in authority never came out well for Tiffany. Her good looks objectified her, and many men found her too ambitious, too haughty, too shrill. She, on the other hand, thought that by and large all men were jerks. Selfish, immature, condescending, weird, egotistical, insensitive, demanding—her list of adjectives for the opposite sex went on and on. Tiffany was in the 'I'm done with men' group of women.

"I'm a dedicated, serious music educator, and a pretty good pianist too," she told Hennessey. "No one at CAN thinks so, or treats me with any respect. All they're interested in is money. Money, money, money. They resent the music schools, and me as the director of the music schools, because we don't turn a profit. As if that's the purpose of them!

"That cockeyed idea about moving the music campuses to some pie-in-the-sky new performing arts center... reee-dick-cu-lous." Tiffany accompanied her syllabic emphasis of the word with one of the largest eye rolls Hennessey had ever witnessed. "And they concocted the whole thing without even asking me about it. Can you believe it, Detective Hennessey?"

Hennessey thought about a response, but didn't share it with her.

I can believe it, Tiffany. I've read Jason Karp's diary. He was filled with frustration and anger about CAN too. Even more than you.

"Frankly," she continued, "I can't wait to move on. I'm now seriously exploring what else is out there for me, what my options might be." Hennessey gave an empathic nod, but his thoughts immediately went elsewhere.

Hmmm. Maybe burning down the music schools was a perfect excuse for Tiffany to move on. What a door opener for future interviews. The sympathy she'd get... I was burned out of my last position. Could she have possibly done it, pulled it off?

As Hennessey put that thought in his mental parking lot, Tiffany mentioned the last time she saw Karp—the executive committee meeting the day he was fired, right before he went on vacation. She'd spent most of the committee meeting agreeing with him.

"Believe me, that didn't happen often," she said. She'd had no contact with Karp since then and was totally shocked by the news of his death. A sadness came over her as she thought about it.

Killed by a shark? Eww. The feeling passed quickly. *That arrogant prick.*

By the time Hennessey finished interviewing Tiffany, she found herself thinking highly of him. Gentle yet firm, he never let her avoid answering questions, but she never found him threatening, never overbearing or tough. She couldn't help note Hennessey's steely blue eyes, his nice and relaxed smile, and his overall sharpness and politeness. He also seemed normal, something women her age craved and thought about above all else.

What a sincere, good guy. Such a rarity. Handsome, and in good shape for someone his age too. I wonder if he's available?

Lipman returned from his talks with Douward and Hemshaw full of beans. Vice Chair Denise Douward hadn't given him much. "I did pick up a few things from her about the overall picture at CAN though," Lipman told Hennessey. "She tipped off the important stuff with that owl-like smile of hers. Apparently, not many of them liked Jason Karp. They all thought Karp got in the way of CAN's rock star, Massahol. She told me that Karp and Massahol—Double M she calls him—were like oil and water together."

At Lipman's earlier meeting that morning, Greg Hemshaw wanted to know why the BCPD detective was even there.

"You must know that I talked to Detective Hennessey already. I've got nothing to add to what I said to him. What does the fact that our former executive director died, suddenly and horribly, have to do with me, or CAN, or his tenure at CAN? Poor Jason Karp. His poor wife and family."

"What a disaster for the Cape," Hemshaw went on. "Just what the local economy needs. Another high-profile shark attack death." For reasons he couldn't quite put his finger on,

Lipman found Hemshaw's concerns and condolences insincere.

"Greg, tell me about the professional relationships at CAN... give me some background into them," Lipman asked.

"Well, there's serious tension at CAN. Some folks, including music director Emre Massahol, board member George Slavin, Conrad Redlich, who was Jason Karp's predecessor as executive director and now runs the SHLAC project, and a few others, they all want CAN to be split up, with the orchestra, music schools, and theater each going their own way."

Lipman perked right up.

"Jason adamantly opposed splitting up CAN," continued Hemshaw. "It really got ugly. He and Massahol couldn't stand each other. He and Slavin couldn't stand each other either. And Jason was extremely critical of how the SHLAC project was going. He'd been brought in to help lead it.

"We had weekly meetings, Jason and I, by phone, Zoom, or in person. He picked up on things quickly, a very smart guy. Soon after starting at CAN, Jason was convinced that Slavin and Redlich had no idea what they were doing when it came to raising money and developing SHLAC. At least that's what he told me. They had a thirty to forty million dollar project on their hands, and no experience whatsoever as to how to pull it off. Over the past half year, Jason dug his heels in deeper and deeper about keeping CAN together, and became more and more vocal about how badly the SHLAC project was being handled.

"It got to the point where he had to go. I was truly sorry about it. We had no choice. His relationships with everyone—the board, CAN's important patrons, the staff, who by the way found him completely overbearing—were poisoned. Thank God the public doesn't know any of this. Listen, we're having a private conversation, right?" he asked Lipman anxiously. Hemshaw waited for Lipman's affirmative nod before continuing.

"Now look at us," Hemshaw went on, agitatedly. "Right when our executive director is let go, an existential crisis hits. Who in God's name would ever, ever burn down CAN's music buildings and its theater? And the other arts buildings on the Cape? Some fringe, crazy criminal."

"Probably that wacko congresswoman from Georgia," Hemshaw continued, only half-joking. "Seriously though, I have no idea what we'll do. We're having an emergency executive committee meeting as soon as it can be scheduled. I'll now have to spend huge chunks of time helping keep CAN afloat. Ugh."

Getting up to leave, Lipman thanked the board chair for his time. "I really appreciate it, Greg. Let me ask two last questions. What's your view as to whether CAN should be split up, and what's your view on the status of the SHLAC project?"

Hemshaw took time before responding.

"Splitting up CAN... No, I don't think it should happen, although there's nothing really left to split up anymore, now that the two music school buildings and the theater are gone. As to the SHLAC project... it's never taken off, despite the money we've pumped into it. I doubt it ever will."

◊ ◊ ◊

After work, Hennessey took Kelly to the Railroad Bar & Grill, a great, not-very-well-known Cape Cod establishment. Set back off the street, it was easy to drive by and miss if you didn't know to look for it. Bumps and puddle holes the size of craters filled the unpaved parking lot.

"Yeow," said Hennessey, bottoming out in one of them.

"Good food and reasonable prices," he said, holding the scuffed, slightly askew door open for her.

Taking in the ambience, Kelly laughed as they slid into a booth. "You're such a big spender, Hennessey."

Dinner passed quickly, full of smiles and laughs and small talk and smidgeons of seriousness. The door to each of their lives continued opening, cautiously and optimistically. In one of his serious moments, Hennessey mentioned how difficult solving the arson attacks was going to be, at least in his experience. He didn't tell her why he thought so. He also said he knew she wasn't much of a baseball fan, given she'd asked why the runners ran counterclockwise rather than clockwise around the bases. He hooted at that. At first surprised and ever-so-slightly indignant, Kelly looked at him and burst out laughing as well.

Time to leave. "Come spend the night with me," said Hennessey. So she did.

She visited with him six nights running. He never asked. Hearing the car tires on the gravel driveway, he quivered with anticipation. She let herself in, sometimes early, sometimes late, pushing the door shut behind her. Stepping out of her clothes, dropping them on the planked pitch-pine floor, sliding cool and soft and naked against him in bed, her scent and lushness and petiteness overwhelming him. No caution to her at all. Just curiosity and desire and need: unsatiated pent-up need.

On the fourth night, deep into their lovemaking, him inside her and both of them deep into bonding their physical selves and souls, she whispered, for she was a whisperer: "Oh Tim, oh Tim... You're taking me there. Oh yes....ohhh yessss." Kelly, for whom it had been an eternity, came and came and came, long waves of primal and physical release and ecstasy enveloping her.

What a joy it was making love to Kelly. Maybe his somewhat advanced years, his newfound, forced-upon-him maturity, had something to do with it. It was a new world to him. She was adventurous and creative, eager to please and be pleased. More than anything else, she shared herself physically in an authentic and absolute way with him.

Not that he'd ever tell her, but he loved the moment right before her climaxes. One of two things let him know she was almost there. She either sucked in her breath through her teeth, a reverse whistling of sorts, and then held it, or she furrowed her brow deeper and deeper, an intense, concentrated look on her face as if solving a complex math problem. Once there, she dissolved like sugar in hot water—relaxed, satisfied, a beatific look on her face.

At long last, that part of Hennessey lived again.

CHAPTER 14

Saturday, September 11, 2021

The breakout had been planned for months. Joey, Jack Ford, and a new member of the Locust Hill Gang imprisoned for life at MCI-Walpolc. The original third member of the Locust Hill gang housed at the correctional facility was no longer around, the one who'd been there when Joey first arrived. He'd lost it in the communal shower room. Some petty vendetta that got out of hand. Jack and Joey never found out who did it. If they had, there'd have been a reckoning.

They put hand-made mannequins in their beds to fool the prison guards, those dimwits, when sight check rounds were done. Using a hard plastic cleaning brush to knock a hole in the sheet rock ceiling of the communal bathroom where a security camera blind spot existed, they pulled themselves up through the fifteen-inch hole and crawled silently on top of the two parallel two-by-four-inch studs, listening intently for guard noise below them and ending up where they knew there was no perimeter fence. There was nothing between them and the wall of the prison itself.

Kicking out a windowless hatch, the three of them used a rope made of towels and sheets. The towel and sheet combo took care of about ten feet of the drop. The last seven or eight feet were a freefall; they'd been doing exercises in the outside rec area, a lot of jumping off stools and higher equipment when the guards weren't watching, to help prepare and get in shape. The newbie went last, making sure the improvised rope didn't untie from the hatch frame they secured it to. He held the rope at the top, reinforcing it, while Jack and Joey scrambled down before him.

Waiting until right after the exterior prison light swept by like a lighthouse, they pressed up against the prison wall, faces to the bricks. Then, the three of them bolted for the woods, fifty to seventy yards away. All that prison exercise paid off. In the woods, they shed their jail jumpsuits. They had street clothes on underneath. About a quarter mile away, straight through and on the other side of the woods, another member of the Locust Hill gang waited for them out on Thoreau Boulevard.

From beginning to end, the whole thing took twenty-two minutes.

"We'll see each other sometime soon, buddy. Real soon," said Jack, as they scattered to the wind at Southie's Carson Park a short while later. "Count on that."

Joey shook Jack's hand and then gave him a spontaneous hug. He'd have never made it through the nightmare known as MCI-Walpole without Jack's protection and reassurance.

God, I hope we see each other soon, Joey thought. *Funny, Jack helped me in that hellhole the way my older brother Tim used to help me when we were kids. Acted like an older brother to me in so many ways.*

Joey never saw Jack Ford again. His best friend from MCI-Walpole died in a 'you're not taking me alive' gunfight with the police and FBI agents. It took place at his mother's house, less than a week after the breakout.

Freedom. Its sweetness is indescribable. In some countries—Germany, Mexico, Belgium, others—the legal philosophy holds that being in prison is a violation of the right of freedom, and that it is human nature to want to escape. In these countries, prisoners who escape, if caught, and if they have caused no harm to person or property while on the loose, simply get returned to jail. No additional charges. No extra time added to the initial sentence.

Not so in the United States, where escaping from prison is itself a criminal offense, and is almost certain to add significant time to an inmate's sentence. If sentenced to life without parole already, it means the inmate is placed under increased security and spends a lot more time in isolation.

Joey's escape hit Hennessey hard. The news screamed across the radio Sunday morning, right when he got up. He then read about it on social media and in the newspapers. Hennessey dwelled on it and despaired.

That's the end-of-the-line for Joey. No prison escapee ever gets away with it. They are always recaptured, always, even years later, like the Bulger serial killer brother. Or they are killed in the recapture effort.

What drove Hennessey almost crazy was that he and a lawyer friend had been trying to get Joey released, or at least made eligible for parole, based on the new Massachusetts Supreme Court ruling on felony-murder. Now that Joey had escaped, it was all for nothing. Destructive old thinking descended upon Hennessey. The whole unfortunate, malign history of Joey, and of everything else that had gone bad in his life, making him numb and remote and pitch black.

Kelly wanted to comfort him, but he withdrew from life, from her—a turtle pulling into its shell.

"Nah... thanks though," he responded four or five nights in a row to the offer of her company.

Complete silence at first. Hennessey's totally darkened-out window. Then came 'it's the family matter,' giving her a glimpse into his enormous internal struggle and his descent into emotional purgatory. The big hug he gave her out in the parking lot alleviated any doubt she had about the two of them. Its length and strength surprised her. She knew then to leave well enough alone, so she agonized silently and from a distance with him. Their bond of grief: an indestructible bridge between them.

◊ ◊ ◊

Late the following Sunday afternoon, a little more than a week after the breakout, two MA state police troopers visited Hennessey. They had on their formal dress. Light blue top and dark blue bottom, knee-high boots, stiff, round-brimmed hat with pronounced, curved visor. The uniforms made troopers look like high-ranking World War II army officers. Their waist belts defined authority: revolvers, mace, taser, handcuffs, and more. As they approached the house, Hennessey thought about their attire. He'd never worn anything like it as a police detective.

Probably modeled after the Germans. Not sure whether it looks commanding, intimidating, or ridiculous. All three, I guess.

Hennessey had nothing to share with them. "Sure, I visited with my brother regularly. Dutifully. What of it?" he asked gruffly. "If you think I had anything to do with the breakout, you're wrong. I had no idea it was in the offing, no idea at all. Good luck with it though."

There wasn't a snowball's chance in hell he'd help the MA state police recapture Joey. Or capture anyone for that matter. Not then. Not ever. Hennessey of course had his own issues in the past as a member of the Boston Police Department. And he readily conceded some of them were big. But the MA state police?

The latest MA state police scandal involved troopers caught padding their overtime pay and taking featherbedded and ghost assignments. It was also the state police who insisted that only police could safely handle roadway construction details, although other states saved tons of money handling them with trained civilians or municipal workers. The Boston Globe reported extensively on these issues. Nothing ever came of it. Hennessey thought about the MA state police with contempt.

At least I never milked the public teat the way some of

these state troopers do. Year after year they do it. Great for us Massachusetts taxpayers, right guys? What a big, lousy blend of legal and illegal corruption. It's sordid. Know why these guys don't care? Money. The Big Green. They're only in it for the Big Green, after all.

The two troopers at Hennessey's house knew about his past detective work for the Boston Police Department, and his current work for the BCPD. It meant nothing to them. His brother, Joey Hennessey, had escaped from one of the State's maximum security prisons, and was a convicted felon in prison on a life-without-parole sentence. Everyone knew that at some point Joey would contact family.

"You know why we're here, Mr. Hennessey," the older and slightly more senior trooper said. Neither of them came close to Hennessey in age or experience. Hennessey looked down at them from the front porch, standing a foot, foot and a half above them. "Yeah, I know why you're here."

"We'd like to come in and take a quick look around if that's ok with you?" said the younger trooper.

"Absolutely not."

The MA state police were not used to having folks say no to them. Initially caught off guard, the troopers recovered quickly.

"Why not? Mr. Hennessey, it makes it seem as if you're hiding something."

"I'm not hiding anything. Not letting you into my house, either."

The younger trooper started to step directly up onto the porch, skipping over the small two-step stairs leading up. Hennessey filled with anger instantly, an uncontrollable rage. He stepped forward quickly, reached out, and pushed the trooper right in the middle of the chest, firmly and emphatically.

No you don't. No friggin' way.

Taking a few quick pitter-patter steps backward, the young trooper tried to keep his balance and stay upright. Failing, he went over on his backside hard.

The senior trooper had his taser out faster than you can blink. "That was a stupid thing to do, Mr. Hennessey, really stupid."

Looking over his shoulder at his fellow trooper, still lying on the ground, catching his breath and not hurt in any way, he asked "you OK?" The look over the shoulder was all that Hennessey needed. He lightly jabbed his right fist, lightning quick, into the standing trooper's nose. Not hard enough to break it, he knew better than that. Just hard enough to do some slight damage and send a clear message.

Both troopers looked at Hennessey with disbelief and outrage. The older one still had his taser out, the younger one now had his revolver drawn.

"Why you son-of-a-bitch," the senior trooper said, wiping the slight trickle of blood coming out of his left nostril. "We ought to shoot you right here, or at least taser the you-know-what out of you." He stepped forward and raised his taser, getting ready to use it.

His animalistic, primitive rage now behind him, Hennessey shook his head. He put his right hand up, palm facing outward, a 'that's enough' signal to them. It was time for everyone to take a deep breath and stop.

"Not a good idea you two. Not a good idea. See the security camera up there?" he said, giving a head nod toward the right-hand ceiling corner of the porch, where he'd put in a discreet 360-degree state-of-the-art camera. "It's captured everything that's happened out here so far, including your unlawful effort to enter my home, which I had every right to stop. The feed goes to three different places. It's captured you pulling a taser on me, and now a revolver, in response to my exercising my legal rights on my own property. You want to enter my home? Go get a warrant."

The two troopers stepped back and huddled for a minute. Taser and revolver were holstered. "Come get in the cruiser, asshole," the older one said. "You're going for a ride up to divisional headquarters in Plymouth. You'll be needing a shower when you get back."

Hennessey closed the front door to the bungalow. "I'll go first, gentlemen," he said sarcastically.

They released Hennessey from the hoosegow early the following morning. He'd been put in a holding cell with a cot and sink and toilet. Nice firm mattress. They'd brought him a sandwich for dinner, turkey and swiss with lettuce and mayo on wheat, along with a small bag of Cape Cod potato chips and a Coke.

There'd been no communication at all between him and the troopers who brought him in, or anyone else at divisional headquarters. At 7:30 a.m., a young female trooper came and unlocked the holding cell.

"Your ride back to the Cape's waiting for you outside. Get outta here." No charges. Nothing.

"Hey, a great way to start your week, Hennessey, huh?" asked Lipman. He'd arrived in his BCPD cruiser, in case they needed to cut through traffic on the way back. "I won't ask. Please don't tell me the details... ever."

"Listen, Phil, do me one more small favor," said Hennessey. "Don't tell Kelly where you picked me up this morning or what happened, ok? Thanks, and thanks for coming to get me."

"No problem, Hennessey, no problem."

◇ ◇ ◇

Despite Larry Sylvester's prayers and the hard work of the Chamber of Commerce and Cape municipalities to put a pollyannaish spin on things, the bad news piled up. The tale of Karp's demise had a long tail. How could it not? Its sensational aspects guaranteed it. Where was his head? Where were his other body parts? How had a finger and a foot made it to shore, but nothing else? Would another unsuspecting vacationer or local stumble upon and be traumatized by discovering another part of Jason Karp? Or worse, have a face-to-face encounter with one of the ocean's mightiest predators, a great white shark, in near-shore waters at a Cape beach?

Last week, Race Point Beach in Provincetown closed due to a great white sighting. It happened twice at Head of the Meadow Beach in Truro over a three-day period. A fisherman in the water off North Beach near Chatham saw a monster of a great white—sixteen to eighteen feet long. Someone fishing for stripers and blues from the shore at Nauset Beach actually had one on his line—fifteen yards off shore—before the shark twisted its head dismissively, snapping the line the way a small twig snaps in a winter ice storm.

The worst sighting was at Marconi Beach, where stunned and terrified beachgoers watched as a great white shark, thirty to fifty yards out, tossed a seal into the air before devouring it, blood spurting in every direction as it caught its prey in an instantaneous death vise. It was like watching a young girl show off by throwing a jellybean or marshmallow into the air and catching it in her mouth. Great white sharks were everywhere, in every nook and cranny of the Cape. There'd been twenty-four sightings from shore this month alone. The sharks were so assured of their dominant place in the Cape's marine hierarchy of life that some even took to breaching, the way humpback whales do.

Larry Sylvester was really anxious. How he wished a rat poison existed for the great white shark, something that didn't harm or kill any other flora or fauna on his beloved Cape Cod, only the damn sharks.

What made matters worse was how news travelled these days. Not only was everyone aware of Jason Karp's death, everyone also knew about last week's great white shark attack out at Grey Whale Cove State Beach in California. The attack almost killed a young man, a very strong swimmer who somehow managed to survive and make it to shore. California closed Grey Whale Cove State Beach and several other beaches until a full and time-consuming assessment of the situation could be undertaken, in the effort to pinpoint precisely where the great white sharks lurked. Sylvester and his Chamber colleagues would never advocate for that; he thought they'd gone crazy out on the west coast.

Those foolish Californians. Terrible for the economy.

There was also the recent video of the hammerhead shark at Panama City Beach in Florida. A drone camera caught the shark circling, circling, circling around two young girls out for a swim, blissfully unaware that another oceanic apex predator was onto them and that death could arrive any second. Sylvester had just one thought when he saw the video.

Thank God they didn't know it was there.

The guest speaker at this month's Chamber of Commerce lunch was none other than Darlene McCoy, the regional state marine biologist. McCoy forgot she had a lunch talk when she headed out to work that morning, and left her dress shoes at home. So she wore her girly rubber boots to the speaker's lunch, the ones she wore when dissecting sharks and other large sea creatures.

Better than my flip-flops, she thought.

Sylvester and other Chamber members wanted to hear first-hand what a scientist had to say about the presence of great white sharks on the Cape, so they could ascertain whether there was anything else they needed to do to make life easier and safer for everyone.

"Listen, folks, here's what I recommend. I know the list is long. Please, write it down, or email me and I'll send it to you. If you have any other questions, send them to me too. Larry will give you my email address."

McCoy's list was a good and practical one. "Stay aware when in the water—always. Stay close to shore—always, not that it necessarily helps. Stay in a group. Avoid areas with seals—really avoid them. Avoid schools of fish too—I know they're super interesting to get close to, but avoid them. Avoid murky water. Don't splash, and finally, listen to and follow closely all lifeguard instructions."

Sylvester couldn't help but think *blah blah blah blah* as

McCoy good-naturedly went about her business. The room was polite and full of good karma, even though someone in the back corner of the room muttered "oh brother" when McCoy mentioned avoiding murky water. There was nothing on Cape Cod except murky water.

McCoy turned next to talking about the great white shark itself and its habits.

"It's a fish, which surprises some people. Yes, all sharks are fish. And it is an apex predator, like us and a few other mammals. Think lions and tigers and bears, oh my!" McCoy giggled at her own silly reference to the Wizard of Oz.

"The great white shark is at the top of the ocean's food chain. Its presence in Cape waters," she said earnestly, "is an indicator of a healthy ecosystem at work."

McCoy's statement about a healthy ecosystem at work elicited a full-fledged "OH BROTHER" from the same back corner of the room. Not to be outdone, the other back corner volleyed forth with "SWEET JESUS… Save the kids, for Chrissakes, not the sharks!"

Agitated, and using his chairman's prerogative, Larry Sylvester jumped up and into the fray with the question on everyone's mind: "Darlene, how do we get rid of these great white sharks? Could we have a hunting season, like deer or turkey hunting season here in Massachusetts?" It seemed like a great idea to him.

McCoy gave them her best 'oh dear' grin. "Everyone… overall, the great white shark population is in serious decline, even if the numbers are booming here on Cape Cod. It's a protected species under federal and state law. I wouldn't ever advocate for culling or removing great white sharks from the Cape's waters through hunting or any other means," she said, proud that her belief in science trumped all else. "Nor will any other marine biologist worth their salt. It's the opposite. These magnificent animals need all the protection they can get."

That was enough for Sylvester. Above the rising hubbub caused by McCoy's provocative statements, his voice cut through like a fog horn: "But one of them KILLED Jason Karp. Tore him to shreds. Poor Karp! His poor family! And think about last year, one death and another serious attack. We've gotta get rid of 'em... Gotta get rid of 'em NOW!"

Sea Interlude #4

There is no question whatsoever that in the battle for supremacy in the ocean, great white shark versus human being, the great white shark loses. It seems unlikely that its current inexorable slide into extinction will be reversed. Human beings have too much say in the matter and don't really care enough to do anything about it.

It's probably too late anyway. Climate change is here to stay. It will be with us way into the future, and will continue to wreak havoc on our ecosystems and all creatures within them.

We've already changed the great white sharks geographic territory and its diet. Seals are back as a mainstay, having been a special dinner feature for the great white during the decades we humans slaughtered seals and made them a rarity in Cape waters, primarily for the vanity of wearing fur coats.

On the U.S. west coast, great white sharks are also on the move, as the northern Pacific's water temperatures become warmer and more hospitable to them. Entering new territory (a new restaurant may be more a propos), these fearsome predators have now decimated our Pacific sea otter population. In Monterey Bay, the number of sea otters—those adorable, playful creatures—plummeted by eighty-six percent in the past ten years. Scientists attribute it in large part to the hunting of sea otters by great white sharks.

Still, the great white shark is no match for us. Found in the stomach of dead ones is the ignominious: plastic bottles, fishing gear, shish kabob sticks, license plates, athletic gear, GoPro video cameras. All signs that in ways large and small, we affect them much more than they affect us.

Should we even try to save this apex predator of the oceans? Where did it come from? What is its history, its purpose on our planet?

Think about it: Our time in and on the ocean would be much more pleasant should the great white shark no longer exist. Mothers and fathers would have much lower anxiety levels as their children played and swam in the surf. Surfers, snorkelers, and scuba divers would eliminate entirely the long odds of a tragic encounter.

We could pull it off. Get rid of the great white shark completely. Why not?

CHAPTER 15

Monday, September 20, 2021

Something was terribly wrong at CAN. Hennessey knew it. He just couldn't put his finger on it.

The high-strutting conductor and music director, Massahol, always got his way. The earnest music school director, Tisdale, felt aggrieved and wanted desperately to leave. The board, led by Hemshaw, a decent but weak person, seemed paralyzed and was dominated by an aggressive board member, Slavin, who was failing miserably at CAN's most important project, the development of SHLAC. Although good at what he did, the abrasive and arrogant Jason Karp got sacked due to his inability to resolve issues regarding the proper way forward for the organization. That put his leadership skills in doubt. Enormous tensions existed as to the right direction for CAN, with very different opinions about it among the organization's leaders. Karp's diary and CAN's board meeting minutes made that abundantly clear. As Hennessey analyzed the CAN situation, a series of thoughts, of questions, floated to the surface.

Deadly tensions, maybe?

That was the backdrop. Confronting the two detectives was a series of arson attacks that destroyed all of CAN's real estate assets, everything except the rented administrative offices in Yarmouth. Everything owned by CAN had been destroyed, and only CAN lost its entire portfolio of buildings, even though serious damage had been done to other arts organizations too.

How do you figure?

The icing on the cake: After disappearing to Europe for several weeks, the recently fired Jason Karp showed up here and there on Cape Cod. No, it wasn't a hectic, jam-packed professional and social life that had him here and there. Bits and pieces of his body literally showed up here and there, apparently dismembered by a great white shark.

What's going on?

With each passing day, Lipman felt an increasing urgency to go public with the backstory to Karp's demise; he wanted it known there was a distinct possibility Karp's death wasn't caused by a great white shark. There was now big tension between the two detectives.

It pained Lipman tremendously to witness the terror gripping Cape Cod. He was a local after all, born and raised there, not someone who moved to the Cape late in life, like Hennessey and others. The graphic and upsetting great white shark pictures and other warnings at the beaches, the somber discussions at town meetings, the rancorous disagreements about what to do. Psychologically the region was in turmoil. Everything and everyone was changing. Lipman noticed it.

"Look at how cautious we have to be, and how scared we always are these days," he said to Hennessey.

"My sister, who used to be a porpoise in the ocean, won't go swimming anymore, at least not on the Cape's open ocean side. Our way of life is being changed, permanently and significantly, by those monsters. We've got to let the public know that Karp's death might not have been caused by one of them."

"Phil, please," said Hennessey. "We've been over it before. What good would it do to let everyone know we found GHB and alcohol in Karp's body, and that his lungs were filled with water, huh?"

"I can't believe what I'm hearing from you," snapped Lipman. "It'd do a lot of good and you know it. Everyone would be relieved, overjoyed really, to learn that there hadn't been another fatal shark attack. You're being a pain in the ass about it. Overly cautious."

"Absolutely not," barked Hennessey, pissed off that Lipman would think such a thing, let alone say it.

"I want you to tell me what good it will do to go public with what we know," Hennessey asked. "Will it make people less nervous about the great whites that are out there? Twenty-four of them sighted already this month. Will it stop the beach closures—Race Point, Nauset, Cape Cod National Seashore, Meadow Beach, and others? Thank God the towns and feds are closing them. A little common sense goes a long way."

"The advantages of keeping it under wraps still outweighs telling everyone what we know," continued Hennessey. "If Karp killed himself—I don't think so, but if he did—his body was nevertheless turned into mincemeat by a great white shark. Already dead, or attacked and killed by it, a big chunk of Jason Karp was found in that shark. The nuances don't matter. And, on the off chance we're dealing with something worse, letting people think a shark killed Karp might get us somewhere. If something else happened to him, whoever was responsible might relax and let their guard down."

Hennessey had just finished researching GHB, the drug the regional crime lab director Bernie MacKenzie found in Karp's torso and foot. Infamous as a date rape drug, GHB acts on the central nervous system. Its effects are wide-ranging: euphoria, increased sex drive, tranquility on the upside; sweating, nausea, amnesia, hallucinations, loss of consciousness on the downside.

GHB is available as an odorless, colorless drug, in liquid or powder form. Easy to mix with alcohol or any drink really—orange juice if you wanted. After gaining notoriety and widespread use through the years, the U.S. Food and

Drug Administration issued a formal advisory declaring GHB unsafe and making it illegal except under FDA-approved, physician-supervised protocols. It now holds the strictest classification under the federal Controlled Substances Act.

"That's worked really well, hasn't it?" said Hennessey. "That banning of GHB? They got all that crap right off the street, quickly and permanently, don't you think? Ha-ha-ha. What a joke. I wonder which pharmaceutical company, or Sackler-like family, is making billions off of the misery known as GHB?"

Hennessey continued filling Lipman in on what he'd found out about the drug. "Wanna know something else interesting about GHB, Phil? It's sometimes used to commit suicide, although I guess taking a mega dose of any drug will kill you."

Hearing that made Lipman even more adamant about going public with the news. "I'm not taking 'no' for an answer. Look, the guy killed himself. Loss of job, loss of prestige and income. People do it all the time under those circumstances. Here's how I see it. Jason Karp makes himself a nice strong drink, tequila or something else, and laces it with GHB. He walks down to Craigville Beach, a stone's throw away from their Hyannisport home. At the beach, he takes off his shoes, drinks his special cocktail, and walks out into never-never land."

Hennessey looked at Lipman with true understanding. His response had an unusual softness and ambiguity to it, as if questioning internally the position he'd staked out in the argument.

"Phil, you may be right. How unfortunate if that's what happened. Beyond unfortunate… it'd be tragic.

"Something's not letting me get there yet. Read the guy's diary again. Think about what others have told us about him, even people who hated him. Jason Karp was full of vim and vigor. Enjoyed a good, public-facing life, accomplished a lot, had a beautiful, extremely wealthy European wife. I don't see him killing himself over getting fired at CAN. Not at all.

"Maybe there was something else going on with Karp," continued Hennessey. "We haven't heard about anything else, though, nothing at all, from anyone. Not a peep since we've had our noses to the grindstone on this one.

"Let's do one last thing before we go public with the forensics. Let's call Ulrike Baten-Karp again. See if we can get anything from her on whether her husband might've killed himself."

"I'm game," said Lipman. "What a delightful talk that's gonna be."

◊   ◊   ◊

Ulrike wasn't particularly upset hearing from Hennessey and Lipman again. She expected that sooner or later they'd get back in touch, although not this soon.

"I am never coming back to your wretched country," she told them, right off the bat. "And as for Cape Cod... the sooner climate change washes it all away the better. I am never, EVER, going back to that horrid place." Other than that, she seemed relatively composed.

The two detectives plunged right in. "Eh, Ulrike," said Lipman. "Pardon me for asking... We're trying to tie everything up regarding your husband's death as tightly as we can. Is there any chance, do you think, any chance at all, that he'd have harmed himself as a result of losing his job at CAN? Or for any other reason?"

"That's ridiculous," she snorted. "Absurd. You told me Jason was killed by a shark. What's going on?"

Lipman looked at Hennessey, who shook his head quickly, indicating Lipman shouldn't tell her the backstory regarding her husband's death.

Glaring at Hennessey, Lipman continued, "Oh, it's nothing really, just that the pathologist... the pathologist found alcohol and some drugs in Jason's body. We're trying to piece it all together."

Sobbing could be heard over the phone. Ulrike Baten-Karp took a moment to compose herself, then responded with as much dignity, grace, and clarity as she could muster. "Detectives, gentlemen… Know that my husband would not in a million years, is that how you Americans put it, would not in a million years kill himself. Jason loved every second of his blessed life, and would never ever have wanted it to end it until God, if there is one, wanted Jason with him." She wept openly now, the discussion making her confront what a few short weeks ago was totally unfathomable: Her beloved, dear husband was dead.

"Thanks for taking our call, Ulrike. We're really sorry to have upset you by raising the issue. We had to run it to the ground—another American cliche," said Lipman. "Is there anything we can help you with at the house in Hyannisport? We'd be glad to do anything we can."

"Thank you, gentlemen. You've been a pleasure to deal with. No, I'm handling things at the Hyannisport house from here in Switzerland. I've hired a local lawyer, so the situation is under control. I've given him a power of attorney to sell or otherwise get rid of everything we left there, including the cars."

"Wait a minute, Ulrike," Hennessey jumped in, speaking for the first time. "There's only one car in the garage, a VW convertible beetle."

"That's absurd," she responded sharply. "The VW convertible beetle, the powder pink one, that's mine. There's also an almost brand new cobalt blue VW Atlas. Jason's car."

They could tell by the quiver in her voice that she was beginning to lose it again.

"Don't you worry, Ulrike," said Hennessey, reassuringly. "We'll get to the bottom of it as soon as we can. You have our word."

CHAPTER 16

Friday, August 6, 2021

Sun glitter danced and sparkled on the water. Its hypnotic effect captured all three of them as they headed out of Chatham Harbor. The first ten minutes of the boat ride were spent watching the brilliance of it, taking it all in. It was almost impossible to stop looking at it; something about it pulled the eye and mind toward it.

Mother Nature's fireworks, thought Jason Karp. *As dazzling as what we humans pull off.* A barely discernible breeze blew, adding freshness and vitality to the afternoon. With the temperature at seventy-four degrees out on the water, it felt like a delicate, soothing caress, a lover's fingertips running gently across the skin.

They saw a fin in the distance and hurried over to try to identify the creature it belonged to. There was no sign of it when they got there, no sign at all. A great white shark, who knows? Could've been a dolphin or another small mammal.

Karp saw no reason to refuse Slavin and Massahol's invite for a last boat trip out onto the waters of the Cape before he and Ulrike left the area. He'd spent his summers on the Cape as a young child before his serious teenage interests— wilderness camp, chamber music instruction, sports leagues,

European travel—pulled him away. He loved Cape Cod dearly and would miss it. The Outer Cape's sense of space and ruggedness, its eternal play between sea and sky, especially at the Cape Cod National Seashore, never failed to capture him. The Upper Cape's lush vegetation and that still well-kept secret known as Buzzard's Bay. It all amazed him. Hyannis? Well, he wouldn't miss Hyannis.

Karp had recently finished re-reading Henry Beston's *The Outermost House.* Part of him grieved that he would no longer have the opportunity to marvel at the Cape's gifts, as Beston once did. Karp related completely to what Beston wrote almost a hundred years earlier, during his Thoreau-like time on the dunes of the Outer Cape: "As the year lengthened into autumn, the beauty and mystery of this earth and outer sea so possessed and held me that I could not go."

"Jason," said Slavin, cutting the engine to his boat, the *Tranche-Two,* and speaking in his usual puffed-up voice. "I really hope there are no hard feelings among any of us. I think, and know I speak for Double M here as well, that you did a lot of things right at CAN. Especially your handling of Tiffany, such a strong-willed woman. Wow, what a handful. It's really only that some of us saw things differently than you. That's all there is to it."

"You'll get whatever recommendations you need from us, you know that," he went on. "I've already talked to Greg and Denise about it. I don't think for a second, not a second, that you'll have any trouble landing on your own two feet, with or without our help."

"Let's celebrate," continued Slavin, excitedly. "There's a little lemonade to be made out of the lemons too. You heard about the fires, the terrible fires that happened while you were away. The initial insurance claim numbers are in. We'll have enough money to buy the golf course and endow Double M's chair… at long last."

One of those irrefutable, instantaneous insights into truth hit Karp all of a sudden, a blinding and brilliant light flashing in his mind.

"You did it," Karp said.

"What do you mean? What do you mean, we did it?" asked Slavin.

Karp looked at them intently. "Why wouldn't you? You both wanted to do away with the music schools and theater. Now they're gone. Literally. You burned them down, or had them burned down. It makes perfect sense." Karp felt a little uneasy going down the path he was on.

Look... there's Slavin's flush.

"Oh stop it. You're delusional," scoffed Slavin. "C'mon let's celebrate." He turned away from Karp and Massahol for a long moment, then turned back, handing them full flutes of champagne.

Massahol took the moment to say, quietly, "Don't be silly, Jason."

"Bottoms up," Slavin said, his own glass in hand. "May our dear friend Jason Karp find a bigger and better place in this world than on tiny Cape Cod. I have no doubt at all that he will."

With Slavin leading the way, they chugged their glasses of Piper Heidsieck.

"Ugh, I am not feeling so good," Karp told them two minutes later, and put a couple of hors d'oeuvres in his stomach to try to calm it down. "Mixing champagne and a boat ride isn't going over too well with me," he continued. Karp slumped against the side of the boat. Out cold.

"Quick, help me get this scuba diving weight belt on him and get him overboard."

"What are you talking about?" said Massahol, incredulous and horrified. "What are you doing? Are you crazy? No way. Stop it George, stop now! I'm not touching him!"

Riding back to Chatham Harbor, Slavin said to the shell-shocked Massahol, "It had to be done. He knew. You heard... you saw. He knew. Whatever you do, don't say anything to anyone about it. Don't ever, ever talk about it, admit it, say anything about it. Ever. Got it?"

CHAPTER 17

Hennessey quickly climbed the stairs at his home. He'd spent the evening at the Land Ho! watching the Bosox drop a close one to the Toronto Bluejays. Despite that, he was in a great mood, thinking Kelly would be waiting for him. Since coming out of his recent blackness, things between the two of them had been better than ever.

Oh yeah, oh yeah, oh yeah. Did she ride her bike over tonight? She's cuter than a button on that bike of hers. Especially that baby blue helmet—goes so well with her eyes.

Hennessey was filled with eager anticipation.

It wasn't Kelly waiting upstairs in his bedroom. It was Joey. Sitting in the dark, in the big leather reading chair off in the corner of the bedroom. The shock, a big one, wore off quickly.

"How'd you get in?"

"Don't ask. Saw the front porch and back door security cameras though. Don't worry, I'm not on them. Wearing rubber see-through surgeon's gloves too. They're a dime a dozen since last year's pandemic. So no fingerprints or other traces of me here." "Look" said Joey, grinning and pointing to his just-shaved head. "No hair to be left behind for a DNA analysis either."

"They've been here already," said Hennessey with a grimace.

"I know. Yesterday afternoon. I watched from the woods on the side of the house. A little wet in there, nothing I couldn't deal with. Amused by how you dealt with those two troopers, big brother."

"You've been scoping out my place?"

"Yeah. Wanted to think through how to get in without leaving a sign. Wanted to make sure they didn't come back, too."

"How'd you get down to the Cape?"

"An old buddy brought me over by boat. I'm not going to tell you who. You know them though. Not a bad trip from Carson Beach in Southie. Dropped me off at Beach Point east of Barnstable Harbor. I worked my way here from there." Joey looked gaunt and exhausted. He had for years, thought Hennessey.

No different from my last visit with him at MCI-Walpole.

"Fucking A, Joey. Fucking A. What a fucking mess you've made of things." Steel in his voice, one of Hennessey's increasingly infrequent waves of anger surged through him. Joey couldn't remember hearing his brother speak that way before.

"We've been trying hard to get your sentence reduced, to even get you paroled. I should have told you that on one of my last visits. I didn't want to get your hopes up though." Hennessey was filled with angst and bitterness about it.

"That recent Supreme Judicial Court ruling on felony murder opened the door for it," he continued. "So I hired a lawyer, a guy who specializes in this stuff, to file a motion on your behalf. Things looked good, really good."

Joey shook his head and frowned. He stared down at the floor, squeezing his forehead between his left hand thumb and other fingers, finding it hard to believe that once again he'd turned potential good fortune into bad.

"Well, the gang wanted the three of us out. Didn't say

why, just wanted us out and told us how to do it," said Joey. "Some sort of a statement, maybe, to the Governor or Attorney General or the great Commonwealth of Massachusetts. I couldn't say no. Not after what they've done for me. The protection I got from Jack and others."

Joey, you owed them nothing, nothing at all, thought Hennessey. *They got you into your hellhole of a life.*

Small talk took over, the way it often does when people in crisis don't want to deal with what's before them. After ten minutes of it, Hennessey brought them back to reality.

"You gotta get out of here. Fast," he said. "Off the Cape. People here notice everything, know everyone. Gossip travels like lightning. The exit routes are limited and can be watched easily.

"For God's sake, Joey, be smart. Go somewhere where no one knows you, where no one cares about your past. Go out west to a small city, not too small though, where you can blend in and not be noticed. Get a real job. Doesn't matter what it pays. New name. New life. Did they give you a new name? A new social security number?" he asked, thinking the Locust Hill Gang would've taken care of it all for Joey.

Looking glumly at the floor, Joey shook his head no.

They sat in silence for a while. Then Hennessey walked over to his bedroom bureau. Opening up the top left hand drawer, he rooted around in it and took out a flip phone, an old Motorola RAZR. A true rarity these days. The phone number was taped onto the screen at the top, readable through the transparent scotch tape that held the post-it to the phone.

He handed it to Joey.

"No one knows about this phone. There are two numbers saved. Call as soon as you can, when you know you can talk for a minute or two without being noticed. It doesn't matter what time it is. Tell them Hennessey told you to call. They'll ask for confirmation. It's three plus three equals six. Understand? Three plus three equals six. Tell them you need a new name and new social security number quickly. Tell them where you want to pick it up, not the other way around. Don't let them tell you where to come get it, and when they deliver it, stake it out beforehand—make sure it's not a sting.

"Tell them to put it on Hennessey's account. Then take the SIM card out and throw the phone and SIM card away. Whatever you do, don't tell them your name. Ever. I've got seven, eight grand in my Bank of America checking account," Hennessey continued. "It's set up so there's no daily limit on the amount I can withdraw. I'll use the debit card first, take out fifty bucks or so, then I'll drop the card a few yards outside the ATM booth. Bright red—you can't miss it. PIN is Claninsah. C-L-A-N-I-N-S-A-H. I'll call it in lost first thing in the morning. Don't look at the security camera. Keep your hat on and face hidden. Walk with a fake limp. Let's go."

Filling a gym bag full of clothes and food for Joey, including his favorite Bosox cap, Hennessey put his brother in the trunk of his Chevrolet Impala. They drove a couple of miles to the stand-alone Bank of America booth at Yarmouth's Beach Wind shopping center. Popping the trunk from inside the car was the signal. Joey was out and had the trunk closed faster than a blink.

Hennessey drove away without looking back. He was now an accomplice to his brother's latest crime. He didn't care about that though, couldn't give a shit about it. The sole thing on his mind: having to tell his unlucky youngest brother to get lost forever. Mulling things over, it brought him unbearable heartache.

The gods look unfavorably upon Joey. It's almost mythological, the poor guy. Me? Nothing I haven't dealt with before. Seen it, felt it, dealt with it before.

Defiance trumped all in Hennessey's heart and soul.

Jason Karp's cobalt blue VW Atlas had been impounded from the Chatham Harbor parking lot, where a no parking rule was in effect from 11:00 p.m. to 5:00 a.m. On its fourth day in the harbor parking lot, Smittie's Towing came and took it away, carefully, since it was an almost brand-new car, to the company lot in Yarmouth. No one knew. No one cared.

Smittie's didn't care how long the car stayed, and made no effort to identify and contact the owner. More money for them. It pissed Smittie's off royally when Lipman, after tracking the car down, told them he was taking the vehicle—no ifs, ands, or buts about it—and that they weren't getting paid the substantial storage fee owed on it.

"Call the BCPD police commissioner about it. Feel free to file a complaint against me too," Lipman said derisively. "Here's my badge number. Here's the commissioner's phone number. Get at it."

Hennessey and Lipman went through Karp's car with a fine-toothed comb. Before moving it, BCPD specialists examined it for fingerprints, hair, and anything else that would leave a human DNA footprint or other forensic evidence. There were plenty of fingerprints, and enough elbow skin and body oil on the armrest of the driver's side door to take a DNA snapshot. Otherwise, the interior of the car was spotless. Probably Ulrike's influence and the fact it was almost brand new. There was no calendar, no note, no empty coffee cups, nothing. A small bottle of hand sanitizer and some breath mints were in the middle console. That was it.

Out at Chatham Harbor, Hennessey and Lipman had the inimitable pleasure of meeting harbormaster William Johnson for the first time. "Call me Harbormaster Willie," he told them. "Everyone does."

Johnson's family went back generations on Cape Cod. It was a venerable family, part of the group of settlers who kept themselves alive fishing, whaling, farming, and bartering with Native Americans. Some of these families still prospered, while others had long since seen better days. Harbormaster Willie's family fell into the latter category.

"Not much of a position," he conceded to them, "but I rule the roost here at Chatham Harbor." His harbormaster hut, occupied daily by him for the past twenty-seven years, sat at the end of the parking lot where the piers began. Its contents couldn't really be described, nor its odor.

God, thought Hennessey, *it smells almost as bad as Karp's refrigerator. Lucky me. Two great olfactory experiences in one week.*

"Of course I know George Slavin. George's boat, the *Tranche-Two,* is right over there," Harbormaster Willie said, gesturing with his hand to a nearby boat slip. "Not much of a boat," he went on. "Don't tell George I said so. He's awful proud of it."

"Has he been out in it recently?" asked Hennessey.

"Let me look," replied Harbormaster Willie. He opened the harbor logbook on his desk—a desk piled high with all sorts of junk that looked ready to tumble to the floor at any moment.

Lucky it doesn't all end up down there every day, thought Hennessey. *Probably does.*

"Well, he went out by himself the last two weekends," said Harbormaster Willie. He flipped methodically through earlier pages in the logbook. "Back toward the beginning of August, it looks like he went out with a couple of friends."

"How do you know that?" asked Lipman, more seriously than he wanted to.

"See here? The date and time is noted—August 6, 2021 at 2:30 p.m. I record the boat owner and the number of people going out: George Slavin and two guests."

"Their names aren't noted. Do you know who George was with that day? His wife?"

"Nah, his wife almost never goes out on the boat. Last time I saw her here was last year. And only once at that, if I remember right."

Harbormaster Willie thought about it for a minute. Then his face lit up in a huge grin, revealing teeth that had definitely seen better days, including a few that had taken a walk and not come back.

"Now I remember, come to think of it. Sure I do. George

had that famous guy with him. That's who went out with him."

Harbormaster Willie rummaged around on his desk. Miraculously, nothing fell. He came up with a recent *Cape Cod Today*, the monthly glossy covering all things Cape Cod. On the cover was Emre Massahol under the caption, "The Sound of Joy." In the photo, Double M leaned casually over a wooden fence in his concert tuxedo, blowing a huge bubble gum bubble.

What a picture, thought Hennessey. *How ridiculous.*

"It was this guy," said Harbormaster Willie excitedly. "Look, he signed the cover for me."

"Keep up the joy!" Double M inscribed, before illegibly scribbling his signature.

"It's Emre Massahol, the regional orchestra's music director," said Hennessey. "That's really good that you remember him, Harbormaster Willie. How about George's other guest?"

"Never saw him before."

Hennessey took out the photo of Jason Karp he'd taken from the Hyannisport house. No one was ever going to miss it.

"Was this the guy?" he asked.

Harbormaster Willie took the photo and stared bug eyed at it carefully.

"Take your time," Hennessey and Lipman both said, verbally stumbling over each other.

"Sorry guys, I don't know. Maybe yes, maybe no. I was so focused on the famous musician and getting his autograph, I'd just read the issue of *Cape Cod Today*, that I didn't really pay attention to George's other guest.

"Funny thing, though. That gentleman didn't come back with them. I asked where he was. His car was here, after all. George said they'd cruised the Cape Cod National Seashore that afternoon, all the way up to Provincetown. Said the gentleman wanted to get off up there, in P'Town, have dinner with a friend, and be driven back later.

"I told them as long as he was back by eleven p.m. when the parking lot closed. Well, not only was he *not* back by then, he didn't come back at all!"

Harbormaster Willie gesticulated wildly, his arms spinning like windmills. "So, his fancy car was towed!" Giving them his huge, gaping grin again, and a big wink, he added, "I guess he was having too much fun up there in P'Town, huh?"

"Yep," clipped Hennessey, reflecting on the grim irony of Harbormaster Willie imagining Karp cavorting in Provincetown when in reality he was dead.

My guess too, thought Hennessey. *He was simply having too much fun.*

Lipman went over to his BCPD cruiser. He came back wearing latex gloves and carrying a plastic evidence bag, which raised Harbormaster Willie's eyebrows and dropped his jaw simultaneously. Looking at the disheveled desk, and eyeballing an empty A&P concentrated orange juice can converted decades ago into a pen and pencil holder, Lipman zeroed in on a black Sharpie fine point pen.

"Is that the pen the music director used to sign your magazine?"

"Yeah, I believe so," said the harbormaster.

Lipman put it into the plastic bag. "I need to take the signed *Cape Cod Today* too, Harbormaster Willie. Your logbook as well. Start a new logbook as of today. We won't be needing that. If possible, I'll get it all back to you when we're done. I can't guarantee it though."

◊ ◊ ◊

Hennessey and Lipman waited for Greg Hemshaw to finish interviewing a managerial candidate for Hemshaw's Woods Hole liquor store before barging in. They'd arrived unannounced. It annoyed Hemshaw. His afternoon was pretty clear though, and it was the police after all. His only requirement was that he make his 4:00 p.m. tee-off time at the Sacconnesset Golf Club. It was his favorite local course.

"Good to see you again, Greg," said Lipman. Hennessey nodded hello too.

"We want to take you up on your previous offer to make everything at CAN available to us. We can of course get a warrant for it all, but it's easier and quicker if you voluntarily make it available. We'd like to review CAN's books and other documents that might be relevant to our investigation."

"Detectives, I'm completely confused," said Hemshaw defensively. "I know I offered it before, but why do you now want to look at CAN's books? What can possibly be in them for you? What do CAN's books have to do with the arson that destroyed our two music school buildings and our beloved Lowlands Theater? Where do the investigations stand, anyway, may I ask?"

"Sure," said Lipman. "We'll always tell you what we can. CAN's the victim here after all, and you're the chairman of the board. Some of the worst crimes possible have been committed against you, including a felony murder. That poor guy, what was his name... Warbles? Doesn't get any worse than that. You're entitled to whatever information we're able to share with you."

Hearing that made Hemshaw feel better.

"As to the arson investigations," Lipman continued, "nothing to hide. They're going slowly. The attacks seem to have been pulled off by a real professional, or team of professionals. It might've been a copycat situation too, the second fires being an imitation of the first ones, done by some completely separate whacko. We're hoping that a review of the books might lead somewhere. Who knows? And other documents in CAN's files too: irate letters from unhappy parents, or students, or concertgoers; board conflict of interest forms; recent visitors to the buildings, that sort of thing. We'll get there, but we've got to broaden our thinking a bit."

That's not very promising. I wonder if they know what they're doing, thought Hemshaw.

"Any news on your end, Greg?" Lipman asked.

"Not really," Hemshaw replied. "We're still absolutely stunned by it all. We have some really big decisions to make. Quickly. Look at everything that's happened to CAN over the past month. The executive committee met again, the emergency meeting I mentioned last time we talked. The full board meets next week, even though it's never had an emergency meeting before."

"And?"

"Hold your horses, will you?" said Hemshaw, perplexed and slightly put off by how keen the two detectives were to learn about what was going on at CAN.

"CAN's got some big internal decisions in front of it," he continued. "First of all, we've got to find a new executive director, pronto. I can't and don't want to play the role much longer. The executive committee is also recommending to the full board that the insurance proceeds from the fires be used to buy the golf course property for SHLAC, and to endow Emre Massahol's chair as music director of the Philharmonic."

"We won't be using the insurance proceeds to rebuild the two music schools and the theater," said Hemshaw. "Tough decisions. In the end, though, they make sense to me. Double M has done so much for CAN over the past decade. He's put his heart and soul into our little Cape Philharmonic."

"So interesting, Greg," said Hennessey, beating Lipman to the punch and interrupting Hemshaw before he could go on. "So very, *very* interesting." The detectives stared at Hemshaw with an intensity that made him uncomfortable.

"How exactly were those decisions made? How did they come about? Who led the discussion about how the insurance proceeds should be spent, and pushed for what the executive committee came up with?" asked Hennessey.

"Who do you think?" said Hemshaw with an air of resignation. "George Slavin, of course. It should've been me. I'm the chairman of the board after all. But you know George. Always taking charge of things."

The three of them talked a bit more about CAN's future

and Hemshaw's role at the organization. His board chairmanship ended next year. Every four years, someone new got to put the CAN board chair feather in their cap. Hemshaw planned to stay on the board and help any way he could, despite the reservations he had about the direction CAN was heading.

"I'll call Tiffany. She's in Karp's office for the time being. I'll tell her you're on your way there and want to look at CAN documents. Books, letters, expense accounts, visitor log-in records, anything else you want to go through. Be my guest, detectives, for whatever it's worth."

"You know what, Greg," said Hennessey. "Come to think of it, you're right. There's no need for us to visit the office again and go through that stuff, at least for now. We'll let you know if we change our minds about it."

CHAPTER 18

Tuesday, September 21, 2021

Slavin's wife answered when Lipman rang the doorbell. She didn't actually know if George was home. The spacious house provided each Slavin with plenty of room to exist in separate universes. They liked it that way. Sometimes they didn't see each other for days on end, except at meals when they happened to be eating at the same time. They did still share a marital bed. It was a California king, the size of the Titanic, so they could slip in and out without disturbing each other.

'I'm sorry, detective... What was your name again? Blipmann?" she asked with a silly smile. After spending several minutes looking through the house for her husband, she said, "George doesn't seem to be in right now." Just as she finished telling Lipman of her husband's absence, Hennessey came from behind the house, George Slavin marching in front of him.

Hennessey and Slavin spoke at the same time. "Look who I found," said Hennessey.

Slavin growled, "I was starting my afternoon beach walk. Out the back door as usual. What's the meaning of this? Why are you here, officers?"

"We'd like to talk to you, George. There are a few things we'd like to go over with you down at the BCPD. There's some privacy there," Lipman said. When Slavin started objecting, Lipman leaned in and whispered, "You know, we can either handcuff you and put you in my cruiser out front, or you can drive yourself there, with us following. Completely up to you... you decide."

Slavin got into his Mercedes C-300; Lipman and Hennessey followed behind in the unmarked cruiser. Despite being told by the two detectives they simply wanted to have an informal talk with him, when he arrived at the BCPD headquarters, Slavin insisted on calling Richard M. Fishley, one of Boston's preeminent criminal defense lawyers.

"I'll get there as quickly as I can, George," Fishley said. "Two, three hours at most. Don't say a thing to them until I'm there with you. Not one word. Don't even tell them your name." Fishley then told his assistant to clear his calendar for the rest of the day.

Slavin had used Fishley before. Years ago, he'd been charged with securities fraud, accused of running a ponzi scheme to finance his private equity firm and lifestyle. Slavin looked back fondly on his acquittal, attributing it in large part to Fishley's brilliant work. He knew who his go-to lawyer was for any hot water he found himself in: Dick Fishley.

"George," said Fishley, settling into the lawyer's chair next to his client, after tersely introducing himself to the two detectives. "Don't answer anything until I tell you it's okay to do so."

Hennessey remembered reading about Fishley and some of his cases in the papers, and hearing about him from Boston Police Department colleagues years ago.

I've heard of this guy. Super smart, unpleasant, fiercely aggressive. No scruples at all. Comes with the territory for criminal defense lawyers, especially the successful ones.

"Gentlemen, what's George Slavin doing here?" Fishley started right in. "And tell me this, if you wanted to talk to him, why didn't you call him and ask him to come in, rather than going to his house and then following him here in your cruiser? I'm sure half the Cape knows by now. Was that your intent? To harass him? Hurt his reputation? Have everyone down here think George Slavin is in trouble with the law?"

This is gonna be torture, thought Hennessey. He knew that Fishley would interrupt and object and talk too much, all aimed toward ensuring the detectives didn't get a clear understanding of whatever it was they were rooting around for.

"George," Lipman started, but was immediately interrupted by Fishley.

"That's Mr. Slavin please, Detective Lipman. Mr. Slavin."

"George," Lipman continued slowly, while staring straight at Fishley, "it turns out you and Emre Massahol were the last two people to see Jason Karp alive. In fact you were the last two people to be with him."

"And?" said Slavin, his quick glance at Fishley telling his lawyer he felt fine mixing it up with the detectives. "What does that have to do with anything? The poor guy," he continued, making reference to Karp and his untimely demise.

"Detectives," jumped in Fishley, "we really need to understand what's going on here, what's at stake for Mr. Slavin, or you need to get on with your day and let us get on with ours. It's already been a huge inconvenience."

Hennessey sat there taking it all in. Hidden behind Slavin's bravado, he noticed an underlying unease, a slight inner turmoil beneath the suave businessman-like façade. It meant something.

"Tell us about the arson attacks, and Pat Kimmell too," Hennessey asked suddenly, blurting it out quickly and purposefully to try to get any sort of reaction out of Slavin.

"What are you talking about?" Slavin responded, his face coloring. "The fires? At CAN's music schools and theater, and the other arts organization fires? Is that what you mean? I'm totally clueless. Horrible events though, that's for sure. And as for that person... who was it, Pat Campbell? Pat

Cymbal? I've no idea who you're talking about."

They're never getting anything from me, thought Slavin defiantly. *Never. I'll rot to death in a jail first.*

Every time Slavin had made an installment payment on the job, and there had been three such payments, the instructions came with a photograph. The first photo: his oldest daughter. The second photo: his youngest daughter. The third photo: a picture of his five young grandchildren cavorting together.

Pouncing on the situation, Fishley stood up abruptly. "Detectives, we're done. You've wasted my time and Mr. Slavin's time and money. Can we send the BCPD a bill? For what you've put George through just now? We'd love to do so."

Rising to the occasion, Lipman barked back: "Sit back down, Fishley. No, we're not done yet. If you insist on George leaving, I guarantee that we'll return to his house shortly, police siren and light on, and we'll bring him in again, this time in handcuffs."

Scowling, Fishley took a long moment, then sat back down. "What do you want from my client?" he asked. Hennessey and Lipman took turns telling the story, making sure, as discussed beforehand, not to share with Slavin and Fishley some of the critical details gathered to date.

"George, we know that you and Emre Massahol and Jason Karp went out on your boat together. We know it. We also know that only you and Emre came back in on the boat."

Before Slavin could say anything, Fishley was at it again. "How do you know that? Tell us how you know that."

"The Chatham harbormaster's logbook has every date George's boat went out, and the number of people on the boat. The harbormaster identified a recent trip that George and Emre Massahol went out on. He was really excited that Massahol signed the cover of his *Cape Cod Today*— remembered it clearly. There was a third person on the trip as well. That's what the logbook shows and what the harbormaster said."

"Did he identify Jason Karp?" asked Fishley, interrupting again. "Did he?"

Slavin guffawed and took over. "Harbormaster Willie? That old lush… He couldn't tell you what he had for breakfast two hours ago, let alone tell you who went out on what boat from the harbor last month. He's a drunk, totally unreliable. Nothing he says can be believed. Nothing he enters into his logbook can be believed either. Ask anyone at Chatham harbor, anyone who knows him. His mouth isn't the only thing missing a few things. Anything he told you, forget about."

Listening intently to what his client said, Fishley bore down. "Did the harbormaster identify Karp?"

"No, he didn't," said Hennessey, slowly and reluctantly. "Karp's car entered the Chatham Harbor parking lot that day and didn't leave when the parking lot closed for the night. The car never left the parking lot. It was impounded four days later. Jason Karp was dead by then."

Fishley inhaled and tapped his arched fingertips together in front of him, taking in everything he heard. Then he jumped up out of his chair again.

"Gentlemen, we are *indeed* done." Fishley stressed 'indeed' and looked at Lipman again, daring him to challenge an experienced, top-notch criminal defense lawyer asserting his professional authority over law enforcement in an ambiguous situation.

"The Chatham harbormaster, apparently an unreliable drunk, didn't even identify who you're talking about, who you say might've been on George's boat that day. Who cares that his car was found there? Let's go, George. Detectives, I advise you to be very careful before dealing with Mr. Slavin again.

"A terrible story about this Jason Karp," said Fishley as he departed with his client. "A great white shark attack… What the hell."

A similar routine played out at Massahol's place. Except, unlike Slavin's abode, there was no rear door to the Maestro's one-bedroom Yarmouth condominium from which to slip out for a late afternoon stroll. The look in Massahol's eyes when the two detectives introduced themselves said it all: like a deer in the headlights.

Stravinsky played in the background. Double M planned on leading the Cape Philharmonic through *The Rite of Spring* next season. The savage, wildly accented passage early on in the piece blasted in the background—*bum bum bum bum bum bum bum bum bum BUM bum BUM bum bum bum bum bum BUM bum bum BUM bum bum bum BUM bum bum bum bum BUM bum bum.* Hennessey tapped his foot along.

Equally savvy and sophisticated as Slavin, indeed light years more so when it came to cultural matters, Massahol now faced a distinct disadvantage: He'd never had a serious run-in with the law in the past. Because of his law-abiding history, he didn't have a Dick Fishley at his beck and call. Of course, Massahol never for an instant thought he'd find himself staring at two detectives who'd just knocked at his front door.

"Do I need a lawyer?" Massahol asked, sitting down in the BCPD's shabby interrogation room, hoping his anxiety wasn't too evident. He took a deep breath and reminded himself of how he needed to feel and act.

I don't want to send the wrong message, get off on the wrong foot by having a lawyer here. Have to avoid that at all costs. I'm here for a casual talk with the BCPD. That's all.

"You tell us if you need a lawyer, Maestro," said Hennessey. "What happened out on George's boat? Three of you went out. Two of you came back. What happened?" The bluff was on. Hennessey and Lipman charted it all out beforehand.

Massahol hid his fear well. It wasn't for nothing that he was an experienced, successful concert hall performer, always the leading performer on the orchestral stage when he stepped out onto it. What he experienced now was like his stage fright of yesteryear.

What do they know? Massahol wondered. *What can I tell them?*

Feverishly processing what he thought Hennessey and Lipman knew, and remembering what he and Slavin agreed to on the horrible boat ride back, he decided, spur of the moment, to stick to the story told to Harbormaster Willie.

"Well... yes." A pause filled the air. "Jason Karp and George and I went out on a farewell boat ride for Jason. On George's boat, the *Tranche-Two.* We thought it would be a nice gesture, a good way of seeing him off after his dismissal from CAN. We wanted to show him that we thought highly of him, despite the hassles of the past."

Hennessey concentrated intensely on Massahol. The content of his statement, the words he used and inflections made, each and every nuance of his body language. After all, Massahol used body language, gestures large and small, to make a living. He conducted orchestras.

He either looks down at the table, or over our shoulders, noted Hennessey. *Why isn't this guy looking at us? What's he looking at up there, over our shoulders? Is Slavin there? The ghost of Jason Karp? Does it help him concentrate, help him remember... or help him make up a story?*

"After leaving Chatham Harbor, we cruised north along the Cape Cod National Seashore," Massahol said. "Small talk and hors d'oeuvres and best wishes to you Jason, let us know how we can help. That was it.

"When we got up to Truro, Jason suddenly said he wanted to get off in Provincetown—had a friend there he wanted to look up and dine with if possible, before leaving the Cape. Frankly, I was glad to see him get off. It prevented the airing of unspoken matters. The whole trip was a bit of forced fun."

A minute of silence passed. An eternity. Tension built up in the room like steam in a pressure cooker. "Why don't you tell us what really happened?" Hennessey said at last.

Massahol flung his head down into his hands dramatically, elbows on the table. He cried out, practically sobbing: "I told you what happened, I just told you what happened. That's all I know!"

◇ ◇ ◇

They'd gotten nothing out of Slavin. His lawyer Fishley made sure of that. But Massahol gave them essential information. Karp went out on the boat with the two of them. Big news. Huge news, even with Massahol maintaining the 'he got off in Provincetown' tale, which is what they'd heard from Harbormaster Willie. Neither detective bought it.

"No, we're not calling Ulrike Baten-Karp again," Hennessey said forcefully to Lipman, who suggested they reach out to Karp's widow to ask who she and Jason knew in Provincetown. "Think how she'll react to that, and what she'll ask us. Let's do the legwork ourselves."

They focused on bartenders and restauranteurs. Even in September, a pretty busy month, Provincetown was fairly discrete. It was not as if a canvassing of all Boston or Cambridge bars and restaurants needed undertaking. Karp hadn't been well known out at the spit-end of Cape Cod. His home in Hyannisport was at least an hour away. Still, no one in Provincetown had seen Karp on the day, or the day after, Slavin and Massahol said they dropped him off. The photo of Karp used by Hennessey and Lipman got a little dog-eared. They left copies of it at many Provincetown establishments, asking that it be shown around, and that the BCPD be contacted if anyone remembered seeing or talking to Karp.

"It's the guy killed by the great white shark, isn't it?" they heard time and time again. Photos of Karp had appeared in the papers and on the news after his body parts were identified.

"The poor guy. And poor us, having those beasts around now and fearing them so much," someone said to them.

"Why are you asking about him?" another person asked.

"We're simply trying to piece his last day or so together. That's all," replied Hennessey.

Lipman, chafing at holding back all of the information

they had about Karp's death, understood Hennessey's rationale for doing so, and reluctantly went along with it. After three full days of canvassing in Provincetown, the possibility existed that they still hadn't met the right person, or that Karp's photo hadn't circulated broadly enough. It was unlikely though. Very unlikely.

"You're telling me, Detective Lipman, you suspect a murder's taken place here?" Judge Wolcott Brennan asked somewhat incredulously. Brennan read the newspapers, Boston and Cape Cod, and knew all about the sensational aspects to Jason Karp's death. "I'm not persuaded by what you've presented to me."

Search warrants issued by judges or magistrates are based on affidavits, sworn statements from police, police informants, or private citizens. The police need to present probable cause that a crime occurred and that evidence exists at the location they want to search.

Judge Brennan took several days in deciding whether to grant search warrants for the Massahol residence, the Slavin residence, and Slavin's boat, the *Tranche-Two*. He called Lipman into his chambers twice to discuss the legitimacy of the ongoing police effort.

"Your Honor, I've worked with consulting Detective Hennessey on the matter for weeks now," Lipman said, giving a nod over his shoulder at his colleague.

"I know of Hennessey," said Judge Brennan, bluntly and sourly. "I certainly hope he's been of use to you, a good use of our taxpayer dollars." The Judge's dour comments surprised Hennessey.

Hmm. Maybe my recent dust-up with those MA state troopers somehow made its way to Judge Brennan, thought Hennessey. *Or he heard about my less-than-stellar Boston Police Department record. Might be known down here by the powers that be.*

"He's been indispensable, Your Honor," Lipman stated

firmly.

"You know, you two," continued Judge Brennan, "you've got one of the flimsiest sets of facts and crime theories ever presented to me in a search warrant request. So, Karp goes out on the boat with Slavin and Massahol and doesn't come back. So what? What they say, about his being dropped off in Provincetown, seems reasonable. I know, I know, you've been up there a couple of days asking around. That doesn't add up to a hill of beans. It's not as if there are only a hundred people in Provincetown. Think of how busy it is this time of year. You probably didn't find who he visited with. Maybe he wanted it that way.

"And maybe Karp was a drug addict. You'd be surprised who is these days," the judge continued. "GHB is a powerfully addictive drug. Maybe he took it with alcohol, swam, and ended up drowning. That's one way to read the forensic report... if it's to be believed in the first place. Often, the forensics aren't worth the paper they're printed on—you both know that. So Karp drowns... Then a shark gets at his body."

Judge Brennan grimaced, thinking about a great white shark dismembering Jason Karp. "Or the poor guy was attacked and killed and savaged by a great white while out for a swim." Brennan winced at that possibility too.

Hennessey stepped up next to Lipman. "Your Honor, may I explain more fully why we think what happened to Jason Karp wasn't an accident, and why we also think he didn't kill himself?"

Judge Brennan nodded.

Hennessey started right in. "Cape Now, known as CAN, is one of our region's leading arts and culture institutions. But it's floundering, strategically and financially. Our interviews with people at the organization, Your Honor, indicate there's great discord within CAN about the future of the organization. And we've looked at CAN's books. There's serious financial trouble on the horizon.

"Emre Massahol and George Slavin are aggressively

leading a group of insiders who want to get rid of the money-losing music schools and theater as soon as possible. Jason Karp vehemently opposed doing so. It was one of the reasons he was fired. On top of all that, CAN's most important project, the new SHLAC performing arts center project, is failing. George Slavin is in charge of the project, but no money has been raised for it, and no property acquired for it yet.

"Then, Your Honor, the two CAN music schools, not one but both of them, burn to the ground. CAN's theater burns to the ground too. Detective Lipman and I know we're dealing with arson attacks. There's no question about it. It's also been confirmed by a guy named Ben Maisky, the chief investigator for CAN's insurer, Archduke Insurance Company. I've worked with Maisky in the past and have nothing but respect for him and his work.

"Here's where it gets interesting. The CAN board, urged on by board member Slavin—you might say, at his insistence—decides to use the insurance proceeds from the fires to buy a site for the SHLAC project and to endow Emre Massahol's conductor's chair, *not* to rebuild the music schools and theater. So, Massahol and Slavin get the two things they always wanted. CAN's music schools and theater are gone, and they have the funds on hand to pursue their own pet projects. All as a result of the arson attacks.

"I can't help but believe, Your Honor, that Karp knew or suspected that Massahol and Slavin either committed the arson attacks themselves, or masterminded them, and confronted them about it. They killed him to silence him."

Clearly and earnestly, dispassionately and logically, Hennessey told the story brilliantly.

"I'm dubious, really doubtful. But I'll grant the search warrants," said Judge Brennan. "Be careful where you're treading."

"Sure, be my guest," Emre Massahol told Lipman, after

receiving a copy of the search warrant by email. He was at his permanent residence in San Antonio, Texas, where he spent most of his time. "I'm fine with you guys going into my condo," he said, confident there was nothing of any interest to Hennessey and Lipman there. The condominium association president had keys to all of the units in the complex, in case of an emergency. She let Hennessey and Lipman in. Nothing.

Slavin called Dick Fishley before opening up his home to the two detectives. It was Fishley's impulse to move to quash the warrant. He insisted Lipman photograph it using his cell phone and then email it to him so he could examine it. Fishley noted it was signed by Judge Wolcott Brennan. Trouble. Battling a search warrant signed by Judge Brennan was an uphill battle, and not good for future appearances in the Brennan courtroom. Not good for Fishley's future business either, and his cash flow these days was as good as it had ever been. He thought about the unlucky saps he might have to defend in the near future in front of Judge Brennan.

"Of course not," Slavin told Fishley, when asked if there was anything incriminating at home.

"Let the jerks in then," responded Fishley.

"Gentlemen, be my guest," Slavin said, opening the front door.

At the *Tranche-Two*, still moored in Chatham Harbor, Lipman insisted Slavin wait on the dock, while he and Hennessey boarded and went through the boat. Hennessey was in an intense place mentally.

The boat's the key to it all. Karp went out on the boat... and never came back.

Working methodically, the two detectives started in the hold. The *Tranche-Two* was nicely equipped, although nothing special. There were no indications or signs of the trip Karp, Slavin, and Massahol took.

"Nothing down here," Lipman said tersely. "Let's head up on deck."

Things seemed perfectly in order on deck too. Seagull

guano here and there. "Take everything apart, everything we can," Lipman said, donning a new pair of latex gloves and handing Hennessey a new pair. "Let's start at the bow and work our way back."

They reached the three-sided seating area in the back, behind the helm and in front of the stern. One by one, Hennessey removed the vertical backseat cushions and looked in the crack behind each.

"Phil, come here," he said. "Bring an evidence bag." Behind the last of the seat cushions, jammed down into the crack, was a small empty vial with a screw-on black top, roughly the size of the first joint of a forefinger.

Could be for anything, thought Hennessey. *I've seen these used as drug vials a million times though. Cocaine or another illegal substance, maybe GHB.*

"Yes indeed, yes indeed," said Lipman, swooping in on Hennessey's discovery. He picked it up gingerly with gloved hands and placed it in the plastic evidence bag hanging from his belt.

Watching from fifteen feet away, Slavin exclaimed, "Wow! No idea what that is, gentlemen. And no idea how it got there or who it belongs to."

◇　◇　◇

The MA southeast regional crime lab folks were getting to know Hennessey and Lipman well. Not in a good way. In short order, the two detectives had submitted three emergency requests for analytical work. This last time on a small glass vial with a black screw-on top. They needed it analyzed for fingerprints and DNA, and for traces of past contents.

The request to do another immediate analysis caused considerable grumbling at the lab. It was about to get a 'wait your turn' response—one of the lab technicians suggested a 'shove it up your ass' response. A call from the Massachusetts Lieutenant Governor, however, who happened to be close friends with the BCPD Commissioner, made clear the need to advance the vial's analysis to the very front of the class.

Hennessey and Lipman had their results three days later. The vial contained traces of two drugs: cocaine and GHB. Slavin's fingerprints and DNA were on it. No one else's.

CHAPTER 19

Tuesday, September 28, 2021

Like a bright young child learning to read, Hennessey soaked up everything about Kelly. Eagerly and openly, he took in everything. Virtually nothing about her annoyed him. Certain things really surprised him. Underneath her demure and somewhat subdued exterior was an adventurous, playful woman who was full of life. It completely captivated him.

Amazing. Never been with anyone like her before.

Over the weekend, and after an early autumn swim and lunch at Longnook Beach, Hennessey had just begun his new book, Leif Eisner's *Peace Like A River*, when Kelly leaned over, nibbled gently on his ear, and whispered enticingly, "Let's go visit the dunes, Mr. Hennessey, what do you say?"

The magnificent sand dunes of Cape Cod, where lovemaking followed swimming and eating in the buff as naturally as the sun came up every morning. "Thought I'd experienced it all," he said to her, holding her hand while carrying in his other the beach blanket that had served as witness to their sweaty, torrid, marvelous coupling. She looked over at him, giving him a 'you haven't experienced anything yet' grin, as they walked back to their spot on the beach.

"I think we'll have to make it a regular occurrence, Mr. Hennessey, how about you? What do you think? Longer lovemaking next time though, huh? Up for it?" she said, giggling wildly at her own double entendre.

"How can I not be? It's what the beach is named for, after all. Longnook."

◇ ◇ ◇

"We told him that malarkey to get him to mind his own business." Back in the hot seat in the BCPD holding room, with Dick Fishley sitting next to him listening intently, Slavin explained why he and Massahol told Harbormaster Willie that Karp got off the *Tranche-Two* in Provincetown.

"Look, the guy's an eccentric lush. You saw his harbormaster's hut, there are signs of it everywhere. We thought we'd put it to bed, Karp not being there, by telling him that. The fact he remembers anything we told him, remembers anything about the day, stuns me."

"Why don't you tell us what really happened, George?" asked Hennessey.

"You won't believe me when I tell you. Here it is. We're out on the boat making nice with Jason Karp. Why shouldn't we, after all? The engine's cut, we're drifting, not too far out, the coast easily in sight—the National Seashore. Anyway, Karp's telling us a bit of his life story, we're telling him some of ours. He says how disappointed he is that things didn't work out at CAN. He seemed despondent about it. We tell him no worries, he's got a great future ahead of him. We have a drink or two, and Double M and I go down in the hold to get the food. We brought a pretty nice spread along with us."

"All of a sudden, we hear a big splash. I remember thinking *what was that?* Probably takes us thirty to sixty seconds to stop what we're doing and get up on deck, another twenty to thirty seconds to look around and get our bearing. Massahol doesn't know the boat, after all. Karp is gone. Nowhere to be seen. My scuba diving weight belt is gone too... not sitting in the corner of the stern where it usually is. Jesus, the horror of it. We didn't know what to do."

Sitting stone-faced across from Slavin and his lawyer, Hennessey noted the insistence on we. *We this, we that... we, we, we. The hangman's hanging a crowd or none at all.* Hennessey also noticed a redness to Slavin's face as the story came out.

Too much sun probably, he thought.

Glancing at Lipman, who was seated next to him, Hennessey spoke calmly and neutrally. "So, Jason Karp impulsively killed himself. Extraordinary. Why didn't you radio it in? A man overboard SOS? Why didn't you report it when you returned to shore? Why didn't you ever report it?"

"Well," said Slavin, rubbing his left thumb up and down over his right thumb, his other fingers interlocked, "we were panicked, absolutely panicked. The blasted boat radio didn't work—I know, I know, every boater's bible. The water visibility... you know what it's like off the Cape. Seven, eight feet at most. We cruised the area for what seemed forever, circling round and round, hoping it was all a big mistake, that it hadn't really happened. On the way back, once the initial shock wore off, Double M and I talked about it. Talked about how horrible it would be for the Cape to know one of its young leaders killed himself at sea. We thought since so few people knew the Karps, since Ulrike was out of the country and probably wasn't ever going to come back—that's what Jason told us at least—it'd be better, it'd be better to let people think he'd moved to Europe." Listening closely, Hennessey's thoughts turned dark.

Sure you talked about it. Talked about an alibi. What a great opportunity to come up with one.

Fishley, who'd been uncharacteristically quiet, knew from experience that his client Slavin was in trouble. He reverted to form. "Detectives, if there's nothing more, we'll be leaving. Again. No more of these ridiculous fishing expeditions, got it? You either charge my client, with who knows what, or that's the end of it."

"George... the arson attacks," Hennessey said loudly and suddenly. "Tell us your role... tell us how you know Pat Kimmell."

Slavin and Fishley spoke simultaneously, filling the room with combustible noise. "I know nothing about the attacks, absolutely nothing! And who the hell is this Pat Kimmell you keep mentioning? You tell me!" Slavin's face colored again, clearing in a couple of seconds.

Fishley spoke even louder: "Enough already, ENOUGH. Not appreciated at all, Hennessey, not one bit. Who the hell do you think you are? C'mon George, we're out of here."

Lipman had the last word. "No, George isn't going anywhere. We found GHB in the vial from the boat. We found George's fingerprints and DNA on the vial—only George's. We found GHB in Karp's body. The three of them went out on the boat together, only two came back. We're booking George Slavin for the murder of Jason Karp. He's not going anywhere."

◊ ◊ ◊

With Slavin isolated in the BCPD holding cell, nothing stopped Hennessey and Lipman from going right at Erme Massahol. They had Slavin's far-fetched story about Karp killing himself in hand.

"Let's see what we can get out of him, unsolicited," Hennessey said to Lipman. "With these common alibi situations, the story almost always breaks down at some point. One of them will say something wrong, some detail will be off, whatever. That'll be our opportunity."

Lipman smiled. "Absolutely."

Massahol arrived, this time with a lawyer, Brian Bucknell, who, while not in Dick Fishley's league, was no one's fool either.

"Maestro... May we call you that, Maestro?" asked Lipman. "We'd like to hear more from you about dropping Karp off in Provincetown. Where was it exactly? What time was it?"

Despite decades on the performance stage, an uncontrollable, underlying fear gripped Massahol, unlike any stage fright he'd ever experienced. No direct eye contact again. That said it all to Hennessey.

Here's someone who communicates all the time with his eyes, to the ninety musicians in front of him, hour after hour. Yet, he can't even look at us.

"I've no idea where we dropped him off. I'm not from the Cape. You know that. I don't know Provincetown at all. We pulled up to some small, non-descript dock and cut the engine for a minute or so while Jason hopped off. The town was off to the right in the distance. That's all I remember."

"What time was it?"

"Oh please, I don't know that either," said Massahol nervously. "My guess is between four and five in the afternoon. The sun was still warm, still making exquisite patterns on the water. We got back to Chatham Harbor an hour later and I was home by seven, even after our grand encounter with the Chatham harbormaster." Massahol opened his eyes wide and put on a big forced grin. He was trying to appear at ease, trying to make it seem as if his memory of the exchange with Harbormaster Willie was warm and humorous.

"Who told the Chatham harbormaster that Jason Karp got off in Provincetown, George Slavin? You? Both of you?" asked Lipman.

"Detectives, I don't see where you're going with this," said Brian Bucknell, finally getting his legal sea legs and recognizing his client needed some bolstering.

"How does it possibly matter," Bucknell went on, "that my client can't remember specifically where Jason Karp got off of George Slavin's boat in Provincetown, or the exact time it was? Or who said what to the Chatham harbormaster? You're not making any sense to me. My guess is you're not making any sense to my client either. Please, if you're not going to ask anything important, let's wrap it up."

Hennessey and Lipman stared at Massahol without saying

anything. "Maestro, I know we asked last time," Hennessey finally said. "Why don't you tell us what really happened?"

"That's enough of that," Bucknell objected. Lipman waved him off with a quick, violent back-of-the-hand gesture, stopping Bucknell in his tracks.

"This interview room's a funny place, don't you think?" continued Hennessey. "So sparse, so dreary, a room that by its non-descript appearance and furnishings should be meaningless. A room where, given its outward appearance, nothing important could possibly take place. How incredible then, that, to the contrary, each and every aspect and dimension of human existence, from the agony to the ecstasy, has played out in this room. These walls have witnessed yelling and tears and laughter, threats and joy and despair, truth and lies. These walls have heard it all."

"Just recently, Maestro," Hennessey continued, "these walls heard George Slavin say that Jason Karp was not dropped off in Provincetown. They heard George Slavin say Jason Karp died at sea. What do you say to that, Maestro? What do you say to what these walls recently heard from George Slavin?"

"Don't answer that question. Do NOT answer it," said Bucknell, almost yelling. Massahol didn't need to answer it. The look on his face said it all. A look of guilt and shame and desperation all brought together into a facial expression that spoke more clearly than anything he could say.

Massahol sighed. A long, drawn-out sigh packed with meaning. Relief. Resignation. Recognition. A welcoming was on the near horizon, an absolving, redeeming welcoming. Erme Massahol began crawling out of the deep hole he found himself in.

"It was Ge..." Massahol stopped suddenly, falling right back into the hole. "He killed himself, the poor guy. It was horrible. He was nowhere in sight. Must've jumped overboard and drowned himself when we were down below. We didn't know what to do. So we didn't do or say anything. To anyone."

◇ ◇ ◇

Hennessey settled back in his seat. He was in row forty-two toward the back of the Airbus A330. He was on the aisle, good for someone tall and gangly like him, with no one sat next to him. Swissair Flight 53 left Logan at 9:50 p.m., arriving in Geneva at 11:00 a.m. the next morning. He didn't expect to get much shut-eye on the flight. Other than a few trips to Mexico, he'd never been out of the United States.

Although he kept his passport current, it was due to expire in four months. That wouldn't do for the Swiss authorities. Anyone with a passport expiring within six months wasn't allowed into the country. The Swiss feared people staying in the country with expired passports, triggering the country's deportation process.

Those anal bastards.

Hennessey thought the situation humorous now that it was behind him. The BCPD came through with flying colors, Kelly at the helm. The new passport arrived a few days before his mid-week departure, thanks to the 'needed urgently by law enforcement' message accompanying the expedited passport application.

"You get yours, too, and we'll use them sometime soon," Hennessey said to Kelly when she mentioned she'd never had a passport. "The place of your choice," he said. She beamed.

Makes my day, that smile of hers, he thought. *Always.*

He was on his way to try to talk Ulrike Baten-Karp into coming back to the good ol' USA. Not only to watch the murder trial, as they sought justice for her and her late husband, but to serve as a key witness. Getting Lipman over to Europe on business proved too difficult; the BCPD needed a county board resolution authorizing him to travel outside the country. So they sent Hennessey instead. He simply expensed the trip as a consultant. It was all above board. The BCPD police commissioner loved the idea. It was hers, after all.

The Baten family compound sat outside of Bern, the capital of Switzerland. Written up in all the captivating Swiss tourist brochures as "Pretty Little Bern," the city became the capital of Switzerland in the mid-1800s, chosen to avoid creating a concentration of power in the much larger and more important cities of Geneva and Zurich. Hennessey read up on Bern on the flight over.

The Aare River flowed through and around three sides of Bern. It was a bilingual city, French and Swiss-German being the official languages. Like most Americans, Hennessey spoke neither, which both bothered and amused him.

Oh well, I'll get by. Wonder if they speak Southie?

Enough people did speak English for Hennessey to get by, including the Batens. As a banker, Mr. Baten had to be fluent in English, the international language of the business world. He made sure his two daughters spoke it flawlessly as well.

The Baten compound spread out over seven acres and consisted of a mix of lightly wooded land and sloping meadows leading gently down to the Aare, which ran along the northern boundary of the property. A stone and iron gate stood at the main driveway entrance. Once within the gated entrance, the driveway split into three—the center route leading to the main residence, the left leading to Ulrike's house, and the right to her sister Anna's place.

Hennessey had been told to come to the main house. It was like stepping back into another century. A miniature castle without the turrets. Heavy stone and thick wooden doors throughout, yet completely modernized for the twenty-first century, at least as much as was possible without damaging the character and aesthetic integrity of the place.

"The Batens are waiting for you on the veranda. Please follow me," said the doorman, or butler, or valet... whatever the gentleman's official title might be.

Well, that's a first for me, thought Hennessey. *I'll have to work on getting greeted that way more often. Maybe Lipman... or Kelly... or even the BCPD commissioner.*

Beyond the veranda's low stone wall, a freshly mowed meadow led down to the river in the distance. Wisps of steam rose, the waters of the Aare slightly warmer than the air at this time of year, the beginning of autumn. The sweet smell of just-cut hay filled the air; its crispness and cleanliness intoxicated Hennessey.

This is heaven, he thought. *Who would ever leave it for America?*

The two Baten daughters stood behind their seated parents with their hands on the back of the wrought-iron patio chairs, Ulrike behind her father, Anna behind her mother. It was a family portrait that could have hung in one of the finest museums in Europe or the United States.

Hans Baten got up as Hennessey stepped out onto the veranda. Tall, with terrific posture, piercing hawk-like blue eyes, a full head of silver-grey hair, and a thin pencil moustache, he looked like a businessman's version of Christopher Plummer.

What a good-looking family, thought Hennessey.

"Detective Hen-ah-see—did I pronounce that right?" asked Mr. Baten. "A pleasure to meet you, despite the occasion being such a terribly upsetting one." He spoke English perfectly, with an underlying Swiss-German accent.

"Yes, a pleasure to meet you, Detective," said Mrs. Baten, introduced herself next, "and thank you for coming." Having also gotten up, Mrs. Baten then promptly excused herself.

Odd, thought Hennessey. *Although I know she hasn't been well. If I'm remembering right, visiting his ailing mother-in-law was one of the last things Jason Karp did.*

"I hope you haven't wasted your time coming over. Not that a visit to Switzerland, for any reason, is ever a waste of time," said Mr. Baten. "I understand you want Ulrike to return to the U.S. for the trial of the two butchers accused of murdering Jason." There was no small talk here, no pleasantries before getting right into it.

"I am utterly opposed to her doing so," he continued. "Why should she subject herself to the agony of it, to the trauma? She's been through enough already. Why should she ever set foot in the U.S. again, the murder capital of the developed world? A country where guns seem to be valued more than human life." Hans Baten spoke dispassionately, although the topics were inflammatory ones. His command and presence made clear his position in life, socially and professionally.

"Papa, Papa, let me speak... please," said Ulrike, inserting herself into the conversation.

With their mother gone, Anna, the younger of the two by a few years, moved over to be next to her sister. Unlike the tall and willowy Ulrike, Anna was a wisp of a woman, petite, with large, shiny doe-like brown eyes and a perfect aquiline nose. You could tell they were sisters by the nose, and their pearl white, perfect teeth.

What beautiful young women, thought Hennessey. *Exquisite really.*

"Good to finally meet you in person, Detective Hennessey," Ulrike said. "It is always the best, although I guess Zoom or Skype is better than nothing. I'm sorry to say, I agree with my father. What could possibly be gained by my returning to the U.S. to watch the trial of those monsters? All it will do is make things worse for me." Her slight tremble made clear to Hennessey she was doing her best to keep her emotions in check.

"Ah, my dearest Ulrike, don't fret over it," said her father. "Detective Hennessey, I don't think there's any way you'll get Ulrike back to watch one of those circus-like trials you Americans call justice. And why should you need or want the victim of the crime there anyway? Please, tell me, is that how the U.S. criminal law system works?"

How interesting, thought Hennessey. *Hans Baten views his daughter, not Jason Karp, as the victim. Says a lot. I guess they're both victims— of course they are.*

Hennessey agreed with many of their points, no matter how acerbic and critical they were of America. He decided on the spot to give them his perspective on the American justice system, and an unvarnished one at that.

"Yes, Mr. Baten. Some criminal trials in the U.S. have a public, I think you said circus-like, setting to them. Most do not. And yes, the upcoming trial has already caught the attention of the national press. That's unfortunate. That doesn't mean it will be a circus, not at all. The press and publicity will be controlled quite carefully by the judge and court administrators. It's really not like you see on American TV shows."

Setting the record straight, Hennessey went on. "You raise a great question as to whether the victim's family has to be there, in fact, whether anyone needs to be there at all. No, there's no requirement that you be there," he said, looking at Ulrike. "But to be honest, it can help a lot. The jury is made up of all sorts of people, coming from all sorts of backgrounds. Having the victim's family in the courtroom allows them to personalize what came of the criminal behavior. A widow, in this instance."

Ulrike began to tear up. Her sister first took her hand, and then swung around and gave her a hug. Hennessey felt terrible.

"I'm sorry, Ulrike, so sorry. But yes, it humanizes the courtroom to have the victim's family—you in this instance—there during the trial. It allows the jury, the judge, everyone, quite frankly, to understand the loss more clearly."

He saw a deep sadness in Ulrike that bore out what he suspected. Her father, and probably her mother—although Hennessey knew this was a family ruled by the father and not the mother, nor ruled equally by both—hadn't liked Jason Karp. So Ulrike carried her loss by herself. The family did not share in it, making it infinitely harder on her. Perhaps sister Anna felt some of the loss and helped Ulrike grieve; sibling acceptance and love of spouses is never on par with parental acceptance and love.

They probably just tolerated him, thought Hennessey. *Perhaps not good enough for their daughter. Poor Ulrike, going through this alone.*

"There's another reason for you to come, too," Hennessey went on. "George Slavin and Emre Massahol claim that Jason killed himself, that they had nothing to do with his death." Before he could continue, a firestorm broke out.

"Putain, j'y crois pas! Vous entendez ça? Ces salauds veulent faire croire que Jason s'est suicidé! C'est impossible! Je le sais et vous le savez. Putain…"

"Calme-toi, Ulrike," interrupted Hans Baten, trying to settle his daughter down, "Calme-toi, cherie."

Hennessey didn't need a French translator to understand what Ulrike said. He got it all.

"You said 'not in a million years' when Detective Lipman and I talked to you before, Ulrike. We need you, really need you, to testify at the trial. You'll be acting as a character witness for the prosecution. It's Slavin and Massahol's only defense. If you don't come and convince the jury that Jason would never have killed himself, they may get away with it."

Ulrike looked at her father, then Hennessey, then her father again. Without looking back at Hennessey, she said, "When do I need to be there? Papa, I want Anna to come with me."

CHAPTER 20

Monday, November 29, 2021

Brenda Schnabel, the Barnstable County District Attorney, and known as DA Schnabel, took on the Slavin and Massahol murder trials herself. It was an indication of the publicity generated by the charges, the stakes involved, and how razor-thin, from an evidentiary perspective, the cases were. Schnabel didn't usually step down into the ranks to handle actual trial work. Her fingernails were already bitten down to the cuticles. Still, she exuded confidence.

I'll pull it off, no problem.

Serious criminal charges against the wealthy and well-educated came about once in a blue moon on Cape Cod. Not counting white-collar financial crime. There was plenty of that, and the consequences of which, if caught, was almost always a light prison sentence at a federal country club. Look at Martha Stewart. She served her enormous five-month jail sentence at the Alderson federal prison, also known as Camp Cupcake.

Cape Cod buzzed with the news. Agog. By and large, the region's business leaders looked positively on the publicity coming from having two prominent members of the community charged with murder. Throughout the country, people read about and followed the trial, like the OJ Simpson murder trial of yesteryear. The Cape was on the minds of everyone; the story popped up ceaselessly on social media apps and news links on smart phones, tablets, and laptops. It pleased Larry Sylvester tremendously.

What great publicity for us, Sylvester thought. *And Jason Karp NOT killed by a great white shark. Eaten by one, yes, but not killed by it.*

Sylvester almost wept with joy. Other members of the Chamber of Commerce were equally delighted.

Massahol and Slavin pled not guilty at their arraignments. Fishley and Bucknell gave the usual 'our clients look forward to being fully exonerated' statements on the steps of the Barnstable Courthouse. Bail was set at $250,000 and came with conditions: The two defendants had to relinquish their passports and wear ankle monitors. Massahol blanched. Slavin thought nothing of it.

I've worn one of these damned things before.

"Your Honor, we'd like defendants Slavin and Massahol tried together." DA Schnabel made the request of Judge Brennan, the judge who'd issued the search warrants leading to the arrests. "Considering the circumstances," she continued, "this matter's perfect for a joint trial. They're each charged with murder based on the same exact facts." *They're equally culpable, equally guilty,* she also thought.

Schnabel hoped Judge Brennan agreed. It was his call, not hers. As the presiding trial judge, Brennan had broad discretion whether to hold two separate trials or join them together into one.

Look, he's a judge who loves efficiency, Schnabel thought. *Here's hoping his calendar is already too full. That'll sway him.*

Dick Fishley and Brian Bucknell argued strenuously against a joint trial. "It really does not fit here, Your Honor," said Fishley.

"I agree, Your Honor," said Bucknell, jumping right in. "There are no conspiracy or RICO charges here. No group criminal behavior, as usually seen in joint trials."

A joint trial was the last thing the two criminal defense lawyers wanted. "It'll make things much easier for the DA's office, for Brennan too," Fishley said to Bucknell, right before their meeting with the judge on the issue.

"Yeah, I know," replied Bucknell. "And it'll make things more difficult for us, trying to coordinate everything as best we can."

Fishley and Bucknell were fine criminal defense lawyers, Fishley the best money could buy. They argued strenuously that separate trials be granted to their clients.

"Listen, gentlemen," said Judge Brennan. "Three men out on a boat, two men back. Your clients claim he committed suicide. DA Schnabel claims they murdered him. Neither of your clients has an inconsistent story. I'm joining the trials together."

The next day, Fishley and Bucknell filed motions with the MA appeals court challenging Brennan's decision. They lost.

"Fine. I knew Brennan would want it that way," Fishley told Bucknell. "We'll be fine. Plan everything out together, spell each other during the trial, build on what each of us says—like tag team wrestlers." He smiled at that one.

What a great image. Lawyers as tag team wrestlers.

So began their complicated, high-stakes criminal defenses of Slavin and Massahol. Challenging work for even the most experienced, skilled lawyers. Together, Fishley and Bucknell moved forward relentlessly toward their unified goal: acquittals. No pleas by their clients. Out of the question. It was scorched earth time.

Right away, the trial was off schedule, much to Judge Brennan's consternation. Jury selection took longer than expected; some of it was Brennan's own doing. The meticulous New Englander in him, combined with his reverence for the constitutions, federal and state, resulted in his making sure that jurors in his courtroom understood completely that in a criminal case it was the prosecutor's burden, its burden alone, to prove guilt beyond a reasonable doubt. And that it was also a defendant's constitutional right to remain silent.

"Funny as it may seem to you," he told the juror pool, "our Founding Fathers thought it so important, so fundamentally important, they made the right against self-incrimination a constitutional right. It's the Fifth Amendment to the U.S. Constitution. At the state level, it's set forth in Article 12 of the Massachusetts Constitution."

For years, Judge Brennan tried to tone down his professorial manner, his use of big, arcane, multi-syllabic words when talking to prospective jurors about rights, responsibilities, and duties in criminal trials. He also tried his best when talking to the jury during and after a trial, when giving it answers to questions that arose, and when discussing jury instructions. Nothing worked. Brennan never really got better at it, never developed a down-to-earth, common vocabulary for speaking in his own courtroom. Thinking about it made him glum and incredibly grumpy.

Maybe that's why I'm just a Superior Court Judge. I'm stuck here. Forever.

Brennan had the ability though, a gift really, to read people quickly. It allowed him, after chatting ever so briefly with a prospective juror, to know they shouldn't sit. He also knew, once the jury was seated, when he'd lost someone. Two weeks into his last big trial, he dismissed a juror for doing Sudoku while listening to lawyers argue about biotechnology patent infringements. The juror insisted she could do both, saying that solving Suduko puzzles while sitting on the jury actually helped her concentrate on the trial.

"I don't think so," Brennan said, his exasperation and frustration apparent to all. "You're dismissed. Step out of the jury box. Who's alternative juror one? Please join the rest of your fellow jurors in the box, and please... pay close and constant attention to the proceedings at hand. *At all times!*"

No wonder Wolcott Brennan had a reputation as a short-fused judge.

As the Massahol-Slavin joint murder trial got underway, Judge Brennan dismissed a healthy handful from the venire, the panel of prospective jurors, based on their antipathy, lack of understanding, or even slowness in responding to him. Although concerned, DA Schnabel and First Assistant DA Scott Bach didn't let on.

What's he doing? He's dismissed way too many of them already! Schnabel and Bach thought the same exact thing.

"I'm fine with it. You?" Fishley asked Bucknell when the two defense lawyers had a moment together.

Bucknell nodded in agreement. "I'd never challenge Brennan on any of these juror dismissals," he said. "We'd be nuts to do so, unless he dismissed all women, or black, or Hispanic potential jurors. And even then..."

Judge Brennan next took up the issue of publicity with the remaining jury hopefuls. While proud to be presiding over a trial that attracted national attention, he was wary of what it meant for the jury's impartiality. Brennan knew that no matter what he told the prospective jurors, and what they said in response to his questioning, there wasn't a chance in the world they weren't consciously or subconsciously influenced by the publicity surrounding the case. The best that Brennan and the lawyers could hope for was that empaneled jurors understood what they were charged to do, and ignored as best as possible the barrage of news about the case.

"How many of you read or heard about this case?" Brennan asked. "In the Boston papers, or in our own Cape Cod Times, the national news, or on social media? I want you all to remember," he went on, "that there's a lot of junk on social media, that relatively new purveyor of instantaneous and often highly inaccurate a news. That's why it's known as disinformation."

Brennan slipped into his intellectual, professorial mode. His use of words like 'purveyor' and 'instantaneous' and 'disinformation' left a few potential jurors behind in the dust. The Hyannis public works maintenance guy, who'd shown up to perform his civic duty, was now scratching his head.

What's this judge saying anyway? I don't understand!

"How many of you have watched the Monomoy Island Foot video?" Judge Brennan went on. Of the remaining twenty-five potential jurors, four slowly and tentatively raised their hands, the urge not to do so, which would guarantee making it through to the next round of the jury selection process, outweighed by the solemnity of the proceedings and the desire to be decent, honest citizens.

"No, don't get up," Brennan said in response to one of the four standing to leave the courtroom bench where they all sat. "I'm not dismissing you."

Instead, he held up the front page of The Phoenician, Boston's weekly newspaper, for the remaining members of the juror pool to see. On the cover was a caricature of a conductor, using a grossly elongated shark's tooth as a baton, with blood dripping onto a music score. The caption read: "A Shark... Or The Maestro?"

"How many of you have seen this, or something similar?" Brennan asked. This time a good one-third of the remaining juror pool responded affirmatively. A few of them let loose with an enthusiastic "oh yeah," making all the members of the legal community in the courtroom wonder, really wonder, whether anything Judge Brennan had told them over the past ninety minutes registered at all.

"This is nonsense," Judge Brennan said, shaking The Phoenician at them and displaying his full authority through the tenor and volume of his voice. "Worthless information. Every bit of it. Let me re-emphasize that." The poor Hyannis public works maintenance guy scratched his head again:

WHAT? Re-emphasize?? What the heck!

For the next ten minutes, Brennan told the prospective jurors, in what seemed like five different languages, that nothing they heard or read about Jason Karp's death outside the four walls of his courtroom mattered.

"You don't know anything about this case," Brennan told them. "Neither do I. That's because no courtroom evidence has been presented yet. None. You might find the Monomoy Island Foot video humorous, or grotesque for that matter. It has no role whatsoever in this courtroom of mine. Neither does anything else you've read or heard. Like this rag," he said, shaking The Phoenician at them again.

"As of today, those of you who end up on the jury are not going to read, or listen to, or watch anything about the case outside of this courtroom. Nothing. Understood?"

◊ ◊ ◊

Like all elected district attorneys, DA Schnabel was as much a politician as a lawyer. With the help of First Assistant DA Scott Bach, she hoped to build an underlying emotional case for the prosecution by presenting the more sensational and salacious aspects of Jason Karp's death. The finding of the finger by a young boy, the finding of the foot by an octogenarian woman, the discovery of the torso in a great white shark—Schnabel and Bach wanted it all heard by the jury.

Fishley and Bucknell would have none of it. They filed motions asking Judge Brennan to suppress certain evidence before the trial began, seeking to prevent the prosecution team from making an impression on the jury with it.

"Listen, Your Honor," Fishley said at the pre-trial hearing, looking at Bucknell for support, "there is no reason whatsoever, *whatsoever*, for evidence concerning the finding of Karp's body parts to be heard by you or the jury. It's irrelevant and it's highly prejudicial to our clients."

"I agree completely, Your Honor," Bucknell piped in.

"I disagree," retorted Bach. As First Assistant DA, Bach played as large a role in the trial as Schnabel. Frankly, he was a more experienced and better trial attorney than she was. "The link is critical between when and where Karp's body parts were found, and what the forensic evidence tells us was in some of those body parts."

Fishley frowned upon hearing it. "No, Your Honor. It's irrelevant information, where the damn foot was found, or the finger, or the torso. And by whom. Who cares? It's eyebrow-raising and extremely prejudicial for the jury to hear. The photos? The Monomoy Island Foot meme? Out of the question, Your Honor."

Bucknell nodded vigorously in agreement. "What's the point?" he chipped in.

Fishley continued. "Listen, Your Honor, Attorney Bach, I haven't discussed it with Attorney Bucknell here, but as far as I'm concerned, we'll stipulate as to the facts surrounding the discovery of the body parts, provided the DA's office writes up the stipulation to our satisfaction. And no photos or graphic descriptions provided to the jury at any point in the trial. None whatsoever."

Before anyone could say anything else, Judge Brennan said, "I like that solution."

◊   ◊   ◊

The courtroom was packed and tense. The defendants and their lawyers sat at the front left table, DA Schnabel and First Assistant Bach sat on the right. Behind the prosecution team were the prosecution's witnesses, including Hennessey and Lipman. Then came the spectators.

Thinking about the national attention the trial had already received, Judge Brennan banned cameras and video equipment from the courtroom. The media was assigned ten balcony seats. They had to determine how to divide them up.

"The Cape Cod Times always gets one of the ten seats," Brennan said, watching out for the hometown member of the news. "Each and every day."

Slavin's wife attended. Neither of his daughters came in from out of town. Massahol's wife, his fourth, and an architect with a busy practice in Texas, took time off from work and arrived from San Antonio the day before the trial. The two wives sat together a few rows behind their defendant husbands, even though they didn't know each other.

Electricity filled the room when Ulrike and Anna Baten arrived, European aristocracy in the form of two beautiful young women. The determined, intense look on Ulrike and Anna's faces showed they expected justice for the taking of a family member, even a non-blood family member. Heads held high, emotions fully in check. Everyone knew what their presence meant.

"Makes things more difficult," Fishley muttered to Bucknell upon seeing them.

The first day Ulrike wore all black, and her sister Anna, a gorgeous paisley dress custom-tailored in London. Without flaunting it, the Baten sisters always dressed and comported themselves so as to reveal their standing in life. And they had a statement to make.

Yes, you've killed Ulrike's husband. An incomprehensible loss for her. But know this: your American lifestyle means nothing to us. You have no class, you have no style, you have no culture. You Americans know nothing about what it means to live. Nothing at all. Look at what you call food, and how you shovel it in at your office desks. Look at your political system. A functioning democracy? What a joke. The environment? You've ruined just about everything worth saving, especially here on magnificent Cape Cod. It'll all be gone soon—watch. American exceptionalism? Please... don't make us laugh.

Hennessey was awed at the arrival of the Baten sisters, and so grateful that Ulrike had come. To him, it was evidence of a personal characteristic that he valued highly, especially in the face of true adversity: undaunted courage.

CHAPTER 21

Friday, December 3, 2021

"This case," started DA Schnabel, "is about murder and greed. Plain and simple."

Fishley was on his feet instantly. "Your Honor, I object." He spread the word 'object' out quite a bit, emphasizing the second syllable and putting air into it to lengthen it. "What's greed got to do with it?"

Judge Brennan's short fuse immediately came into play. "Sustained. Let's not hear that word again, DA Schnabel."

Schnabel and Bach shared the prosecution's opening statement. Between the two of them it was well done. They lamented the untimely, tragic death of Jason Karp, discovered only fortuitously by the illegal landing of a great white shark by one of the Cape's commercial fishermen. They focused on the forensic evidence, so critically important, and urged the jury to listen carefully to what the State's forensic experts told them. They discussed the Big Lie—that's what Bach called it, the Big Lie. Judge Brennan overruled Fishley and Bucknell's objection to the term.

"You'll hear testimony that the defendants first said that Jason Karp got off the boat in Provincetown to dine and visit with a friend. Please, spare us. Then, when they were caught, the defendants made up something even more outrageous: Jason Karp killed himself. Please, spare us... again. Together, it's the Big Lie." Bach quickly revved up the prosecution's case.

DA Schnabel then stepped in. Although less experienced than Bach, she had a politician's ease and presence when talking to the jury. The jurors responded well to her.

"You may be thinking, why would these men murder a former colleague? What could be their reason for doing so?"

"To protect themselves," she went on. "That's why. To prevent Jason Karp from telling people about their arson attacks."

Fishley and Bucknell leapt up quickly. "Your Honor!" they exclaimed, almost in unison.

"I know, I know," said the Judge. "Please, Schnabel, please. None of that. No more, understood?" Judge Brennan stared hard at Schnabel and addressed her without the courtesy of calling her DA. His look said two things: You know better than that, and you're getting yourself in hot water with me.

"Jury, disregard what the District Attorney said. I want you to disregard it completely. The defendants are charged with murder here. There are no other crimes at stake, despite what you heard. Do not think about anything else."

First Assistant Bach finished up the prosecution's opening statement. He took the jury through the cast of characters on the prosecution's team, like the cast of a play or movie, explaining the role they would play. Bach presented it all with a cool, detached seriousness. A little understated, perhaps, but he'd prosecuted important criminal cases for years now and had an excellent read on how to go about it. The bizarreness of the discovery of Jason Karp's body warranted a cool, detached prosecutorial manner. Bach hoped the dressing down his boss got from Judge Brennan reinforced that.

It's an unusual case, thought Bach. *It needs a toned-down approach. Body parts everywhere; a great white shark as a*

*member of the cast? No thanks. I'm staying away from that...
completely. Focus, focus, focus. Three men out, two men
back. Serious antagonism, hatred even, between the two who
came back and the one who didn't. That's the crux of it.
That's the story.*

After the prosecution's opening, Judge Brennan took a
short break. Hennessey moved back a few rows. "May I sit
next to you?" he asked Ulrike Baten-Karp, sandwiching her
between himself and her sister Anna.

Strange things going on right here, thought Hennessey, as
he observed the Baten sisters up close.

Ulrike stared like a laser beam at the back of Slavin and
Massahol's heads, never once moving her gaze. Her sister
Anna pivoted her body a little and stared across the aisle at
Slavin and Massahol's wives. She never wavered in her stare
either, except to infrequently whisper something in French or
Swiss-German to her older sister. Massahol's wife initially
misinterpreted the gesture, giving a little smile and wave in
return. By the middle of the second day, it totally unnerved
her. After the lunch break, she moved to the balcony to get
away from Anna's relentless, withering gaze.

Swiss-style justice. I like it. Hennessey smiled almost
imperceptibly.

◊ ◊ ◊

Brian Bucknell opened for the defense. How sorry he was,
and knew they all were, about the untimely, tragic death of
Jason Karp. It wasn't at the hands of his client, Maestro Emre
Massahol, though.

"Maestro Massahol has spent well more than a decade
now, ladies and gentlemen of the jury, making the Cape a
richer, better, and more peaceful place," said Bucknell.

Bach responded quickly, like a snippy dog. "Your
Honor... Relevance? Where's the defense going with this
platitude? What's its purpose, and what on earth do
defendant's professional doings on the Cape—good, bad, or
indifferent—have to do with his deadly behavior?"

That statement, heard by the jury and made for their benefit, bent everyone out of shape. Fishley threw up his hands dramatically in a you've-got-to-be-kidding-me gesture; Bucknell, almost shouting, exclaimed, "Oh, c'mon now, Your Honor!"

"The objection is overruled," said Brennan, looking first at Bucknell and then glaring at Bach. He called the four lawyers up to the bench and took the proceedings off record. Judge Brennan resisted, with every bone in his body, the impulse to yell. Loudly. *It's way too early in the morning for this,* he thought. *I should've expected it, though, from these four pseudo-gladiators in front of me.*

"Gentlemen, DA Schnabel," Brennan hissed, "I can't believe what's going on here. These highly inappropriate comments being made in front of the jury, the objections raised, during opening statements! It's unbelievable! Almost unprecedented! What the hell is going on? What do you think you're doing?"

"Attorney Bach," continued Brennan, quickly and sternly, "I thought I made it abundantly clear that I'll have none of these inflammatory gratuities in my courtroom. Not from either side, understood? I won't hesitate to sanction any of you next time. Got it? Or I'll hold you in contempt—that'll impress the jury, huh? Think you're too big and important for me to do that? Try me. Now get on with it."

The four lawyers returned to their stations, wearing the faces of scolded schoolchildren.

After Bucknell summarized how every bit of evidence presented by the prosecution could and would be refuted, Dick Fishley finished the defense's opening statement. He had on a perfectly cut and tailored blue, double-breasted suit with wide pinstripes. Not navy blue, slightly lighter, and whose color changed subtly when he moved. His pocket square matched his lovely J. Press necktie. As always, Fishley dressed to impress, to show his stature in the profession.

"This has all been a terrible mistake," he said, building on the foundation Bucknell laid out for him. "Of course, everyone grieves for the loss of Jason Karp. Our deepest condolences to his widow." Fishley looked out and nodded to Ulrike Baten-Karp. She continued staring at the back of the two defendants.

"Sure," said Fishley, in his smoothest, most persuasive voice. "You'll hear the DA's office present what they say is irrefutable evidence. Your job is to ask yourself, is it really irrefutable?

"They found a drug in Mr. Karp's body, and traces of the same drug in a small vial on Mr. Slavin's boat. So what? And as to the small vial, how long was it on the boat: a day, a week, a month, a year, ten years? It could've been on the boat for years and years. So what?

"You'll hear that Mr. Slavin and Mr. Karp never saw eye-to-eye, and that Mr. Massahol and Mr. Karp never saw eye-to-eye either. So what? A lot of folks who work together, especially in the emotionally charged arts and culture world, don't see eye-to-eye. The whole purpose of the boat trip was to make amends and to make sure everyone let bygones be bygones. Could such a boat trip end up in murder? Of course not."

Fishley's last statement prompted a subdued "objection" from DA Schnabel.

"Sustained," said Judge Brennan. "Strike that from the record," he instructed the court reporter. He'd really had enough of the throwing gasoline on the fire.

"I'm sorry, Your Honor," said Fishley. After a reflective pause, he continued. "Members of the jury, let me address something that must be on your minds. It's this: Why didn't Mr. Slavin and Mr. Massahol report what happened, either while they were still out on the boat or upon returning to shore? And why make up a tall tale about Jason Karp getting off the boat in Provincetown?"

Hennessey focused like a hawk on what was being said.

This guy Fishley is good, really good. Schnabel and Bach should've hammered home the fact that Slavin and Massahol didn't report Karp missing, didn't report that he'd gone overboard. Bach's talk about the Big Lie didn't do it. It wasn't enough and wasn't directly on point. So now, Fishley gets to frame the issue. He's too good a lawyer to let the opportunity pass.

"So, my client and Mr. Massahol didn't report anything," continued Fishley. "Do you know, members of the jury, strange as it may seem, bizarre as it is, it is *not* a crime to not report a suicide. Let me put it another way. You don't report a suicide you're aware of? *Not* a crime." Fishley spoke with a flourish, emphasizing every 'not' as strongly as he could, and glancing at Judge Brennan to make sure he wasn't stepping out onto thin ice. Seeing no indication that he was, Fishley plowed ahead.

"Yes, my client George Slavin and his colleague and friend Erme Massahol failed to let anyone know. The boat radio was broken. A big deal, I know, we all know, especially when out on the Cape's unpredictable waters. So, they couldn't radio it in. Then, shell-shocked on their return, they get the tipsy, nosy Chatham harbormaster asking where their buddy is. So they make up a silly and innocent enough story about dropping him off in Provincetown.

"Morally wrong? Ethically wrong? I suppose so. But not, I repeat, *not*, a crime. There was no crime here. There was tragedy. Jason Karp killed himself, or went swimming off the boat while the others were making lunch and got attacked and killed by a great white shark. Those are the only two conclusions you'll be able to reach after hearing all the evidence. I thank you for listening to me."

Fishley finished on a high. Out in the audience, Ulrike, without changing her facial expression a bit, quietly took her sister's hand when Fishley started his suicide spiel. The second time Fishley mentioned Karp's suicide, she took Hennessey's hand too.

What an unbelievable grip, thought Hennessey. *This must be absolute torture for her.*

Hennessey recognized the profound injury and loss Ulrike

Baten-Karp faced, and watched her intently as she battled valiantly to overcome her interior darkness, her interior doubts, with whatever courage she could muster. Squeezing her hand right back, Hennessey knew that Ulrike shared that special place where bonds of grief exist. Ulrike was there, with Kelly and him, the three of them separated from all others in a space as great and vast as the Grand Canyon.

The prosecution's case was purely circumstantial. No eyewitnesses, no murder weapon, nothing—unless one considered the small, empty drug vial a murder weapon. And Fishley made clear the defense's position about the drug vial in his opening statement.

It could've been on the boat for years and years.

During their pre-trial strategy sessions, the two defense lawyers by and large agreed about everything. Bucknell, though, thought they should just let the DNA evidence in without challenging it.

"Dick," Bucknell said, "we're not going to claim that what washed up on the beaches, and what was found in the shark's stomach, weren't parts of Jason Karp. Let's stipulate to it and get it behind us."

"I agree we're not going to say it's not Jason Karp," said Fishley. "That'd be foolish. On the other hand, we have to sow doubt about everything, absolutely everything. If we can, if that jackass Brennan will let us, let's bring up the fact that DNA testing isn't the be all and end all everyone thinks it is. It'll help with what follows."

Fishley pulled from his briefcase a recent New York Times article titled, "You Think DNA Evidence is Foolproof? Try Again." He handed it to Bucknell. "Here, read this," he said. "Even DNA evidence can be gotten wrong."

So Bucknell brought up the issue of the fallibility of DNA evidence during his cross-examination of Bernie MacKenzie, the regional crime lab director. Bach objected quickly and forcefully. "What's the evidentiary foundation, Your Honor, for Attorney Bucknell's attack on the science of DNA? Bucknell shrugged and mumbled a response. It wouldn't be good lawyering to say he was relying on a New York Times article about it.

"Sustained," said Judge Brennan forcefully. He used his gavel, which he rarely did, to reinforce his ruling. That was that. There would be no questions about the legitimacy of DNA as evidence in Brennan's courtroom.

The drug vial provoked an interesting battle too. With MacKenzie still on the stand, Fishley got a little ahead of himself, asking a series of questions that hurt his cause, a highly unusual mistake for Fishley to make.

"It's your opinion, Mr. MacKenzie, that the vial found on the boat had traces of GHB in it, as well as traces of cocaine?"

"It's not an opinion. It's a fact."

"I see... I see. A fact. Does GHB have a shelf life?"

"Yes. A long one. But it can be shortened by exposure to the elements. Sun, water, moisture in the air."

"So, you can't tell whether the traces of GHB found in the vial had been there a long time—a day, a month, a year, ten years?"

"No, I can't."

"And can you tell us how long the vial had been on the boat—a day, a month, a year?"

"I can't answer that either. Why don't you ask your client?"

Simultaneous eruptions burst forth from Fishley and Bucknell, making it hard to hear either of them.

"Your Honor!" shouted Fishley. "Your Honor... strike that response."

Bucknell said, "I object, I object strenuously to that statement, Judge Brennan! Totally uncalled for, totally prejudicial! You must strike it from the record."

Judge Brennan sighed wearily. "Yes, it's stricken."

Then, he stared at the regional crime lab director

intensely, as if casting a spell on him.

"Mr. MacKenzie. I'm surprised. You've been an expert witness in my courtroom before, several times as I recall. You know what's going on, you know how to comport yourself... and you definitely know better than that." Judge Brennan sounded aggrieved. *What is it, something in the water these days?* Judge Brennan fretted. *I pray the jury isn't totally confused.*

On his best behavior, MacKenzie continued. "Our analysis came up with traces of two drugs, cocaine and GHB, in the vial found on the boat. I stand fully behind our test results, and the process through which we arrived at our results." Outlining in detail how the analysis was undertaken, MacKenzie didn't budge in his certainty as to the vial's former contents.

MacKenzie turned next to the Karp pathology report, to the finger, foot, and torso that had turned Hennessey and Lipman's world upside down.

"Yes, the blood tests we ran detected GHB in Mr. Karp. We ran them twice to make sure. No, the GHB in Mr. Karp's body can't be linked directly to the GHB traces found in the vial. There's no way we, or anyone, could do that," MacKenzie said. "GHB is GHB. There are no chemical variations of the drug. It's not like marijuana, with numerous different strains that can be individually identified. Traces of GHB were in Karp's body, traces of GHB were in the vial. That's what our crime lab work shows, and I stand behind it one hundred percent."

Done with the cross examination, Fishley dismissed Bernie MacKenzie from the witness stand. He was steaming mad though.

That schmuck, Fishley thought. *I should've cut off MacKenzie's cross-examination much earlier.*

Fishley and Bucknell's attempt to lacerate Harbormaster Willie's testimony, to turn it into farce, failed too, even though the harbormaster's appearance lent itself to their effort. He arrived in his overalls and gumboots. Apparently had not bathed either. Attendees sitting right on the main aisle in the courtroom noticed. Someone bring a herring sandwich with them for lunch? No, it was Harbormaster Willie striding by, heading to the witness stand.

"Sure, I had a beer or two by the time that afternoon rolled around," he retorted in response to Bucknell's question about his daily drinking habits. "What of it? I do that all the time. A man needs his refreshments, needs to keep hydrated too." All Bucknell could do was shrug and roll his eyes for the jury to see.

"Yes, I keep my annual logbook the same way, every year. Yep, they're accurate... I know it. Please, Attorney Bushmill... that was it, right? Your name?" Harbormaster Willie had his favorite Irish whiskey squarely on his mind. That didn't stop him though.

"Attorney Bushmill, show me any wrong entry in them books of mine, and I'll gladly fix 'em. I can vouch for them being right, though. I know it."

"No, I didn't know him, didn't recognize him," the Chatham harbormaster responded when asked if he knew who went out on the *Tranche-Two* with Slavin and Massahol. "I didn't know him either," he added, gesturing toward Massahol seated at the defendants' front table. "Until I got him to sign my copy of *Cape Cod Today*. I know what I heard and what they told me. That the guy hopped off the boat up in Provincetown."

Harbormaster Willie perked right up thinking about it. He grinned widely, showing the entire courtroom the full extent of his dental needs.

"I remember it crystal clear," he went on. "I told George and the Maestro over there that the guy had to be back by eleven p.m., when the parking lot closed. He wasn't. Not that night, or the next night... or the next."

There was nothing for Fishley and Bucknell in their cross-examination of Harbormaster Willie. Nothing at all.

◇   ◇   ◇

"Yes, I found his diary in the house. It was in the master bedroom on the bedside table. No, I didn't think twice about taking it," Hennessey said, somewhat surprised by Fishley's question. "We were investigating a missing person matter. It was the missing person's diary."

The defense team objected to the diary being admitted as evidence, and objected vehemently to entries from the diary being read to the jury by Hennessey or anyone else.

"Overruled," said Judge Brennan swiftly and firmly.

Well, thought Hennessey. *If the judge says I can read from it, I'll read from it.*

Hennessey, who'd participated in his fair share of criminal trials before, was a bit surprised at the ruling. With a strong and measured voice, he shared what Karp's diary revealed about the deep animosity between Karp, Slavin, and Massahol.

He also testified about the drug vial.

"Yes, once Detective Lipman and I discovered it on Slavin's boat, the *Tranche-Two,* we followed all the proper procedures for collecting and delivering it to the State's regional crime lab."

Hennessey was merely reinforcing what Lipman had testified to earlier about the discovery and handling of the drug vial. He went over in detail each and every step the two detectives took in getting the drug vial from Slavin's boat to the lab. "To my knowledge, and in my experience," Hennessey concluded, "the chain of custody was handled appropriately for this evidence."

Nailed that one, he thought proudly.

Hennessey reflected on the critical nature of chain-of-custody issues in criminal cases. If the police or prosecuting office cannot account for the location and handling of important evidence at all times, it calls into question the validity of the evidence. If something's wrong with the chain of custody, the evidence may be thrown out. Criminal cases collapse sometimes because of chain-of-custody issues.

Bucknell finished the cross-examination of Hennessey. "Mr. Hennessey, you've lived here on the Cape for twelve years now, right? And before that you were a detective with the Boston Police Department, right?"

"Yes. Correct on both counts."

"Tell us... why did you move to the Cape? Was it because you were thrown off the Boston Police Department for abusing informants, drinking on the job, and other serious behavioral problems?"

"Objection, Your Honor," said Bach. "Detective Hennessey's past has nothing to do with this case, or the limited matters he's testifying to."

"I'll allow it," said Judge Brennan, thinking it might shed light on Hennessey's penchant for truthfulness. "Answer the question, Detective Hennessey."

Hennessey expected it, expected to have some of the nasty, unpleasant aspects of his past dredged up. He insisted Kelly not come listen to his testimony. It also really upset him that Schnabel and Bach hadn't wanted to raise his checkered background on direct examination; they didn't want to spend valuable court time doing so.

They could've controlled and spun my story, Hennessey thought glumly.

"During my time with the Boston Police Department, I did some things I wasn't proud of. Not proud of at all. One included hurting a police informant. Badly. At the end of my time with the Department, I struggled with my drinking. Stress, divorce, my youngest brother being in jail, other family matters. It all added up to my drinking too much. Way too much, I'm sorry to say.

"I also did some serious damage to police property," he continued, "and to the property of other people as well. I'm ashamed of it, I am. And I'll have to live with it for the rest of my life. It's with me every day. Every single day."

Bucknell moved to enter as evidence photos of the damage Hennessey described, including a photo of the severely injured police informant Donnie Zimmer, the guy

Hennessey handcuffed to his cruiser and dragged, ultimately causing a leg amputation. It was the defense team's total scorched earth approach.

"I object, Your Honor," said Bach. "These photos put into the record... Why? They're completely irrelevant."

"I agree. Sustained," said Brennan, giving Bucknell a look that indicated he didn't want to hear a word about it. Impressed with Hennessey's candidness about his past foibles and struggles, and the way he looked at and spoke earnestly to the jury when discussing his past problems, Judge Brennan wrapped it up himself. "You're done, Detective Hennessey. Thank you."

Once Hennessey had returned to his seat out in the courtroom, Ulrike took his hand again and squeezed it. Hard.

◊ ◊ ◊

The entire courtroom was transfixed when Ulrike Baten-Karp headed to the witness stand. Her beauty and composure radiated like the sun. She walked with assurance and confidence in her two-inch, black Manolo Blahnik heels. She wore a pure silk, light grey, velvet Yves St. Laurent suit and a white silk blouse, with a modern Hermes scarf around her neck whose colors contrasted and complemented the rest of her outfit. Stunning. And all business.

"Ma'am," asked DA Schnabel, "will you please state your name and address for the record?"

"Certainly. I am Mrs. Ulrike Baten-Karp. I reside at 55 Chemin de Vallee, Bern-sur-Aare, Switzerland."

"And what was your relationship to the deceased?"

"He was my husband. We were married for twelve years—twelve wonderful years."

Fishley started getting up to object to Ulrike's characterization of the marriage, then changed his mind. The defense lawyers knew they needed to give her some leeway. They didn't want it to look as if they were picking on or needlessly badgering the widow. Judge Brennan was going to ensure that anyway.

"Did your husband commit suicide?" asked Schnabel, speaking forcefully and a bit more quickly than usual, so as to get the question out before the storm arrived.

"Your Honor," Fishley and Bucknell said simultaneously, echoing each other.

"A leading question," continued Bucknell, "and highly objectionable for other reasons as well."

Judge Brennan paused for a long moment. "I'll allow it. Overruled." He knew the risk in letting Ulrike Baten-Karp testify this way. The appellate court might well reverse him on it, but he was interested in getting to the bottom of what happened, what really happened, and knew she could help do so.

"Absolutely not," Ulrike answered emphatically. Sitting out in the audience next to Anna Baten, Hennessey let out a big, albeit quiet, breath.

Bravo, he thought. *She's on her way.*

"Mrs. Baten-Karp," DA Schnabel went on, thinking carefully now so as to avoid further interruptions from Fishley and Bucknell. "You've made the long trip across the Atlantic to participate in this trial. It's quite extraordinary, and all of us in this courtroom are grateful to you for it.

"Please, and take your time, please... Can you describe your husband's personality to us. Describe him to us as fully as you can. Who was Jason Karp?"

Shrewd lawyering, thought Hennessey. *Schnabel took the cue from Brennan after he overruled the defense on that last objection. Ulrike's got an open field ahead.*

Ulrike Baten-Karp spent the next twenty minutes telling the jury, judge, and courtroom audience what a privilege it had been to share life with Jason Karp. Sure, there were ups and downs—what relationship, what marriage didn't have them? Jason was always full of life, larger than life really, which meant he could be overbearing, even with his wife on occasion. They were happy together, though, really happy. She was happy. He was happy.

"His optimism was infectious, absolutely infectious,"

Ulrike told them. "One of his many American traits that I loved so much. His emotional maturity too, how I loved and admired it. He could talk about anything with me, anything, in an open, unreserved, let's figure it out way. It's not a trait many of us Swiss share."

"And what an idealist he was," she continued. "I adored that about him. Jason always thought about making things better, and what could be done, concretely, to make things better. He believed in our world, so so much. He believed in making it a better place, not just here in the U.S., everywhere."

"I loved him so, and miss him so," she said, finishing her portrayal. It was the only time during the twenty minutes she choked up, her voice cracking, her eyes glistening.

She used the word 'loved' a lot, thought Hennessey. *What a loss.*

Ulrike looked right at the jury when telling the tale of her late husband. No haughtiness or pride to her at all. She looked at and spoke to each and every juror. Despite the chasm between Cape Cod working-class jurors and European aristocracy, when she was done she'd brought them into her life, making them believe completely in the authenticity of her relationship with Jason Karp. She was easy-going and relatable and clear, resolutely clear, about who he was, about who she was, and about what they had been as husband and wife.

It took awhile for DA Schnabel to regain her composure following Ulrike's deeply moving testimony. She was a bit too emotional to get right back at it. After a long moment, Schnabel continued.

"Thank you. Thank you so much for sharing that beautiful and special portrait of your late husband with us, Mrs. Baten-Karp. Again, and based on your knowledge of him as his wife, was your husband suicidal?"

"Objection, Your Honor," said Fishley, jumping in quickly. "Despite her eloquence and insight about her late husband, how can Mrs. Baten-Karp possibly speak to his state of mind?"

"I'll allow it," said Brennan. "Overruled." Fishley shook his head in disbelief.

"Mrs. Baten-Karp, was your husband suicidal?"

"No, absolutely not," said Ulrike firmly. "During all our years together, and we knew each other two years before we got married, I never once heard him speak of suicide. Not once. I never knew him to be seriously depressed, despite life's ups and downs, despite the state of the world, despite the unbelievably difficult time he had at CAN. Suicide was not a word in his vocabulary. Not ever."

CHAPTER 22

Wednesday, December 8, 2021

The prosecution's case wrapped the day before. Ulrike Baten-Karp did most of the damage. Other witnesses, including Hennessey, caused some damage too. The vaunted legal defense team hadn't been able to cast much doubt on what happened out on the *Tranche-Two*, hadn't been able to make much of a dent at all, despite the purely circumstantial nature of the case. Slavin and Massahol were in deep trouble.

"Judge Brennan's really screwing us. I can't believe it," Fishley said to Bucknell. "He's allowed in evidence that should never, ever have come in. Baten-Karp's opinions about her husband? She shouldn't have even been allowed on the stand! Harbormaster Willie's crystal-clear recollection of the discussion when they got back to Chatham? There was no evidentiary foundation established for that at all!

"And then not allowing us to challenge any of it? He's so clearly biased. We've got two, three grounds for an appeal already." Equally frustrated, Bucknell agreed.

The trial made for long days and nights for the two defense lawyers. After each day in court, they first debriefed with their clients individually, going over the day's testimony and events, getting Massahol and Slavin's thoughts, insights, and factual corrections as to what transpired. Then Fishley and Bucknell met, sometimes late into the night, to plot out their joint legal strategy for the upcoming day.

They knew that if they lost the case, it would be an uphill battle getting the verdicts overturned. Even if they showed on appeal that, during the trial, Brennan acted more like a cheerleader for the prosecution than an impartial judge. Making matters worse, Massahol and Slavin weren't being represented by harried, overworked, underpaid public defenders, those lawyers whose efforts on rare occasion could only be described as marginal. No, they had two of the top criminal defense lawyers in Massachusetts slaving away for them, and were paying top dollar for the privilege. It all added up to intense pressure for Fishley and Bucknell.

"It takes a leap of faith to pull it all together," Bucknell ruminated. "In my view, they've pulled it off so far." He and Fishley were experienced and realistic enough to know it.

"Yeah," replied Fishley. "Hard to believe, but they have. Ulrike Baten-Karp crushed us. Who wouldn't believe someone with her force of personality and conviction? And the Big Lie our guys told… What a mistake that was! In his own way, that stinky, half-addled Chatham harbormaster was as convincing as Baten-Karp."

They sat and thought for a while.

"GHB in the vial and in Karp's body," Bucknell said, breaking the ice. "That's the key to it all. Maybe the vial's connected to what happened that afternoon, maybe it isn't. With the GHB in both places, it's easy to make the leap of faith Schnabel's asking the jury to make. And Brennan is certainly paving the way for it to happen."

"Let's put them on the stand," said Fishley suddenly, referring to Slavin and Massahol. Bucknell raised his eyebrows and cocked his head, caught off guard by the suggestion that their clients waive their Fifth Amendment rights and testify.

"I know it's risky," Fishley continued, "but they're persuasive, experienced, public speakers. They'll be witnesses for each other. I can't think of another way forward, can you? The jury needs to hear two more stories, one from your client Erme Massahol and one from my client George Slavin."

"Hmm. Such an unusual thing to do," responded Bucknell, pinching his chin with his left thumb and folded-in forefinger. "Let me chat with my client about it. They're still under Brennan's gag order too, so they can't talk to each other. That makes things difficult."

"Not really," responded Fishley. "They don't need to talk to each other. Just make sure your client has the story straight. They're in the hold together, prepping lunch, the trip a success so far, then they hear a big splash. By the time they're back up on deck, Karp is gone, nowhere to be seen. It's all been said before. Got it?"

◊ ◊ ◊

The performer in Massahol came out naturally on the witness stand. He was somber and ever-so-slightly humorous. He was anguished and eager, humble and clear in thinking and speech. He showed it all at the appropriate time, as if going through a music score's different movements, making his way through his testimony fast and slow, loud and soft, deliberate and impulsive.

"What a tragedy, Jason doing this, what a tragedy," he sighed, finishing up his direct testimony and looking out at Ulrike Baten-Karp when saying it. She continued her emotionless stare at the back of Slavin's head.

Listening carefully, Hennessey had his own thoughts about Double M's testimony.

What a phony. He reeks like Harbormaster Willie. With him, though, it's the stench of insincerity.

Bach led the cross-examination. DA Schnabel knew how important the cross-examinations of Massahol and Fishley would be. She put her substantial ego aside and let her more experienced first assistant handle the questioning of the two defendants.

"Mr. Massahol, explain to us why it took two of you to go down and get food ready. There were only three of you eating, after all."

Massahol looked to see if Bucknell would object to what he viewed as a frivolous and irrelevant question. Not seeing his lawyer kick into action, he came up with a response.

"Well... I thought I'd help George out with any prep that needed doing, that's all. I brought some of the food too. Hummus and pita bread, and Turkish pastries, delicious ones known as baklava... know them? I wanted to make sure things went quickly and smoothly."

"What does the hold of George Slavin's boat look like, Mr. Massahol?" Bach asked. "Where's the kitchen, where are the dishes and everything else kept?"

"Your Honor... Objection."

Bucknell had done nothing during the cross-examination of his client so far. As he and Fishley discussed previously, with Brennan firmly in the prosecution's camp, he didn't want to do anything to bend Judge Brennan further out of shape. So he stepped gingerly, but enough was enough.

"Where is the prosecution going with this? Where can it possibly lead?" Bucknell asked. He had also objected—an ancient strategy of the experienced trial lawyer—to give his client time to get his thoughts together.

"Overruled."

"Your Honor," whined Bucknell. "May I approach the bench so we can discuss it?"

"No. The objection is overruled. Sit down, Attorney Bucknell."

"I... I... I don't really remember what the hold looks like... its set up," stammered Massahol. "The kitchen galley was straight back... I think. Not sure about that though. George took charge of everything, I merely helped a little bit."

Massahol had no idea what the hold of Slavin's boat looked like. He'd never been down into it, not on the fateful trip with Karp, and not on his previous trips out on the

Tranche-Two with Slavin. His conductor's composure began to crumble.

"You don't remember the layout of the hold? You don't remember anything about it?" Bach scoffed sarcastically, abandoning the subdued, toned-down mannerism he'd sworn to himself to use throughout the trial. "Maybe, Mr. Massahol," he continued, with great drama, "maybe you never went down into the hold?"

"Your Honor!" exclaimed Bucknell. "Objection, please! He's badgering the witness, and he's putting words in the witness's mouth. This has to be stopped…"

"Overruled," said Judge Brennan. "Answer the question please, Mr. Massahol." Bucknell was stunned.

"No… I… of course I went down into the hold. It's only that all boat holds look the same. At least to me. Seen one, seen them all." Massahol responded with nervousness and defensiveness in his voice.

Bach went over to the prosecutor's table, picked up a folder, and then came back to where he'd been standing in front of Massahol. The folder contained photos of the hold and kitchen galley of Slavin's boat. Prior to the trial, the defense team's effort to exclude the photos as evidence failed. As a result, there were a dozen or so photos of the *Tranche-Two's* hold in the evidentiary record.

"Mr. Massahol, is this the hold and kitchen galley on the *Tranche-Two*?"

"I guess so. If you say it is. As I said, I can't remember. You tell me."

"Mr. Massahol, can you indicate to me and the jury which of these three cabinets held the plates? Which held the glasses? Where the utensils were located?"

"I… no, uh, no, I can't. George took charge of getting everything out, and I don't really remember anything about the kitchen galley or what was where." Massahol glanced pleadingly at Bucknell, a look that said I desperately need your help.

"Your Honor," said Bucknell, getting up again, and

somewhat tentatively for an experienced criminal defense lawyer. "Don't you think some serious badgering is going on here?"

Judge Brennan looked out at the back of the room, way beyond the back, as if he was searching for something in the distance. He daydreamed of being almost anywhere else but there, in his own courtroom, with his judicial robes on and in his judicial capacity.

"Yes," he said at last. "You're done with this, Attorney Bach. The objection is sustained. We're taking our lunch break now. Move on afterward, when we're back in session."

◊   ◊   ◊

During the break, Bucknell worked feverishly to bolster his client. "Listen, when you answer him, just say 'yes,' 'no,' 'I don't remember,' 'I couldn't say.' That's it. Keep your answers, your storytelling, to an absolute minimum. I know it's not in your nature to do so. But do it. You have to. I insist."

Bach's dance with Massahol continued. He zeroed in on the return to Chatham Harbor, circling tighter and tighter, like a great white shark on the scent of its prey.

"So, Mr. Massahol," Bach said, "let me get this straight. The two of you get back to the harbor, and when Harbormaster Willie asks you where your third party is, you tell him he got off in Provincetown, right?"

"Yes, George said that." Massahol regained the composure he'd lost earlier, when it was apparent to all in the courtroom that the wheels were falling off his car.

"Tell us," Bach continued, "why did you tell everyone that Jason Karp got off the boat in Provincetown? How can we believe anything you say, after you told the Big Lie?"

"Your Honor," pleaded Bucknell, on his feet again instantly. "Objection! Mr. Massahol is under oath. For Attorney Bach to suggest he is telling anything but the truth right now is unacceptable. I ask that you strike that from the record and direct the jury to disregard it. And it was George

Slavin who said it, and only to one person, not to everyone."

Bucknell was livid. What dirty pool the prosecution played. Bach's highly inflammatory suggestion was further grounds for an appeal: prosecutorial misconduct this time, not the trial judge's error. The damage was done. The jury heard everything Bach said, and understood what it implied. It floated around like poisonous gas seeping through the air.

"Sustained," said Judge Brennan. "Jury, you are to disregard completely that statement, as if it was never made and you never heard it." Staring silently at Bach for a good thirty seconds—an eternity in a court of law—he then called all four lawyers up to the bench again, out of hearing range of the jury, and off the record.

"This is the second time I've had to call the four of you up here. What the hell is going on? Any more malarkey, a polite word for it, any more malarkey from any of you and I'm going to end the whole thing. Understood? That means you, DA Schnabel and First Assistant Bach. That means you, Attorneys Fishley and Bucknell. None of you, not one of you, has taken my earlier 'got its' seriously. Where do you think you are?"

Judge Brennan was beyond furious. "I'll tell you where you are, you're in MY courtroom. I will NOT tolerate any more of it. I'll direct the verdict, one way or the other, if this keeps up. Don't think I will? Try me. Now get back out there and finish this mess up. You ignore what I say at your own peril. Understood? Got it? For the last time?" Breaking from the lawyers huddle, Bach smiled in a calm, friendly way at the jury as he headed back to his spot in front of Massahol.

I'll be damned if I let them see that the Judge reamed me out, Bach thought. *Time to get back to my initial trial strategy persona, though. The low-key, affable Scott Bach.*

"So, Mr. Massahol, you told the Chatham harbormaster that Jason Karp got off the boat in Provincetown, yes or no?" His changed tone of voice indicated that a new and gentler First Assistant Bach was now in the courtroom.

"Yes. That's what George told him."

"Did he get off the boat in Provincetown?"

Massahol looked down slightly and shook his head no. Judge Brennan stepped in: "Mr. Massahol, please give a verbal answer for the record."

"No. He did not."

◊   ◊   ◊

Although George Slavin appeared confident and relaxed when he stepped up into the witness stand, he was anything but. He'd been a defendant in a serious criminal trial before, and with Dick Fishley as his lawyer. In the previous trial, the Ponzi scheme case where he got off, Fishley grew more and more confident as the trial progressed, and communicated as much to Slavin. This one was proceeding differently. There were no such signs of confidence coming from Fishley.

It caught Slavin off guard and alarmed him when Fishley changed course and said it was probably in his best interest to take the stand. Both Judge Brennan and Fishley previously told him he didn't need to, that it was his constitutional right not to testify. Fishley told Slavin that Massahol was testifying too and that they wouldn't be allowed to hear each other's testimony.

"Stick to the same story, always. Like putting that Mercedes Benz of yours on cruise control." Fishley reviewed with Slavin the questions he'd ask him on direct, explained why he planned to ask them, and helped Slavin get ready for the onslaught: Bach's cross-examination.

"Although you didn't see your buddy testify, you've got to learn from Massahol's mistakes. Bach really got under Massahol's skin. Don't let him get under yours. Don't let him box you in. And whatever you do, don't seem confused or frightened. It makes you look guilty. If you need time to think about something, I'll know and try to get it for you, or you can always say, 'can you please repeat the question?' Ask twice if you need to."

"When I'm questioning you on direct," Fishley continued, "give me big, long-winded answers. When Bach has you on cross-examination, give the shortest answers possible. Always. And look over at the jury in a friendly way. Don't stare at them when telling your story. That seems contrived. Look around—at them, at me, the judge, the courtroom audience. Make sure you give the jury plenty of attention, though, and be earnest about it. "

Although it wasn't new to him, getting on the witness stand was an out-of-body experience for Slavin. He seemed split in two, one half of him watching the other half stand up at the defense table, straighten his tie and button his suit coat at the middle, and march to the witness stand.

Who is that person? Slavin wondered. *What is he doing here? Where is he going? Why is he going up there? How uncomfortable. How surreal. Like a bad drug experience. Yes, it's like a bad drug experience.*

Fishley spent a good deal of time exploring with Slavin the so-called animosity between him and Jason Karp.

"Hmm. I wouldn't call it animosity," said Slavin, taking some time to answer. He wanted it to seem as if he'd spontaneously come up with the response, even though he'd been through it beforehand with Fishley. "I'd characterize our relationship as competitive. Jason and I were very friendly but quite competitive."

"About what?"

"Well, really about everything having to do with CAN. We had a pretty clear course set for CAN before his arrival. Particularly in regard to finishing our new performing arts center, the Seaside Heights Living Arts Center, and where it should be located.

"Jason didn't accept anything about the SHLAC work we'd done. It was almost as if, because he hadn't done the planning, or come up with the ideas, or overseen the progress made so far, none of it was any good. That was the type of competitiveness we had."

Slavin went through everything from his vantage point, including the woeful tale of Jason Karp killing himself. He was feeling good, really good, when Fishley turned to Judge

Brennan and said, "That's it for my direct, Your Honor."

On cross-examination, First Assistant Bach returned to Slavin's relationship with Karp.

"Mr. Slavin, let's return to your friendly but competitive relationship with Jason Karp. You said before that Jason didn't think any of your work on SHLAC was any good. 'None of it was any good,' you said. Your words, Mr. Slavin, not mine. Sure sounds antagonistic, hostile even, not a friendly but competitive relationship."

"Objection, Your Honor," said Fishley, trying to protect Slavin's earlier testimony from Bach's attack. "Attorney Bach is mischaracterizing what Mr. Slavin said in an unacceptable way."

"Overruled."

In a suave, understated manner, Bach pulled the Slavin story apart, as if holding the end of an intricately tied string knot and pulling ever so slowly to ensure it unraveled properly.

"Mr. Slavin, let me now go back to an excerpt from Jason Karp's diary, something that Detective Hennessey read earlier."

Reading from the notes in his hands, Bach went on. "This is from July 10th. 'The money spent on the SHLAC project so far: WTF! '"

A couple members of the jury guffawed.

"Here's more. 'Nothing to show for it. WTFx2! Their favored golf course location: couldn't be worse. WTFx3! The guys have no idea what they're doing. GS putting the new performing arts center project right in the toilet,'" Bach stopped reading.

"GS—that's you, right, Mr. Slavin?" Bach asked. "Seems like a funny sort of friendly competitiveness to me. Wouldn't you agree?"

"And tell me," Bach continued, "how is the fundraising for the SHLAC project going? You're responsible for it, right?"

"Objection, Your Honor," said Fishley. "Relevancy?"

"I'll allow it. Answer the questions, Mr. Slavin. There were two of them."

Slavin felt a weariness setting in. It was exhausting taking a constant pounding from Bach while remaining outwardly calm and collected, and while his inner self worked feverishly to put together answers that didn't seem contrived or inauthentic.

"Yes, I'm responsible for the SHLAC fundraising. And as to your first question, the fundraising is going a bit slowly."

"Slowly, Mr. Slavin?" Bach asked. "That's an understatement, isn't it? I understand you haven't raised anything for the SHLAC project yet. The golf course property alone will cost SHLAC three and a half million dollars. How much of it have you raised so far?"

As he'd been advised, Slavin gave a short answer: "None."

◊   ◊   ◊

At the next break, Fishley went over Slavin like a trainer working on his prize boxer late in the match, and with the decision, ironically enough called a verdict in boxing too, still up in the air.

"Remember my instructions. Don't stray," Fishley whispered to him as they re-entered the courtroom.

Bach returned to Karp's diary. "Mr. Slavin, I'd like to go over another of Jason Karp's diary entries with you, something else that Detective Hennessey read earlier."

Fishley started to get up. There was no need for him to do so. Judge Brennan beat him to the punch: "First Assistant Bach, it better be new, it better be relevant, and it better not be inflammatory."

"It's all of those, Your Honor. May I proceed?" The judge nodded his assent.

"On August 4th, just a few days before his death, Jason Karp writes in his diary 'What an invite!?!' He follows the three words with an exclamation point, a question mark, and then another exclamation point."

Bach was making the point for the jury, not Slavin, and appreciated Judge Brennan allowing him to do so.

"Then Karp writes 'Why not!!' and follows those two words with two more exclamation points."

Fishley was up in a flash. "Your Honor, this isn't relevant. I object. These entries from Jason Karp's diary... so what?"

"Overruled. Go on, Bach."

"Mr. Slavin, Jason Karp was clearly surprised by your invitation to go out on a farewell boating trip. Five words, four exclamation points, one question mark. Not really the response you'd expect from a friend, even a competitive friend, don't you agree—yes or no?"

Slavin's response was a long time coming: "I... I don't know. I guess so, yes." Flustered and desperate to avoid Bach inflicting any more damage to him, Slavin quickly and impulsively went on: "Here's the truth. I was in the hold getting lunch ready... by myself. I heard a heated discussion going on above me, Emre and Jason, followed by what sounded like a fight—punches and kicks being thrown. I heard a big splash and thought I'd better go check to see what was going on. When I got up on deck, I saw Emre at the stern, looking overboard, leaning over. There was no sign of Jason anywhere."

Stunned silence. Suddenly it was as if an improvised explosive device went off in the courtroom. Bedlam everywhere. Disorder reigned supreme.

Bucknell looked at Fishley, shocked and horrified, the look Julius Caesar gave Brutus upon the latter's betrayal and treachery.

He was on his feet instantly, his face dark with anger: "Your Honor, Your Honor, this is an outrage. An absolute outrage. I demand that you declare a mistrial. You MUST declare a mistrial immediately."

Fishley sat there, stone-faced and looking straight ahead.

First Assistant Bach, standing over where he'd been questioning Slavin, was too surprised to react in a meaningful way. *What? What was that? How can this be?*

DA Schnabel, sitting at the prosecutor's table, put her head in her hands. *I can't believe it,* she thought. *WTF. All that work for nothing.*

Massahol, caught completely off guard, at first said nothing. Then he erupted: "No... NO! It was him. HE did it. Not me. HE did it. It was all his idea." The jury, not knowing where to turn or who to listen to, ducked and weaved and bobbed, gabbing among themselves like chickens waiting for their daily feed, confused and wondering what just happened and what it all meant to the exercising of their civic duties.

Ulrike Baten-Karp had the last word. She leapt up roaring: "MURDERER. MURDERERS! You MURDERED my husband! You American Pigs!"

CHAPTER 23

Friday, December 10, 2021

Judge Brennan asked the Massachusetts Board of Bar Overseers to disbar Dick Fishley. After writing to the state entity that disciplines wayward lawyers, he sat at his desk fuming. The pencil twirling between his fingers snapped in two, stinging a bit but not breaking any skin. Brennan was beside himself.

I'll make sure Fishley pays for what he did, that unethical bastard. What a mess. What a black eye. One of the Commonwealth's highest profile murder cases in years, in my courtroom, and right down the drain. A terrible blot on my record.

Brennan knew how bad declaring a mistrial in Massahol and Slavin's joint murder trial looked. He had no choice, though, with one of the two co-defendants unexpectedly turning on the other. Brennan realized it probably destroyed any chance he had to be appointed to a higher court, to the Massachusetts Appellate Court or even the Supreme Judicial Court.

The bad news for Judge Brennan was that, without any concrete proof that Dick Fishley helped Slavin fabricate testimony, there weren't grounds for disbarring Fishley.

There weren't even grounds for sanctioning him, a lighter disciplinary action. There was no way the Board of Bar Overseers could force Fishley to disclose his conversations with Slavin. The attorney-client privilege made them sacrosanct. Slavin could waive the privilege; his attorney could not. So, unless Slavin suddenly found God and came clean about what he and Fishley discussed, no one would ever know if the two of them concocted the stunning testimony that abruptly ended the trial. Unless some sort of miracle happened, it would stay between them, and only them, until their last breaths.

Ensconced in his corner office on the forty-sixth floor of One International Place in downtown Boston, Dick Fishley mulled things over, tapping a finger slowly on his expensive teak desk while gazing out the window at Boston Harbor.

Who knows which story is true? Maybe my client told the truth. I don't know. I don't know, and I don't want to know.

Judge Brennan revoked Massahol and Slavin's bail upon declaring a mistrial, resulting in the two of them spending a couple of nights in the slammer. Brennan had reason to do so. There was no chance that Jason Karp committed suicide. His widow forcefully and movingly cast huge doubt on the notion, and then, when Slavin accused Massahol of the murder, the whole suicide defense was completely undermined. With the 'he jumped overboard while we were in the hold' story out the window, Brennan had at least one murderer, and maybe two, on his hands. He ordered them both held without bail.

The bail decision was quickly reversed on appeal. Wealthy, established white guys with no prior criminal convictions denied bail, even on murder charges? Please. Bail was increased from $250,000 to $750,000, the ankle monitors stayed on, and their passports remained in the vault of the Barnstable County District Attorney. One new restriction was imposed: no boating at all. An escape at sea was the last thing anyone needed. This time, Slavin was the one who blanched; Massahol accepted it nonchalantly.

Back at the BCPD office, the day after everything blew up and the mistrial was declared, Hennessey talked things through with Lipman.

"What a mess," he said to Lipman. "It's beyond sordid. Massahol and Slavin, or one of them, killed Jason Karp. It's all out there in the public eye, for everyone to read about and talk about and analyze. Everyone knows it. But proving it beyond a reasonable doubt? Schnabel and Bach really have their work cut out for them."

The next day, DA Schnabel announced she would prosecute Massahol and Slavin separately for murder, and as quickly as possible. Like Judge Brennan, who would preside over the two new trials, Schnabel's ship needed righting. Talk slithered and snaked about within the Massachusetts Bar: she blew it in a big way. Every lawyer in Massachusetts followed the case, even trust and estate lawyers, those prim and polar opposites of their legal brethren duking it out daily in the armpit world of criminal law. Schnabel should have seen it coming a mile away, her critics carped. Many of her friends and supporters thought so too.

"Easy for Monday morning quarterbacks to second-guess her," Hennessey told Lipman at the office. They thought she'd made the right decision prosecuting Massahol and Slavin together.

"Of course she handled it right," said Lipman, "and remember, the decision wasn't hers, it was Brennan's."

With Massahol and Slavin now pointing the finger at each other, neither detective saw a successful prosecution ahead.

"The facts are too screwed up, the defense lawyers too good, for Schnabel and Bach to pull it off," said Hennessey. "It's waaaaaaay beyond sordid."

Lipman thought so too.

It rained in the night. One of the Cape's soft and frequent rains giving life to the region's rich flora along with the constant, all-encompassing moisture that came from being surrounded on all sides by the mighty Atlantic Ocean.

The curtains kept lifting into the room. It was a balmy evening. Hennessey could hear the patter of the rain on the roof and on the back patio, each making a different noise at a different timbre. After their slow and gentle lovemaking, he held Kelly against him, warm and pale and naked. She now spent the night sometimes. They fell asleep like that, content in their new element.

Hennessey bolted upright in the middle of the night: 3:10 a.m.

"Jesus, how stupid can I be?" he exclaimed.

Kelly, sleeping on her stomach with her petite, outstretched hand resting lightly on his chest, was startled. "Hnn... what's going on?"

"The flush, the flush! How stupid can I be? I get it, I get it now. Karp's diary. He was referring to when Slavin lied. Or was caught making something up. His face turns red. He flushes.

"Did you notice it when he testified at the trial? I did. He got red in the face when he made certain statements. Especially at the end... his testimony that caused the mistrial, when he said he was in the hold of the *Tranche-Two* when Massahol killed Karp.

"Every time I asked about the arson attacks, he flushed when he answered. He always said, 'what are you talking about?' or 'I'm clueless,' or 'Hennessey, you might as well be speaking a foreign language.' But he turned red every time he answered, sometimes slightly, sometimes strongly. He lied about it, lied about not knowing Pat Kimmell too. I'm sure of it. Holy shit. Slavin was in on everything. He wanted the insurance money for his own purposes all along. All along. He's behind the arson attacks, probably hired Kimmell himself. It all makes perfect sense."

Hennessey was wide-awake now.

"Hey, Mr. Perfect Sense, think about it more when the sun's up," replied Kelly sleepily. "Come back to bed." She wasn't thinking about the veracity of Slavin's statements, or his red face. She'd woken up from a wonderful, erotic dream about Longnook Beach, and was now thinking about their next trip there.

"In a little," Hennessey said. "I want to think things through a bit more. I'm going downstairs to jot down some notes. I'll come back to bed shortly." Bending over, he gave her a kiss on the forehead, then on the lips.

Ah, those lips.

◊ ◊ ◊

Hennessey got at it early the next morning despite missing a few hours of sleep. Slavin's involvement with the arson attacks weighed heavily on his mind. He made his way to CAN's administrative office in Yarmouth, planning to start there in his new investigations. His mind raced on the drive over.

Of course Slavin was behind the arson attacks. Had to be. And he knows or is connected to Pat Kimmell too. Has to be.

Upon arriving, he noticed the faint scent of perfume or powder in Karp's old office. The presence of a woman. Tiffany Tisdale. Hennessey forgot little, especially with his days of wandering about in an alcoholic stupor behind him. He remembered Tiffany. Super-long legs, lovely face, prominent cheekbones, big eyes, nice smile, intelligent look, extremely articulate. He appreciated it all.

They talked about the music schools. "How's it going for you, Tiffany, holding your music classes in different buildings and locations, all over Cape Cod?"

"Actually, it's not been as big of a nightmare as I thought it would be. The Cape's churches came through for us in a big way. A number of them have let us use their space, and they all have a piano or two, some music stands too. Nothing was salvageable from our Falmouth or Barnstable campuses," she said, sadly. "So much lost, and although our lessons and classes are going again, who knows what the future holds."

"Any idea, any thoughts at all, Tiffany, as to who might

want to burn down the music school buildings?"

"No. None at all,"

"Has it been a big task, getting in touch with current and prospective students?" he asked. "You were beginning to contact them all the last time we spoke."

"No, it's been easy," she replied. "Our current students are part of the CAN family. We know them all and we're constantly in touch with them, even without a disaster on our hands. And prospective students and parents only visit on Saturdays. We don't have the staff to have a more extensive visitation program. It's too bad, really, because visitor programs are known to work at boosting arts and music class enrollment. Get them in to see the place and they're hooked."

"Can I take a look at the sign-up sheets for your visitors and prospective students?" Hennessey asked.

Tiffany looked at him quizzically. "Sure... Why not? You're lucky. Before this year, the visitor records were kept on campus at the two buildings. They'd be dust and ashes now. Jason centralized all of the outreach work in Yarmouth this past year. I brought the weekend visitor lists here every Monday when I came to the weekly all-staff meeting."

Hennessey thumbed through the Barnstable music school visitor list. He started four months out, a date he picked randomly, and moved forward through the weeks toward the date of the first fires. It all seemed entirely mundane to him, until an entry stopped him dead in his tracks. Someone named Kim Forbes visited the Barnstable music school a month before the fire and listed two addresses on the log-in sheet: a principal address at 220 Brookline Avenue, Apartment 416, Boston, MA, and a secondary address at 57 Algonquin Path, Brewster, MA.

Hennessey's eldest daughter, Nancy, lived at 220 Brookline Avenue in Boston. She was in Apartment 415, right next door to Apartment 416.

57 Algonquin Path in Brewster? It was Hennessey's home address.

Hennessey felt as if he'd been punched hard in the stomach. Instantly, a knot developed, tight and painful, and an emotional flooding swept through Hennessey. He experienced it in the past, when something of terrible personal consequence happened. He spent years working to vanquish it. After a few deep breaths, Hennessey got it under control.

Picking up the CAN office phone, he tried the telephone number left by Kim Forbes. Tiffany started to object, but the look Hennessey gave her told her to butt out. Disconnected.

He called his daughter Nancy next. Luckily, thank God, she picked up.

"Dad, how good to hear from you! It's been way too long. So great to hear your voice. Yeah, I know... I know. I'm not in touch much, but neither are you. I'm fine, how about you? Work's going well. Super excited about my new role in the company. Yes, yes, I'll explain it all to you when I see you next. What's that? Do I know my neighbor in Apartment 416? Sort of a funny question, Dad, don't you think? Okay... Okay Dad!

"Of course I know my neighbor. Neighbors, you mean. A couple of recent Boston College grads. Smart, handsome guys. Real cuties. Already attached though, to their college sweethearts. Too bad for me.

"Am I sure? Dad, what's going on? Of course I'm sure. I'm always careful. Please, Dad, do me a favor. Stop asking that. I'm not twelve years old anymore. Yes I'll come visit soon, I promise. Or you come up here. I'll take you to dinner! Love you too."

Hennessey's terror receded into anger, and then transformed into a steely, analytical calmness.

"Tiffany, the visitor sign-in sheet from Barnstable, this one from one month before the fire, do you remember anything about this Kim Forbes who visited, what they looked like?"

Taken aback by Hennessey's new sternness, Tiffany tried her best to remember who it might have been. She looked carefully at the sign-in sheet and took a long moment before responding.

"Gee, I'm sorry, Detective Hennessey. For the life of me, I can't remember which of the nine people who signed in that day it was. Sometimes parents come with their kids, sometimes not. The kids don't have to sign in. There was someone who came in not long ago, I don't know if it's the Saturday you're looking at, who signed the visitor log-in sheet but kept their sunglasses and a hoodie on the entire time. Said nothing. I couldn't even tell whether it was a man or a woman.

"That's not unusual for us. We get all sorts of artsy people coming in to check us out. The attire, the hair color, the body piercings, the tattoos... To me, some of it's too much. Gothic is back, did you know that? The next Mozart, the next Schoenberg, the next Heifetz—you name it, we get them, with their instruments and purple hair. These days, they're all into that heavy metal cello group, Apocalyptica."

"I really wish I could help" said Tiffany, again making a mental note that for a semi-retired guy, Hennessey, frankly, was a hottie. "I have no idea who that Kim Forbes was though. There's nothing else I can tell you."

Hennessey knew. Of course he knew. It was Pat Kimmell. Thinking back on his frustrating, futile efforts of the past, Hennessey vowed that nothing would stop him now.

I'll get you this time, you motherfucker.

CHAPTER 24

Monday, January 10, 2022

DA Schnabel looked at both Slavin and Fishley across the table. First Assistant Scott Bach took up the fourth seat.

Lipman and Hennessey had begged to be included in the discussions. After all, the two detectives knew more about the underpinnings of the alleged murder, and about the personalities involved, than Schnabel and Bach. No dice. Schnabel, who never thought highly of any rank or category of police, insisted that only defendants and their lawyers participate. No Lipman. No Hennessey.

"That was some story you told on the witness stand," Schnabel said to Slavin. "A whopper of a tale. My sense of it? You're going to jail for a long time. You're looking at fifteen to twenty years minimum. And with what we've got on you, my bet is we put you away for life. Without parole.

"Just because you were the one to break down and give up on the Big Lie, and rat out your accomplice, doesn't mean jack. We've got you right where we want you. Your boat, your booze, your drug vial, your idea. Let's kill Jason Karp."

Speaking coolly and crisply, Schnabel had a detached air to her. Underneath, she seethed like a volcano. Her reputation took a huge hit as a result of the mistrial caused by Slavin's shenanigans, like a beautiful new Tesla being t-boned at an intersection by a beat-up Ford F-150. Her road to redemption involved nailing one or both defendants quickly and mercilessly.

"What my client said on the witness stand was the absolute truth," said Fishley, stepping in. "I won't stand for you intimating otherwise, or for your bullying. And George is prepared to elaborate on it if an understanding is in the works."

"What sort of understanding?" said Schnabel.

Bach leaned in instantly. "No deal until we hear what he has to say," he interrupted. "Then we'll decide." He looked at Schnabel in a way that reminded her that while she was the boss, he was the much more experienced prosecutor. Schnabel was thankful to have Bach with her on this one.

"I need to talk to my client for a few minutes," Fishley said to the two of them. "I'll call you if and when we're ready to continue with the conversation."

◊　◊　◊

Downing his third cup of coffee that morning, Dick Fishley thought long and hard about the hand he and his client George Slavin had been dealt.

Going to trial again will be a disaster. There's no way George will get a fair trial in Brennan's courtroom, not a snowball's chance in hell. That jackass Brennan tried to get me disbarred! How funny.

Fishley also knew the grounds didn't exist to ask that another judge preside over the trial… to have Brennan recuse himself. In a rational world that's exactly what would happen. After the debacle in Brennan's courtroom, it should automatically be assigned to another judge. That wasn't happening though, and even making the request would piss Brennan off more than he already was.

Slavin paced up and down in the DA's conference room— back and forth, back and forth. "I wonder if there are secret recording devices or cameras in here," he asked Fishley, looking around carefully as he started to lap the conference room table.

"Stop that pacing, will you?" Fishley barked. "Sit down. Let's talk."

"I know you don't think it," Fishley continued, "but we've got the upper hand. I say that based on my experience. Look at me, George, look at me. I've got the gray hair of experience. And that bomb you threw in the first trial. Magnificent." Fishley chuckled at his own dry wit.

Looking down at the table, Slavin was about to share something. He had no more than opened his mouth, though, when Fishley jumped on him.

"No, no… I don't want to hear it!" Fishley said, tough and urgent in his message and startling Slavin. "I don't want to hear anything about it. Not now, not ever."

Knowing that his client lied on the stand would put Fishley in an ethical quagmire, one that even he, a lawyer with wafer-thin professional ethics, would be hard pressed to ignore. He'd have to report it to the judge and prosecution. That, or he'd have to step away from representing Slavin. In order to prevent either unwanted scenario from arising, he simply wouldn't ever discuss with Slavin the testimony that abruptly ended the first trial. Fishley knew, though. Of course he knew.

"You've got your story, George. Keep to it at all costs, and for God's sake, don't stray from it. If and when the time comes to share it with others, make sure you tell it with as much detail as possible. Be convincing and earnest," he said.

"There's no turning back now," continued Fishley harshly, responding to the stricken look on Slavin's face. "Absolutely no turning back. You will be crucified if you even think about it. Crucified. Didn't you hear Schnabel? She's throwing the book at you. She's after you big time. You're looking at a looooong prison sentence, maybe the rest of your life, unless your story wins out. Got it?

"You know what it's like in MCI-Walpole? Go ask that stiff, Detective Hennessey, the one who testified against you.

Hennessey's younger brother, Joey, was in there. Broke out, and now he's the subject of an international manhunt. Hennessey visited his brother, I'm sure. He'll tell you what it's like in there. There's one small rectangular window in each cell, the size of cellar windows in old houses. It's eight feet off the ground. Direct sunlight? Not a chance. Indirect light a few hours a day, a dull grey light. Is that what you want? For the rest of your life?

"The blessing, and a true one, is that your buddy Massahol dug himself a deep, deep hole with his testimony. Even the nitwits on the jury could tell he was never in the hold of your boat. And Schnabel, Bach, Judge Brennan—they knew for sure he was lying. He couldn't possibly have weakened himself more. Your story, that bomb you threw, fit in perfectly."

Slavin looked at Fishley with hope, optimism surging through him.

This is why I hire this guy! Yes!!

"What's next, then?" Slavin asked.

"Cut a deal with Schnabel and Bach." When Slavin started to object, Fishley spoke right over him. "No, no, no, no, no. You listen to me. Plead to a charge that doesn't require jail time. I should be able to work that out for you. You'll have to be a witness against Massahol too. That's no problem. You already played that role.

"And know your story. Know your story inside and out. It's the only possible way forward. Look at what your options are."

◊   ◊   ◊

His instinct for self-preservation kicking into high gear, Slavin spilled his guts out when Schnabel and Bach returned to the room.

"I was in the hold, so help me God, when whatever happened, happened. I heard heated words, scuffling, and a big splash, so I scrambled up on deck. There was Massahol, looking overboard. When he turned around and saw me, the first look on his face was like the cat that caught the canary. Then he looked anguished, utterly anguished." Slavin elaborated in detail on his story. Brilliantly. Convincingly.

"On the way back, Massahol pleaded for help and understanding. So we came up with the tall tale that Karp got off in Provincetown, and as a backup, the tall tale that he killed himself."

Schnabel and Bach took in the entire tale. Soaked it up without interruption. When Slavin finished, Schnabel took off her glasses, put them on the table in front of her, and asked with a sigh, "Now, why, George? Why would Emre Massahol murder Jason Karp, huh? Why would he ever do such a thing? And why would you ever make up such a story? Another big lie of yours?"

Slavin locked his fingers behind his head, holding on gently, his bent arms stretched out on either side like large elephantine ears.

"I'm not making up anything. You mean you don't know about the hatred and utter contempt that Erme Massahol and Jason Karp had for each other?

"I thought everyone knew. Massahol hated Karp, from the second Karp arrived at CAN. Massahol had been at the organization for more than a decade. He thought he ruled the roost—no questions asked. Not only did he hate Karp for taking over responsibilities that should have rested with CAN's executive director in the first place, not its music director, Massahol was also absolutely beside himself that the orchestra's budget was being cut so that more money could be spent on the music schools and theater. Massahol said he'd rather die than see that happen. The board went along with it though. Frankly, I was surprised it did."

Slavin took a deep breath; he was in full stride. "Did you know that Massahol also fought tooth and nail with Karp's predecessor, Conrad Redlich? Massahol was responsible for Redlich getting fired too—both of them, Karp and Redlich. You didn't know any of this? Don't take my word for it. Go ask others. Ask Redlich how much he and Massahol hated each other. Ask Greg Hemshaw, the board chair. Ask Denise Douward, the board vice chair. I guarantee they'll all tell you the same thing. Guarantee it"

Fishley said nothing during this part of the interview, except for a few "uh-huhs," "hmms," and other non-verbal signs of acknowledgement and agreement. As he sat there, a deep satisfaction took hold within him.

That-a-boy, that's my boy, thought Fishley. *You tell that story of yours. You tell it.*

◇ ◇ ◇

Schnabel and Bach perked up upon hearing about the intense rift, the hatred, between CAN's dead executive director and CAN's living music director. They had Slavin go through it all again, listening intently for any discrepancies, any inconsistencies in what he told them. There were none.

During the next break, Bach dug around in his office for notes he'd gotten from Hennessey. He remembered something important in them, information Hennessey had received that shed light on what Slavin told them.

"Eureka!" he exclaimed, rushing into Schnabel's office next door. "Listen to this. Its from Hennessey's interviews with Greg Hemshaw, the CAN board chair, and with Denise Douward, the vice chair. Hennessey interviewed each of them before the first trial, back when everyone thought a great white shark killed Karp.

"'Karp and Massahol couldn't stand each other.' That's what Greg Hemshaw told Hennessey during his interview. Denise Douward, the board vice chair, told Hennessey, 'Karp got in the way of our rock star, Double M. They were like water and oil together.'"

Bach finished reading the notes. "So Slavin's telling it like it is," said Schnabel. The look between them said it all, as did the spontaneous, affirmative nods to each other. The path ahead was clear.

Returning to the interrogation room, Schnabel told Fishley

she'd call within twenty-four hours with whatever plea deal she'd be prepared to offer. The two prosecutors then accompanied Fishley and Slavin to the front door, seeing them out.

"Hey," Bach threw out as they walked back to their offices. "Did you see how red in the face Slavin got when telling us what happened?"

"Yeah, I did," responded Schnabel. "Hot in that conference room, wasn't it?"

◊   ◊   ◊

Slavin pled guilty to aiding and abetting in the disposal of a body, a misdemeanor with no jail time associated with it. He also agreed to testify as a witness—the star prosecution witness—at the upcoming murder trial of Emre Massahol. Dick Fishley's role in the debacle was by and large over. He'd only have to attend the day his client testified. Nevertheless, sitting in his plush downtown Boston office, Fishley fretted about it.

God, I pray he doesn't get hammered, thought Fishley. *Or worse, get off his story. That'd be the end of George Slavin.*

Fishley felt no remorse, no pang of conscience whatsoever, about the plea Slavin accepted, or about the fact that with the tables now turned in an extraordinary, cut-throat way, his client would be the chief prosecution witness against his former close friend Emre Massahol. Fishley didn't give a nanosecond's thought as to whether Barnstable County District Attorney Schnabel, and with the active assistance of his client, was treating Erme Massahol fairly in her pursuit of justice. Fishley scoffed at the notion.

Justice... fairness? The sentiments and values of losers. Was it Massahol? I don't know, and I don't care to know.

In Fishley's view of the law, there was no place for right versus wrong, no abstract sense of justice, or searching for the truth, and certainly no room whatsoever for remorse. He had one goal and one goal alone: getting George Slavin out from under a first-degree murder rap. He'd do it any way he could. After years of practicing law, and now at the zenith of his profession, Fishley knew not to think big thoughts. He had only one thought on his mind at the moment.

Next up for dinner: Emre Massahol. A prime meal for our justice system. The way Jason Karp was for that great white shark.

DA Schnabel and First Assistant Bach wanted a conviction badly. Judge Brennan even more so. In the weeks leading up to Massahol's murder trial, Brennan seemed to forget that Slavin had caused the mistrial. He didn't care. He wanted the case over and done with quickly.

"Three days max for this one," Brennan told the lawyers at the pre-trial scheduling conference. "I'm holding you to it," he said sternly.

Behind Judge Brennan's mask of neutrality, which he'd learned to wear so well through the years, he again rooted hard for the prosecution. Of course it was the jury's job to determine who and what to believe and not believe, but Brennan knew Massahol lied during the first trial about being in the hold of Slavin's boat. He had also been tremendously moved by Ulrike Baten-Karp's composure and testimony. That was enough for him. Schnabel and Bach would get free rein.

"Sic 'em, you pit bulls," Judge Brennan muttered under his breath as the trial began.

Armageddon was upon Erme Massahol. He lived a surreal nightmare, beyond description, and from which there was no escape. Opening his eyes each morning proved difficult. The weight and enormity of the situation made it hard for him to breath. A numbing desperation defined him.

I didn't do it. How can this possibly be happening?

Both Slavin and Massahol took the stand again. Slavin told his story beautifully and earnestly. Massahol's new testimony—that it was Slavin who drugged Karp and threw him overboard, and that Massahol in fact tried to stop him from doing so—carried no weight whatsoever.

After all, in the first trial, and while under oath, Massahol said something completely different on the witness stand. DA Schnabel made sure the jury knew. Judge Brennan, through a few highly questionable evidentiary rulings, paved the way for Schnabel to do so.

There was the testimony of a few new witnesses too, such as CAN Board Chair Greg Hemshaw and former CAN Executive Director Conrad Redlich.

"Did Emre Massahol and Jason Karp yell at each other, were they profane with each other, during CAN budget talks?" First Assistant Scott Bach was questioning Hemshaw about the angry discussions between Karp and Massahol on the issue of cutting the orchestra's funding for the overall benefit of CAN.

"Yes. Absolutely."

"As the board chair," Bach went on, "you had insight into it, so let me ask... how was the relationship between Karp and Massahol?"

"Terrible."

Next up was Conrad Redlich, Karp's predecessor as CAN's executive director. Not only had Massahol been responsible for Redlich losing his job at CAN, he had always made Redlich's life miserable. Dressed to the nines in one of his favorite Hugo Boss double-breasted suits, Redlich approached the witness stand with eager anticipation.

Time for Double M's comeuppance, he thought. *How sweet it is!*

"What was your relationship with Emre Massahol like?" Bach asked Redlich, as they got into it.

"I'd use two words to sum it up," replied Redlich. "Abysmal and poisonous."

"Did he ever threaten you, or seem threatening to you?" Bach continued.

"Objection, Your Honor," said Bucknell, Massahol's by-now besieged lawyer. "A leading question if I ever heard one, and one that requires a speculative answer to boot. It can't be…"

"Overruled. Sit down, Attorney Bucknell."

Redlich shrugged and raised his eyes slightly toward the sky, then gave a slight affirmative nod. "Mr. Redlich, give an oral response so the court reporter can get it down," said Judge Brennan.

Sighing, he looked at the court reporter: "Yes, quite frankly… Yes."

The sword through the heart came from outside Judge Brennan's courtroom. On the second afternoon of the trial, Brian Bucknell geared up to introduce the keystone evidence to Massahol's defense: the drug vial found on Slavin's boat. The vial had Slavin's fingerprints and DNA on it—only Slavin's—and it contained traces of GHB, the drug detected in Karp's body.

At the very last moment, however, the drug vial couldn't be introduced as evidence on Massahol's behalf. It wasn't Judge Brennan's decision. It came from the highest court in Massachusetts, the Supreme Judicial Court. The hard-core drug use of a state crime lab technician, who consumed drug evidence rather than analyzed it, caused it in part. But mainly it was caused by years of corrupt, tainted analytics throughout the entire Massachusetts crime lab system.

Deciding enough is enough, the Supreme Judicial Court threw out thousands of pieces of crime lab evidence in one fell swoop. It happened just hours before Erme Massahol's defense was to begin. The Boston Globe had a field day with the news, reporting it under a two-inch headline—the font size usually reserved for declarations of war or the assassinations of presidents. 'The Worsening Massachusetts Crime Lab Scandal: Just The Beginning.'

It was the first bit of good news Judge Wolcott Brennan had received in a long time.

Thank God, Brennan thought. *It's been taken out of my hands!*

Hennessey and Lipman were driving to the Barnstable

County courthouse when they heard the news on the radio. They were scheduled to be the last two witnesses in the prosecution's case.

"Unbelievable," Hennessey said. "The SJC's ruling is supposed to help criminal defendants, not hurt them. Remember... last time, before the mistrial, the drug vial was a key part of Schnabel and Bach's prosecution. They linked the vial to Slavin, and the drug in the vial to Karp's body.

"This time it would've been exculpatory evidence for Massahol. It's really the one thing that might save him, and he can't use it. He's screwed. Royally."

Lipman didn't know what to say. He drove in silence. The two of them pulled into the courthouse parking lot a few minutes later.

Watching the nails being hammered one by one into Massahol's coffin ate away at Hennessey. After all these years acting as a small cog in the wheel, he still clung to an intangible, inchoate belief that the American criminal justice system had merit to it.

What am I, a big rube? thought Hennessey. *Justice about to be served here? What a joke.*

Prior to Massahol's trial, Hennessey and Lipman repeatedly told the two prosecutors that they didn't believe a word coming out of Slavin's mouth. Lipman ended up in a shouting match with Bach about it. "You're arrogant and an idiot know-it-all!" yelled Lipman. Hennessey was equally adamant. "You've got the wrong guy," he exhorted. "Phil and I know you do. We know it."

Schnabel and Bach didn't want to hear it. Not a word of it. Especially not about Slavin's tendency to flush when he lied, something they'd now seen even though it didn't register with them when they witnessed it.

"We're not revisiting things," DA Schnabel snapped at the detectives. "It's too late in the ballgame for that. Way too late. That flush of Slavin's that you noticed... do you think that we're required to turn information about it over to the defense, or that it can somehow be introduced into evidence?

That Massahol can use Slavin's flush to exculpate himself? Think again, detectives, think again."

Disgusted, Hennessey descended into a dark place, agitation growing in him like a sudden windstorm.

The law doesn't give a rat's ass about the truth, he thought. *Those suits up at the tables, the judge in his god-like black robe, none of them care about the truth. All they want is for some arcane, antiquated, byzantine process to be followed. That's all. And as often as not, it results in the polar opposite of justice occurring.*

Dick Fishley descended the courthouse steps with his client George Slavin at the end of the day. Without smiling or looking at Slavin—he didn't want any questionable photos showing up in the press or being posted on social media—Fishley said out of the side of his mouth, "you've got to be the luckiest stiff on the planet, do you know that? And good job with your story today, by the way. Well done."

◊   ◊   ◊

The day after the guilty verdict came down, Bucknell filed notice of the appeal. Rather than denying bail outright, Judge Brennan set it at a whopping $1.5 million.

"I'm not getting stung again," Brennan said to himself, remembering how his outright denial of bail after the mistrial had been reversed with lightning speed. Massahol was out again, this time under strict house arrest, a form of torture for someone confined to a small one-bedroom condominium on Cape Cod.

Two days later, Emre Massahol killed himself. He used the nice little .22 pistol he had picked up years earlier at Artie's Ammo & Guns in the Cape Cod Mall, and which he occasionally took to the Bass River Rod & Gun Club indoor shooting range during down time on the Cape. The pistol was somehow overlooked during the sweep of Massahol's condo when he was put on house arrest.

The bullet hole in Massahol's cranium: small and discreet. Lying next to his body on the floor of his condo, with a little blood flecked onto it, was the score to Stravinsky's masterpiece, *The Rite of Spring.*

"Well, he's not conducting that one next season," Hennessey said to Lipman. "What a loss. That's some penance Double M made, like the sacrificial maiden in *The Rite of Spring.* I'm not sure what music Stravinsky would've come up with for his demise. Something wild and dissonant, no doubt."

Lipman had no idea what Hennessey was talking about. They looked the scene over quickly and left.

CHAPTER 25

Monday, February 7, 2022

Lipman arrived at the office first. Not unusual. Hennessey wrestled perpetually with the morning sun, and having pulled Kelly into his world after they became an item, the two of them were habitually late. Lipman's phone rang just as he sat down to get to work, first and foremost on his medium-sized Dunkin' Donuts coffee with milk and two sugars.

"Detective Lipman? It's Ben Maisky calling. Well, I'll be, we've never met or talked. I run the investigations unit at Archduke Insurance Company. Terrible thing, that Jason Karp murder. Massahol's death too. Listen, we're based up here in Boston. Archduke is CAN's insurer. I've been leading the insurance investigation into the burned down music buildings and theater."

"Good to meet you by phone, Ben," Lipman replied. "Hennessey told me you might be calling. What can I do for you? Got some information for us?"

Lipman was eager to get Maisky's news, thinking that at last they might have a breakthrough on the arson attacks. At the end of the ten-minute call, he stared vacantly at the far wall for a minute. Then he pounded his desk with his fist.

Hennessey, arriving a short while later, entered Lipman's

office in response to the 'come see me' note on his desk. He immediately picked up on his colleague's angst.

Uh oh. Bad news is on the way, thought Hennessey. *The BCPD is out of money and can't use me anymore.*

"Hey," stammered Lipman. "I heard from your old buddy, Ben Maisky, at Archduke Insurance this morning."

"Good... good," Hennessey interrupted. "I told him to call you if he had news to share. Maisky's brilliant at his work." He wondered why Lipman was bent out of shape about the call.

"Yeah," Lipman went on awkwardly. "Maisky came up with something I wanted to share with you first. He found matching cigarette butts at the two sites. One in the Burger King parking lot, the other in Beebe Forest, the woods next to the Falmouth music school and theater. Maisky managed to pull DNA off of the butts and there was a match, the same DNA on both."

"Great!" said Hennessey. "That's great. Now maybe we'll get somewhere."

The longest of silences followed. Lipman wouldn't really look at Hennessey, his eyes darting around his office. Hennessey couldn't begin to understand it.

What's going on?

"Yeah," Lipman continued at last, "except that the DNA on the two cigarette butts. It's yours. Or a family member of yours."

Astonishment froze Hennessey rigid. His brain went haywire, firing off internal responses faster than they could be processed.

Is this some sort of a joke? Can you say that again? Did you really mean what you just said? There's something completely wrong with this picture. Maisky's DNA test must be all screwed up.

Gathering his wits, Hennessey sat down and talked it through with Lipman.

"Think about it, Phil. Have you ever seen me smoke a cigarette? Anywhere? The answer is no, because as you know, I don't smoke. Go check my place if you want. Check my car too. Tell me if you find a trace of cigarettes anywhere. Here's the keys." Hennessey dropped his key ring in front of Lipman, who swooped it up as if he was going to take Hennessey up on the offer. Instead, after a couple of seconds, Lipman handed them back to Hennessey.

"I know it wasn't you. But how can this possibly be?"

"My brother Joey is—or was, I should say—in MCI-Walpole at the time of the arson attacks." It embarrassed Hennessey to talk about Joey's situation, especially since a national manhunt was now underway for one of the country's most famous escapees. "Unless he had night passes for getting out of a maximum security prison, it couldn't have been Joey." Lipman agreed that Joey was off the list.

"My brother Doug lives in Denver. Has for years and years now. He's married, is raising his three teenagers there, and works for Miller-Coors as an IT specialist. He never comes back to the Boston area. Doug's visited with me twice in all the years I've lived down here. Once was when he tacked on a weekend visit to an IT conference he attended in Boston.

"You need to look into Doug," Hennessey told Lipman. Of course Hennessey couldn't do the work himself— investigate his own brother. He also knew it couldn't possibly have been Doug. The idea was so patently crazy it made Hennessey smile.

Doug will have solid alibis for the nights the arson attacks occurred. I'm sure he was thousands of miles away. What would Dougie be doing here on Cape Cod, burning down performing arts buildings?

"Don't worry," said Lipman, equally puzzled and equally convinced that none of the Hennessey brothers was involved in the arsons. "I'll go light and make it quick. Don't worry about it."

"Thanks Phil. We'll get to the bottom of it, I guarantee."

Hennessey took the rest of the day off. The extraordinary nature of the news made it impossible for him to concentrate, to get any work done. Leaving the office, he gave Kelly a big hug and long kiss, the first public display of affection between the two of them. He felt an overwhelming, emotional urge to do so.

God that felt good, he thought. *So good.*

Kelly was surprised, grateful, and a little worried by the gesture. "Everything okay?" she asked as he left. She knew Hennessey well enough by now to know that his showing affection like that meant something was off. Kelly also knew him well enough by now to know there was nothing she could do to help. Hennessey wasn't wired in a way that would allow him to ask for and receive support, even from his partner. It upset her tremendously.

He's entirely alone in his emotional world, she thought sadly. *Like Robinson Crusoe stuck on his island.*

Relieved at the confidence Lipman placed in him, Hennessey nevertheless found his world turned upside down again. Confused. Depressed. Defeated. Back home, he took his favorite magnet off the refrigerator door, the one with Winston Churchill's "never, never, never give up" quote on it. He flipped it over and over with his fingers, manipulating it the way a magician prestidigitates.

"Really?" he said out loud to himself, staring at the magnet in his palm. He'd often been inspired by Churchill's pithy statement. Not today.

◇   ◇   ◇

John Hennessey answered the phone after seven or eight rings. He was slow to do so these days, and getting to the phone in this instance was made more difficult by his being out on the veranda, soaking up some early afternoon Florida sunshine.

"Hey, Dad. Yes, it's me again," Hennessey said to his father. "I know we talked over the weekend. Listen, I've received the weirdest news. I got it through some consulting work I'm doing. Believe it or not, someone out there has DNA that matches ours. It's been found at several crime scenes."

He listened to the voice at the other end.

"Why don't I come down for a visit? Yes, it's been too long... I know that, Dad. Probably a year now." After a pause, Hennessey continued, "Sure I'll come down. That way we can catch up on all sorts of things, including this strange DNA news.

I'll take the next few days off. Why don't I hop on a cheap stand-by first thing in the morning? I'll get there as early as I can. I'm really looking forward to seeing you too, Dad. Love you too. See you tomorrow."

◊　◊　◊

John Hennessey's fifth floor condominium overlooked the sixtcenth hole at Tampa Bay's exclusive Sunshine Forever Golf and Tennis Club. John plunked down some righteous cash for the condominium and the right to golf whenever he pleased, along with the other members of Sunshine Forever.

Hennessey and his father sat out on the veranda. A cool breeze blew. Through the gently swaying palms trees screening the condo from the golf course, the ping of golf club against ball could occasionally be heard. Now and then, laughter, or a swirl of unintelligible talk, wafted into them.

After a few hours, Hennessey noticed something. His father was doing just about everything possible, using all his powers, to avoid talking about the life-is-stranger-than-fiction DNA issue. Ducking and weaving, weaving and ducking, John Hennessey avoided it, wouldn't talk about it. How strange.

"Dad," Hennessey finally said, taking his father by the forearm and holding it firmly. "I didn't come down only for a fireside chat. This DNA business... I've been a detective a long time now, pride myself on my ability to read people. And you're my father. I can read you like a book! I see it all, Dad. What's this about? What's going on? Please, tell it to me straight."

Shame, rearing its ugly head, at first choked John

Hennessey into silence. It forced him to stumble on his words and obfuscate. Breaking through it at last, he poured everything out, clearly and movingly.

"Tim, I loved your mother very much. You and your brothers know that. There was never anyone else for me other than your mother, Mary Greenwood. I hope she felt the same way about me too. But, during a rough spell in our marriage, I strayed." John Hennessey looked down at the veranda deck when he said it. He had an incredibly difficult time talking about it, even decades later.

"I was unfaithful to your mother. She was spending so much time and energy watching over you boys. And whatever leftover time and energy she had, she spent on her anti-busing work, not on me. It was a bad time for us, the worst in our marriage. All marriages have their ups and downs, you know that as well as I do.

"It wasn't with anyone you or your brothers knew. And it ended after a year, after I said repeatedly that I was never going to leave your mother. That ended the affair. The result of it, though, was a child. I didn't know until several years later. It practically killed me when I found out."

The thought of an unknown half-sibling floating around out there for all these years floored Hennessey. "Holy shit, Dad. Holy shit. Does Dougie know? Does Joey know?" Hennessey wondered whether his brothers had kept this incredible family secret from him all these years.

"No, no one knows except you. You're the first. I never met the child, although I provided support as best I could, once I found out. You know me, my dear son," exclaimed John Hennessey, anguish in his voice, tears in his eyes. "I could never let a child of mine be in need, not even a child I never knew or met. That's where much of the vacation money went every year, the trips your mother was disappointed we never took, although she never knew the reason why, never found out, thank God."

Hennessey's emotions bounced around violently from moment to moment. He seethed with anger one second, empathized with his father the next.

"Name... Do you know my half-sibling's name?"

"Pat. Pat's the name."

Hennessey was on his feet, the volcanic rage he'd spent a lifetime learning to control now coursing freely through him like a rampaging wildfire.

"What the hell, Dad? WHAT THE HELL?" Hennessey screamed at his father, who shrank in dismay and fear of his eldest son.

"Great news, Dad. Great news." An icy contempt filled Hennessey's voice. "If you only knew what a mess it all is, Dad. You have no idea. The only thing I can say is this: You can't imagine the mess. It's beyond belief."

Hennessey burst out laughing at the absurdity of it all.

Yes indeed, life is one big joke.

"This Pat, Dad... what do you know about them?"

His father shrugged.

"Well," Hennessey continued, "Let me tell you about Pat. A long time ago, Pat joined one of your other children, Joey, in a life of crime. It's been one hell of a joy ride your Pat's been on. Decades now. Cybercrime, arson, felony murder— remember that rap, that's what they got Joey for—Pat's an expert at all of it. Much worse than anything Joey ever did. Much much worse.

"I have to find and take Pat in, Dad. It's a good thing the two of you never met, because Pat's going away for a long time. Let me have Pat's address, Dad. I'll let you know when it's all over."

His anger behind him, Hennessey's better side, empathic and tender toward his aged and infirm father, re-emerged. He didn't blame his father for the situation, nor did he ever doubt his father's love for his mother, or for him and his two brothers. But what a mess. His half-sibling Pat was into it up to the eyeballs.

Wanting to get the brutal and ugly business of the arrest behind him, Hennessey made to leave. He spent a last few minutes in gentle discourse with his father, and gave John

Hennessey a long kiss on the forehead before departing. Closing the door to his father's condominium, Hennessey shook his head, a gesture of both despair and resignation.

No one needs to tell me about the complexities, the headaches, the ups and downs of relationships and life. I've seen it all. I'm the king of it all.

◊   ◊   ◊

"Pat, Pat? Is that you? It's Dad calling."

"Yes."

"How have you been?"

"I'm fine, Dad, fine. You?"

"I'm fine too Pat. Pat, I've got to ask... What have you done? What have you done?"

"What's this, Dad? What're you talking about?"

"Your oldest brother, Tim, was here earlier today and says he knows all about you. Says you're a big-time criminal. He's coming after you right now. Please be careful, Pat. Please be careful."

"I gotta go then. Thanks, Dad. Appreciate the call. Much love to you."

John Hennessey sat in his red leather wingback chair and counted the brass studs on it for the umpteenth time. He sat in complete silence, crushed by the cruelty of a world that would pit one child of his against another in an upcoming, herculean battle. There would be no winners. He knew that. Getting up, he walked over to his amply stocked bar cart and poured himself a huge shot of Jameson's. It had to be Irish whiskey. He was John Hennessey, after all.

Back in his favorite chair, John opened the prescription bottles sitting on the small reading table next to him. A regular and frequent visitor to these vials, he considered them good friends. Crushing and mixing into the glass of Jameson's enough Ambien and valium to take out a great white shark, John Hennessey downed it in one fell swoop and then placed the glass carefully back on the table. He sighed contentedly.

I made it to eighty-one. Not bad for a run-of-the-mill guy like me. Mary, my one and only love... here I come. I told you I would meet you on the other side. Here I come, my dearest Mary.

EPILOGUE

The apartment was easy enough to find. It was on St. Botolph Street in Boston's South End. After driving himself there from Logan Airport, Hennessey let himself in. It took about ninety seconds to pick the lock.

Pat should know better. I got into this place faster than I can blink.

Hennessey reflected on the difference between South Boston and Boston's South End. St. Botolph Street was the South End's grand old dame.

Similarly named, geographically close, and a universe apart in character: South Boston and the South End. Pat certainly has good taste in streets and neighborhoods.

There wasn't much for Hennessey to discover in the place. Nothing linking Pat to any crimes, nothing whatsoever. The apartment looked just like the old one that he staked out years and years ago, in his different life. Under the bathroom sink cabinet, tucked away in the back behind the toilet and tub bleach spray, was a half-used box of tampons.

Well, well, well. So that's our Pat.

The entire apartment was minimally furnished. The bedroom empty, save for a queen-sized platform bed and

251

bedside table. The bedside table had a Haruki Murakami novel on it and two framed photos. One was a picture of an attractive, youngish woman, jet black hair, light eyes—one could tell even in black and white—with a radiant, warm smile on her face. Hennessey looked at her a long time. The other photo—same size, similarly framed, also black and white—was John Hennessey.

Anger pulsed through him. Then grim fatalism took over. Grabbing the Murakami novel, Hennessey moved back out into the living room. The only place to sit was a red leather wingback chair with brass studs, with a floor lamp hovering above it. He'd seen a similar chair earlier in the day. It churned his stomach.

Hennessey settled in for a long night, figuring he'd have to sit in complete darkness while he waited for Pat to return, in order to surprise her. As he sat in the dark, his mind filled with thoughts about the second criminal in the family, the one he'd never met and never knew was related to him until that afternoon. He grieved for all of them, for his father in particular, even for Pat.

His cell phone buzzed in his pocket. The ringer was off. It was an unknown number with a Tampa Bay area code, where he'd been earlier that day.

Hennessey wished he hadn't answered it. It was terrible news from the Tampa Bay police department. When his father hadn't shown up for a round of golf, a friend went looking for him, and found him dead in his favorite living room chair, apparently by his own hand.

Immediately, the old veil, the old numbness, the black flooding of his mind descended upon Hennessey. Agony and bitterness took over, the pain intolerable. His thoughts locked themselves in a tremendous battle.

I'll never be free of it. Never. Why should I go on? Why?... *My incredible children. The wonderful Kelly Coughlin. Work that means something. The sublime beauty of Cape Cod.*

After calling his brother Doug with the grim news—they wept together over the phone—Hennessey headed out to his car for the short drive back to Logan Airport. He'd book another flight down to Florida from the car or at the airport. Dealing with Pat Kimmell would have to wait.

On the windshield, tucked under the driver's side windshield wiper where Hennessey couldn't possibly miss it, was a note.

"Sorry we missed each other, big bro. Sometime soon. NOT."

"We'll see about that, sis, we'll see about that," muttered Hennessey, crumpling up the note and tossing it onto the front passenger's seat as he hopped into his car. Their father's funeral arrangements beckoned.

ACKNOWLEDGMENTS

There are so many people to thank for their assistance in getting *Dissonance* written, I don't really know where to start.

First and foremost, to my highly accomplished fellow novelists, whose critiques, insight, and counsel proved invaluable: Conall Ryan, Harry Groome, Elisa Speranza, and R.C. Binstock.

Second, a thank you to the top-notch editorial team who polished the manuscript significantly and taught me the intricacies of *The Chicago Manual of Style*: Elaine Ash, Victoria Brock, Sarah Rabel and Sherry Gottlieb.

Third, a thank you to dear friends who provided wonderful writing environments last summer—John and Melanie Clarke, and Bill Cook—and to family and friends who took the time to read and comment on portions of the manuscript: my sister Elizabeth, Mark Becker, Jon Leibowitz, and Randy Hiller, and a huge thank you to Bob Gold.

Fourth, to my dedicated, patient and talented cover designer, Jaycee DeLorenzo, and my guru Paperback Press publishing coordinator, Sharon Kizziah-Holmes, many thanks.

The biggest and final thank you goes to my wife, Nathalie, whose unwavering support—in every sense of the word—allowed me to undertake the arduous task of bringing Detective Tim Hennessey to life. Much love and thanks to you, NFLTK.